INSTRUCTIONS FOR FALLING IN LOVE AGAIN

LUCY MITCHELL

For Catherine and Sue

CHAPTER 1

PIPPA

*M*y eyes settle on the corner of the red notebook poking out from my handbag. Wedged between my phone and a bumper box of Tampax, it has avoided being sucked below into the sea of receipts, lip balms, school letters, spare knickers, tissues, countless hair bobbles, a Macmillan Cancer Support booklet, shopping lists from six years ago, headache tablets, mints, packets of dog treats, trusty child head lice combs, pictures of pretty fairy cakes I've secretly torn out from the magazines in the doctors waiting room, a child bereavement advice leaflet, a colourful pub football team newsletter from five years ago, and a multitude of family photos.

Letting my fingertips trail over the notebook's spine, I think back to how earlier this evening I locked myself in the downstairs toilet and traced his messy handwriting on the front cover. Sounds of my three children arguing over a packet of crisps and the dog barking at my mother, who had come to babysit, drifted through the door as I whispered, 'Dan Browning, I'm holding you entirely responsible for what I'm about to do tonight.'

Everything has gone blurry. I can't find the blasted tissues inside my handbag of chaos.

'Pip – you okay?' asks Emma, refilling my wine glass and then topping up Mel's.

My two best friends – Emma and Mel – and I are currently nestled at the back of our local pub. It seems fitting that us three are sitting here tonight, in the Nag's Head. This old wooden table and the dark timber beams above our heads have been witness to all sorts of life-changing news over the years: marriage proposals, engagements, failed engagements, pregnancy news (all mine), dating successes, many dating failures, promotions, sackings, significant weight losses on new diets, children securing places at good schools, house purchases, a cancer diagnosis, treatment updates, and plans for a charity parachute jump.

Every fortnight we meet up in this pub and mainly dissect what we've already told each other, at length, on *WhatsApp* and texts.

On the agenda tonight is Emma's decision to dump ex-golf captain, Phil, and an update on Mel's affair with a married pilot which resulted in her being fired from her job as a flight attendant. She and the married pilot, Jeff, were caught having sex in the plane toilet on a delayed flight to Malaga.

In contrast to my quiet and hermit-like existence, Emma and Mel have lives which could easily be turned into a popular soap opera.

Emma has spent the last three years completing her dating bucket list. Last month Mel and I were treated to scampi and chips here in this pub by a jubilant Emma who told us all about the last few challenges she faced in ticking off everything on her list. Through one of her PR contacts she managed to get a date with a French astronaut, an *Instagram* contact secured her a string of dates with a Premiership footballer, a local election enabled her to secure a date with an MP in his hotel bar, and her yoga teacher got her a date with a handsome Brazilian yoga instructor. This led to an evening of complicated sexual positions which Emma didn't complain about. A few days later, she met Phil and set herself a new challenge; to stay in a relationship for longer than six weeks.

Mel is the one I worry about the most. She gets herself into some dreadful life messes and is a magnet for bad men, toxic relationships, heartbreak, and disaster. There's a permanent place at the end of my sofa for a sobbing Mel. Over the years she's also got herself into numerous difficult situations on the job front too. From taking underwear shots of herself while working for a wedding photographer and accidentally emailing them to his database of future bridal customers, to going skinny dipping while working as a tour rep and emerging from the sea to find someone had stolen her clothes. She had to run naked past her elderly holidaymakers who had just returned from a coach tour and one old man's pacemaker packed in. Poor Mel was devastated and turned up on my doorstep in a teary mess.

Tonight, I'm going to jump the agenda and tell Emma and Mel my secret. I can't keep it to myself any longer.

With a trembling hand, I put down my wine glass. 'I think it's time for me to start … umm … dating. '

Emma's glossy pink lips fall open in surprise. Mel, who has been busy texting ever since we arrived, drops her phone, sending it clattering to the wooden floor.

Judging by their reaction, they weren't expecting this.

Mel speaks first. 'What's brought this on, Pip? '

Wringing my hands together, I attempt to say what has proven impossible for the last three years. 'Dan's gone.' The words I've been trying to force off my tongue tumble out effortlessly.

Emma's sparkly blue eyes widen, and Mel's sculptured brown eyebrows shoot up her forehead.

I continue with a wavering voice, 'It's taken me a long time to process what happened.'

In a fraction of a second, they fly around the table and reassuring arms are placed over my shoulders and they form what we call a *best friend cocoon*. For a moment we sit in silence. They squeeze and I fight back stinging tears. His name flashes across my mind.

'We know, Pip,' whispers Emma, pressing her forehead against my cheek.

Freeing myself from their embrace, I sink into the leather seat, recalling the agonising times I've sat on my sofa, waiting to hear Dan's key in the front door. Expecting to see him bound into the lounge with a huge grin plastered all over his face and carrying our son, Billy, on his broad shoulders.

I must have spent months wearing Dan's thick, woollen jumper around the house, inhaling every last trace of his scent. It always resulted in me making two cups of tea, laying an extra place at the family dinner table, and putting out his wellies when the kids and I were going on a dog walk.

Waking in the middle of the night shouting his name, I would run my hand across his side of the bed, wondering whether his headaches, those terrifying seizures, and the Stage Four Glioblastoma diagnosis had been part of a dreadful nightmare. The coldness of his pillow and sheets always brought me back to reality.

'I swore to myself when he died that I wouldn't need anyone else in my life.' I sniff. 'How could I replace someone like Dan?'

Fiddling with my messy hair bun, I wonder whether he's listening from the afterlife. Hearing me talk like this would result in that lovable smile spreading quickly over his rugged face, those intense green eyes to twinkle, and a booming laugh to ring out.

'But now …' I mumble, hanging my head. 'Things feel different.'

'What do you mean?' Emma asks, handing me a packet of tissues from her black designer clutch bag.

Taking one, I dab at my watery eyes and stem the flow from my snotty nose. 'He's not here anymore, he's not coming back and …' My voice falters. 'If I'm going to be really honest, I'm lonely.'

Mel gives my arm a gentle squeeze.

'There's something missing in my life.'

'Sex,' Emma says, with a wry smile.

Emma can always be relied upon to bring some much-needed humour into a tense moment. She also has a one-track mind. Sex is never far from her conversations.

Shaking my head, I cast her a mock-stern look. 'No, Emma, that is the last thing on my mind.'

Glancing at her phone, Mel shifts about on her seat. 'Oh God, Jeff's wife has texted me.'

'What does she want?' Emma asks.

After clearing her throat Mel explains, 'She's called Cassandra and she wants my version of events. In the toilet. A detailed account.'

Emma shakes her blonde head in bewilderment. 'Why would she want to read a detailed account of her husband having sex with another woman in a plane toilet?'

Mel pulls at her shirt collar. 'This is not fun anymore.'

Emma nudges me under the table.

'What's wrong, Mel?' I ask as she stares blankly at her phone.

Mel nibbles on her thumbnail. 'Getting sacked and now this from his wife has made me think about my life.'

With a mock horrified glance Emma quickly refills Mel's glass. 'Oh God, you can stop that *thinking about your life* nonsense right now!'

Mel turns to Emma. 'You've never sat and thought about your life?'

I choke on my wine and start to giggle at the thought of Emma assessing her life.

Emma's false eyelashes flicker a few times before she lets out a shriek of laughter. 'Melanie, the only thinking I do nowadays is whether I swipe left or right. Now drink some more wine and you'll feel a lot better.'

I sense something is troubling Mel and place my hand over hers. 'You can talk to us.'

She casts me a weak smile. 'Ignore me, Pip, I'm ruining your news. Carry on with what you were saying.'

I try to get my brain back into gear. 'There has to be more to my life than cuddling up to a cheap bottle of red from the local shop, working my way through a box of Milk Tray chocolates, and browsing through my neighbour's latest cruise snaps on *Facebook*.'

Reaching inside my handbag, I fish out my glossy pink lip balm and apply a thick layer. 'The thought of getting intimate with someone scares the hell out of me. I need someone who will organise nice dates, take me to lovely restaurants, go on long country walks ... but not want anything else.'

Flicking her shiny bobbed hair away from her tanned face, Mel says, 'Pip, you'll struggle with that sort of dating requirement these days.'

My stomach tightens. 'It's only been three years since Dan died. Maybe I should stay single longer?'

Emma's smooth forehead furrows. 'Aren't you forgetting something?' She twirls a strand of golden blonde hair around a manicured pink finger nail. 'Dan actively encouraged you to ...' She strokes her chin. 'Now, what was the phrase he used ... oh yeah ... he wanted you to *rewrite your fairy tale*.'

Spotting the red notebook sticking out of my handbag, Mel sighs. 'I still can't believe Dan did what he did. Jeff told me he wouldn't want his wife moving on with someone else if anything happened to him.'

Emma's ring-clad hand shoots into the air. 'Let me stop you there, Mel,' she says, struggling to keep a straight face. 'Jeff, the married pilot who was having an affair with you, didn't want his wife to find someone else … if anything happened to him?'

While Emma and Mel discuss Jeff's approach to relationships, I find myself staring at the corner of the red notebook.

Dan was Mr Organised. His life revolved around lists and plans, meticulously laid out in spreadsheets. In our kitchen, he erected huge family planners, assigned us coloured pens, and mapped out our days, weeks, and months. He had his work cut out with three kids, a wife, and an old bulldog who all preferred to live in absolute chaos.

We rarely took any notice of Dan's attempts to organise us and happily rebelled against him.

It wasn't a surprise to discover he'd given careful consideration to how our lives would be after he passed away. Before he died and while in an unimaginable amount of pain, he wrote me and our three children instructions, in little coloured notebooks, on how to live without him.

A familiar Dan-shaped lump balloons at the back of my throat. I quickly swallow it away.

There was a notebook for each of us, filled with Dan's personalised life advice.

Our youngest, Billy, was gifted a dark-blue notebook. An appropriate choice given anything other than blue would have been deemed 'girlie' by Billy and promptly hidden under his bed. Billy's instructions were about not spending all his birthday and Christmas money on Power Rangers toys, improving his football skills, and not leaving the house without combing his hair and brushing his teeth.

Libby, our middle child, had a white notebook. From an early age Libby was obsessed with footballs and goal nets. It was apt that Dan's notebook fitted with her passion. Her instructions were to concentrate on her football skills, as out of the three of them, Dan believed she had the most potential. She was told not to adopt small furry creatures from the garden and force them to live in cardboard boxes at the back of her wardrobe. He also forbade her from taking the kitchen scissors upstairs and cutting her hair off whenever she felt like it.

Daisy, our now teenage daughter, got a green notebook. She shares her father's green eyes which she houses under a thick layer of black mascara, so the colour green was fitting. Her instructions were focused around not being sarcastic to me, controlling her temper, and not going to parties on a school night when she was older. He also warned her that being possessive and controlling with her friends would only lead to trouble. At the time of writing the notebook, Daisy, nearly thirteen, was struggling to accept Maggie, her best friend, wanted to go shopping in town with *other* friends. Things almost reached crisis point when Daisy locked Maggie in the shed and text Maggie's other friends to decline their invite.

Mine was a vibrant red colour. Dan didn't write me a set of instructions on how to survive grief, how to change a plug, or how to change the tyre on the car. No. He left me instructions on how to fall in love again, with someone else.

The notebooks were in Dan's belongings from the hospice. Presented to me after he died by Pam, his favourite nurse. She wiped away a tear and said she'd miss Dan's cheeky comments about her choice in football team, Swansea City.

Dan often joked with her about how glad he was she liked football and he was overjoyed to hear she was going to give up supporting Swansea and join him as a Cardiff City fan. Pam would snort with laughter and threaten to do her shift caring for him wearing a Swansea shirt.

The kids and I weren't in a fit state to read the notebooks straight away, so I buried them in my underwear drawer. Life took over. We battled our way through three painful years of grief and heartache. Dan's notebooks were forgotten. A few months ago, I cleared out my underwear drawer and found them, hidden at the back.

After baking a batch of Dan's favourite football-themed fairy cakes: complete with a little green football pitch on top, a tiny football, and a white goal post, I presented each child with a cake and their book. To my horror, Billy scoffed his cake, scanned his notebook, before leaving it on the kitchen table and going to play football in the street. Libby squirrelled hers away in her wardrobe, and Daisy rolled her eyes and stuffed it into her schoolbag.

Keeping mine private, I stashed it in my handbag for safe keeping. Emma and Mel were then summoned for a bottle of wine a few days later. After the kids went to bed, Emma, Mel, and I read Dan's instructions for falling in love.

I swore blind I wasn't ready for romance, although deep down something opened up inside of me the night I first read his words.

A peal of laughter rings out from the bar. It makes us look up.

He's here. The person I've been avoiding since reading Dan's notebook. He's now stood in the pub doorway, dressed as a … *ballerina*. His hairy chest pokes through a tight pink leotard, an elegant ballet tutu hugs his bony hips, and his giant spade feet are stuffed into a dainty pair of ballet shoes. A group of women on the table next to us squeal until their eyes stream at the sight of him.

'The stag party organiser is here!' A chorus of claps and wolf whistles fill the air.

'Oh, Dan,' I groan, 'I think you made a big mistake. '

Nudging me in the ribs Emma points her wine glass in the direction of the ballerina. 'Isn't that … Mikey Stenton, the bloke who Dan suggested you …' It takes a lot to shock Emma and I cast her a worried look when her words disappear.

'Look at that hairy chest!' Mel says, craning her head to get a better look. She returns to her phone. 'Hang on, girls, let me do some social media stalking on this interesting male specimen.

He's friends with me on *Facebook*.' We watch her start to scroll and then present us with her phone screen.

Mikey Stenton's *Facebook* feed makes me gasp. A multitude of photos of him snogging a number of different women, a photo of his bare backside on a moonlit beach in Thailand, one photo of him lounging in a hot tub in Sydney, and another of him and a blonde woman riding a horse in California greet my eyes.

'He hasn't changed then?' I remark, thinking back to all the football social events I attended with Dan. 'All the football girlfriends and wives used to talk about Mikey Stenton.'

'Okay,' says Mel. 'Here's Mikey's *Instagram*.' The sight of him dancing on a table with several half-naked women turns my stomach.

We all turn towards Mikey Stenton talking to a tall man with an elegant quiff, who is also dressed as a ballerina. I take in Mikey's broad shoulders, his messy brown hair, and his boyish smile. He glances in my direction, making me gasp.

Mel notices my attention has been hijacked. 'Pip, don't stare, he might think you fancy him!'

I look at Emma. 'We need more wine. Is it your round?'

Mel's phone pings. Judging by her shocked face it has to be another text from the pilot's wife. I watch Emma weave her way through a group of noisy students and then a couple of middle-aged men enjoying a drink and finally the noisy mass of male ballerinas stood by the bar. I grin as she raises a concerned, pencilled eyebrow at Mikey Stenton, prancing around the bewildered looking stag.

After five minutes Emma returns with three Sex on the Beach cocktails. 'I persuaded Simon to make us these.'

'Hasn't he got enough to do with all those ballerinas?' asks Mel.

Emma giggles. 'Here, drink some of this.' She hands us each a tall colourful glass, crackling with ice.

Once seated, Emma leans over the table. 'Please tell me you're not going to consider Dan's dating recommendation. Let's agree, it was ... how can I put it ... ummm ... rubbish?'

I repeat out loud what Dan had said about Mikey in his notebook. 'I have to look past Mikey Stenton's male bravado, his *Instagram* feed, and his hedonistic ways.'

Emma lets out a shriek of laughter. 'Good luck with that, Pip!'

In the back of the red notebook, Dan listed all the men I should avoid dating. This consisted of half of the local pub's football team, which he used to play for and a lot of his friends at work.

He also warned me off the men from the car wash place, our family dentist, and the butcher, who plays for an opposing team.

To my surprise – and horror – Dan also named someone he thought I *should* consider dating – Mikey Stenton.

I steal a quick look at Mikey Stenton. 'I can't understand why Dan would suggest I date someone like him.'

Grabbing an expensive looking tube of lip gloss Emma smears a thick layer over her lips, before frowning. 'I dread to think who Phil would come up with for me in this situation.'

Mel laughs. 'Oh, Emma, can you imagine Phil doing some matchmaking?'

Emma clamps a manicured hand over her forehead. 'He knows I detest all his colleagues, his golf friends, his badminton acquaintances, and his cycling friends. Maybe that's why I'm getting a strong urge to dump him?'

Placing her phone down on the table Mel lets out a sigh. 'I can't take any more of Cassandra's texts. She wants to know whether Jeff was tired when I took advantage of him.'

'Was Jeff tired when *you* took advantage of him?' Emma takes a sip of her cocktail and grins at Mel.

Mel shakes her head. 'Jeff seemed fine to me.' Shouts and cheers make us look towards the door. A crowd of attractive young women have entered clad in short leather skirts and

11

skimpy vest tops. We watch several long-haired girls make a beeline for Mikey and his tutu clad friends.

'Male tart alert,' whispers Emma. We all watch Mikey break free from a leggy blonde to perform a ridiculous ballet move. Everyone around him shrieks with laughter.

'Idiot alert,' I whisper back.

Mel stares in bewilderment at Mikey's pirouette. 'Dan wasn't well when he wrote that notebook of yours, Pip. Those drugs clearly messed with his brain.'

In an instant, I'm transported back to those last few weeks with Dan. We are all in his room in the hospice. I'm perched on his bed, holding his hand, even though he's losing feeling in it. Pam and I have swept back his thick black hair, using lots of gel, and created his favourite Danny Zuko pompadour style. Sitting up in bed, Dan's greeting everyone with his best wonky smile. He always said out of all the horrid things his brain cancer had done to him, ruining his dazzling smile was the one he was most annoyed about. My mother is busy with her crochet in the corner, Libby is sat on the opposite chair with her colouring pens, Daisy is crouched on the floor listening to her headphones, and Billy is playing a noisy game of Power Rangers under the bed. Dan's trying to stay awake but he's too weak to fight the tiredness.

Back in the present, tears sting my eyes. I find myself nodding in agreement. 'I think you're right. Dan wasn't himself. He put Mikey's name under the wrong header.'

One of the girls stood near the bar who has her back to us shakes out her shoulder-length black hair. From where I'm sat, she looks strikingly similar to Daisy. My heartbeat quickens.

Is my teenage daughter in a pub with a load of grown men dressed as female ballerinas?

Taking out my phone, I check Daisy's text from two hours ago. It informed me she was busy getting stuck into her homework.

Dragging my eyes away from the girl with the long black hair, I notice Mikey Stenton standing in the middle of a circle of excitable and hysterical young women.

'Stay well away from him,' advises Emma, taking out her phone. She reads a text and screeches. 'Oh no, Phil has spotted my profile has gone back up on *Tinder.*'

'What?' Mel and I flick our heads towards Emma.

With a nervous laugh she gushes, 'I only had a little peek. Damn – I must have accidentally put my profile live.'

'Do you think he's got the hint the end is near?' Mel takes a sip of her cocktail.

Emma shrugs. 'He knows I find anything longer than six weeks hard. And, if he's on *Tinder*, he must be thinking the same.'

While Mel and Emma launch into a conversation about *Tinder*, I trace the title Dan gave my notebook with my finger.

Instructions for Falling in Love Again.

After leafing through the handwritten pages, I flick to his message at the front.

My Darling Pip,

If you're reading this, my Glioblastoma has finally won. I'm in heaven. God is enjoying his time hanging out with me, and we're busy organising heaven's first ever football league. I knew there was a reason why God wanted me to come here so quickly.

I hope you're reading this after making the decision to move on with your life.

Battling against my illness this last year has not been great. Chemo sucked and my sad-looking consultant, Mr Rogers, annoyed me with his dire predictions.

Losing all feeling in parts of my body has been depressing and so too was knowing I would soon be leaving you all. You know all this.

However, the worst thing of all has been watching you lot go through all this. It's been heart breaking watching you and the kids fuss over me, helping me move about, and putting on a brave face after our horrendous appointments with Mr Rogers.

You lost your beautiful smile somewhere along the way, Pip. It's not surprising when you think about everything we've gone through with my cancer. So, I've decided you need someone to magic it back. I want to rewrite your fairy tale, Pip. This is why I've put together this set of instructions.

This is really hard. Pam thinks I'm nuts, but I know it's the right thing to do. You know I'll always love you and there won't be a day in heaven where I don't look down on you.

I'm so glad you kissed me during the 80s night in that pub all those years ago. Still can't believe I met the love of my life over a pint of cider and a packet of pork scratchings, with Duran Duran's 'Hungry Like the Wolf' playing in the background. You were some kisser!

When Daisy came along and surprised us both, I cried with joy into our chicken chow mein takeaway.

Proposing to you outside the Chinese restaurant, while Daisy slept in her pram, has to be one of the happiest nights of my life. Then Libs and Bill appeared. We had some good times as a family. All those amazing holidays, our impromptu barbecues in the back garden on a Sunday evening, and all the adventures we went on.

I will always love you, Pippa, but once I'm gone, you'll need to move on with your life.

Before I get onto the point of this notebook, promise me one thing, you will do something with your baking. Your fairy cakes are amazing and wasted on us lot.

I can't believe I'm writing this, but I want you to find someone else and be happy again. Please, Pippa, go out and fall in love.

Over the past few months, I've had a lot of time to think and I've come up with some instructions for you.

Read them and for once, please take my advice!

You deserve to be happy.

All my love forever, beautiful girl!

Dan xxx

PS: I hope you listened to me and didn't paint our entire house Fifty Shades of duck-egg blue after I died. Your fascination with that colour was odd, Pip.

PPS: I also hope you didn't spend a lot of the life insurance on an expensive new kitchen and blow the budget I planned for you.

CHAPTER 2

PIPPA

*S*liding the notebook back into my bag, I take a deep breath. 'Dating is going to be scary. I've only ever dated two men in my life, one of them being Dan.'

Emma grins. 'As I'm days away from getting back into dating …'

'Days away?' interjects Mel. 'Emma, you're already back up on *Tinder.*'

With a chuckle, Emma gives Mel a playful swipe, before turning back to me. 'What I was trying to say before being rudely interrupted by Melanie, is that once she's knocked the affair with the pilot on the head, we can all navigate the world of dating *together.*'

Mel shakes her head. 'I need to sort out my life. The last thing I need right now is more male stress.'

Emma rolls her eyes, ignoring Mel and it an excited voice says, 'It will be like school again. We did everything together back then.'

Fiddling with her gold earring Mel casts us both a puzzled face. 'We all started our periods in the same week so I suppose we can count that.'

'We smoked our first cigarette together at the back of the bike sheds after Biology,' I add, causing Mel and Emma to nod in agreement.

Emma gasps. 'We started going out with older boys who *shaved*, within days of each other. Do you remember boasting about how our boyfriends had stubble?'

With a loud clap Mel laughs. 'We said farewell to our virginity on the same weekend after our exams had finished. Emma, you had sex with that Darren from the upper sixth, Pip did it with Anthony, and I lost mine to Pete, the waiter from the Italian.'

Sending my mind back, I think back to see if there's anything else we've done together. The memory of three sets of parents looking agitated in the school playground while Emma, Mel, and I hung our heads, comes rushing back to me. 'We all got disappointing GCSE results.'

Emma smiles and clinks glasses with all of us. 'We all had our belly buttons pierced and infected within days of each other.'

After we've finished laughing, I point to the framed photo on the cream-coloured wall above our heads. The photo shows us in a plane, wearing brightly coloured goggles, and grinning into the camera, minutes before we did our charity parachute jump. 'A few months ago, we jumped out of a plane together.'

'Your instructor was so fit,' Mel says to Emma. 'I wasn't worried about throwing myself out of a plane, just spent the whole time wishing I was strapped into him instead and you had my instructor with the awful tea breath.'

Emma fiddles with one of her curls and grins at Mel.

'Do you remember my parachute instructor?' I say as we all relive the memory of the white haired, little man who had claimed he was one of the best parachute instructors in the south-west.

'Pip, I was definitely not jealous of you being strapped to … *Grandpa.*' Mel giggles.

Taking a sip of my drink, I watch my two best friends fall

about in hysterical laughter over Mel's nickname for my instructor.

I send God a silent prayer of thanks for these two fabulous women. Emma and Mel, who hugged the life out of us when Dan and I asked them to be bridesmaids. They took it in shifts to hold my hand during labour with each of my children and babysat Daisy in the early months, letting Dan and I spend some time together. They squealed when we asked them to be *fairy* godmothers to our three children, came to live with me and the kids when Dan went on football tours, and put their lives on hold when Dan first became sick.

Since he died, these two have turned up on my doorstep with bottles of wine and chocolates, dragged me to the pub, replied to my emotional *WhatsApp* messages in the small hours, let me use their shoulders to cry on, looked after my kids when I needed a break, and joined me in doing a variety of mad and silly things to help raise money for Dan's cancer charity. I love them both, dearly.

Mel turns to Emma. 'Did you just go back on one dating site?'

A wry smile slides across Emma's face. 'Nope. I *accidentally* put my profiles back up on *eHarmony, Match, Plenty of Fish, Muddy Matches, LoveStruck, Tin Dog,* and *Veggie Romance*. I like to throw my net wide,' she whispers. 'Don't tell Phil. From his recent text, it sounds like he's struggling seeing my *Tinder* profile go back up.'

Turning to Emma, I cast her a confused look. 'How can you be on a dating site for dog lovers and a site for dating vegetarians, when you don't have a dog and aren't a veggie?'

She winks. 'You're going to let me borrow Maria the bulldog for a few dates and Mel is going to write down what she has to eat on a daily basis. Sorted!'

'So, what's it like, this online dating business?' I ask, keen to hear what my new dating advisers have to say.

Mel rolls her eyes. 'A lot will send you intimate photos of themselves after the first email.'

INSTRUCTIONS FOR FALLING IN LOVE AGAIN

I stare in horror. 'Really?'

Emma nods. 'You will see things which will make your hair curl.'

Mel chuckles at me, pointing to Emma's mass of blonde curly hair. 'She's seen a lot of things!'

Emma grins. 'Some blokes will reply to your first email and attach a pic of their private bits.'

Nodding Mel adds, 'Some blokes will only send you a pic of their private bits.'

Emma continues, 'Some stop communicating with you after three weeks of non-stop messaging. They don't give a reason or anything.'

The stag party exits the pub, taking with them the crowd of young women. Our little local pub breathes a sigh of relief. Everyone returns to their quiet conversations and Simon, the landlord, sits down with his tablet to watch the Cardiff City game.

I check my phone. It's nearly eleven. 'I had better be getting home.'

Emma grabs her camel skin coat and Mel pulls on her black leather jacket. They both gesture for me to lead the way. 'We'll call a cab from yours.'

A refreshing night breeze caresses our warm cheeks. Mel and Emma link their arms through mine. 'We are proud of you, Pip,' says Mel. 'It can't have been easy to make that sort of decision.'

Shaking off a cloud of dating anxiety, I pull my two best friends closer. 'I just hope I'm doing the right thing.'

Emma tugs on my sweater. 'I thought you seemed different the other week.' She gives me a knowing wink.

I stop and frown. 'What do you mean?'

'You were gawping at the hunky shop assistant when we were buying shoes.'

Emma and I squeal with laughter.

'He was a bit young for me, but maybe that's what I need?'

Mel shakes her head. 'You need to go for the older man.'

'You mean older, married man,' interjects Emma.

We look at Mel, who pulls us to a stop. 'Come on, let's hear Dan's instructions once more on how to fall in love?'

Leading us to a spot underneath the yellow glow of a street light, Emma gestures for me to get Dan's notebook out. I flick to the first page.

'Okay, the first section is what he calls, *Preparations For Finding Love*, I don't think we looked at this when you came round all those weeks ago.'

'This should be good,' says Emma, leaning against the black railings and shooting me a serious expression. A cackle of drunken laughter escapes from Mel's lips.

I take a deep breath and begin, 'Number one. Don't take dating advice from the following: your mother, your sister, Helen, Emma, or Mel.'

We all find interesting things to look at on the pavement.

Mel lets out a sigh. 'Agree with Dan about your mother, Pip. I wouldn't like to be in the same room as Barbara when you break the dating news to her, and I dread to think who she'd recommend for you.'

My mother's scary face materialises inside my mind. She possesses strong views on how her grandchildren should be raised, so there is no doubt she'll have something to say about dating.

Mel carries on, 'But I'm outraged he's advising you not to listen to Helen, Emma, or me. Does he give some rationale?' She peers over the notebook.

I read what Dan had written. 'I get the feeling your sister would be happier if Rick worked away from home permanently.'

Emma giggles. 'Helen swears Rick working away has done wonders for their marriage. What does he say about me and Mel?'

I take a deep breath. 'Emma is addicted to dating and I foresee nothing but trouble for Mel when she becomes a flight attendant.'

Emma and Mel turn to each other with fake, horrified glances.

'Number two. Get a fringe cut into your hair. You had one when I first met you. It made you look hot.'

Tilting her blonde head to one side, Emma studies my face. 'He might have a point. I did like you with your fringe.'

I place my hands over my ears. 'But I was thinking about getting it cut off and going for a pixie type cut.'

Emma and Mel cast worried looks at me.

'What's number three?' Mel cranes her neck to see what he'd written next.

I look down and groan. 'Don't get a pixie style haircut. You won't suit it and you'll regret it.'

'That's too funny.' Emma laughs.

Mel gestures for me to read on.

'Number four. Try not to go on a date near your period as you make irrational decisions and can be a little ratty.'

'A little ratty?' Jokes Mel, taking out her phone. 'Pip, you're a nightmare when you're on your period.'

I want to put the notebook away, but Emma insists I carry on. 'Number five. Empty your handbag! I've never known someone to carry around so much stuff. Pip – I reckon it's all stuff from the past, probably related to me. This is the time to start afresh.'

Emma chuckles and points to my overflowing handbag. 'To be fair, Pip, if I delve inside your bag, I bet I find something from the past.' Before I can say anything, she's slipped her hand inside and brings out the football newsletter from five years ago. Dan's beaming face is on the front page.

'Carry on.' Mel taps me on the shoulder and gestures for Emma to put the newsletter back in my handbag.

'Number six. Try not to get drunk and let him hear you sing one of your favourite pop hits from the eighties on your first date. I know you like eighties music and I know you think you can sing, but please think about your date. Although, I will say this, the man who falls in love with you will find a way to put up with this.'

Mel looks up from texting. 'I'm loving Dan's feedback.'

'Number seven. Throw away your tracksuit bottoms. Start wearing dresses again. You look amazing in dresses.'

Throwing her arms up in the air, Emma stares up at the star-studded night sky. 'Thank you, Dan, wherever you are. I've been telling her this for years.'

'But, I like my tracksuit bottoms,' I moan, grimacing at the thought of wearing a dress.

Mel gives my arm a playful swipe. 'What's the next one?'

My eyes widen. 'Number eight. Start a business which involves your wonderful cakes. You need to do this, Pip. Follow your baking dreams.'

'Dan's talking sense,' Mel says, with a knowing look.

'Number nine. Take Libby and Billy to a kids' football club. It will get you out of the house and talking to other people. We both know you will have lived the life of a hermit until now. Also, Libby needs to do something with her amazing talent.'

We all go silent at the subject of Libby and football.

Mel removes her leopard skin ballet pump and removes a tiny stone. 'When Libby and I went out for ice creams a few months ago she refused to talk about football.'

Emma nods. 'I still can't believe she gave it up.'

My chest tightens as I recall the football-mad version of Libby. From the moment she could walk Libby insisted on kicking a football. As a toddler all she did was run about the garden with Dan and her beloved football. Her skills at such a young age were astonishing. It was like seeing magic at work when Libby got behind a ball. By the time she started school she was spending all her spare time outside kicking balls into Dan's football nets. Boys in the playground bribed her with stickers to join their team. Libby was so talented at five years of age there was talk of future football academies and Dan's *Facebook* video of her doing kick ups nearly went viral.

When Dan died, Libby put away her ball, threw her boots in the bin, and declared she'd never play again. Wiping my eye with my sweater sleeve, I have a good sniff. 'Wish I was a better mummy to Libby.'

'What?' Mel and Emma chorus in unison.

'A good mummy would have found a way of getting her to go back to football.'

Emma places her arm on my shoulder. 'You're a brilliant mummy. Football reminds Libby of Dan. Remember, she's only nine and has been through something traumatic. When she's older, she might go back to it.'

Mel nudges me to read the next point. I have to read it silently a couple of times before saying it. 'Number Ten. Find the real Pippa again. After years of raising kids and caring for a sick husband, the real Pippa got lost along the way. Go find her.'

Throwing her arms around me Mel places a sloppy wet kiss on my cheek. 'That is the best piece of advice, Pip.'

'Oh, he's being silly, I don't need to find the real Pippa,' I say, letting out a nervous laugh.

Emma wraps her arms around Mel and me. 'You need to have some fun again.'

I shake them off. 'Right, let's move onto his instructions for falling in love.'

Letting out a groan I read out Dan's first instruction. 'Don't go online to find a date. Find someone the old-fashioned way. Become friends first, have a laugh together, and then start a relationship.'

Emma takes out her lip gloss. 'I disagree, Dan. Slim dating pickings on the local front and no one has time anymore for the old-fashioned thing.'

I continue. 'Our kids mean the world to you, Pip, so the

person you fall in love with has to like our kids and at the same time be prepared for excessive noise, tantrums, mess, and heavy sarcasm from Daisy. Our kids are a handful. Make sure your date spends time with the kids and if they can get Daisy on their side, you know you're onto something.' With a disapproving face at what Dan has written, I snap, 'I still don't think they're a handful!'

Okay, Daisy's hormonal most of the time, Libby's grumpy, and Billy can't stop kicking his football through glass windows, but they're not a handful. Wifi and regular batches of my home-made fairy cakes work a treat with them all.

Mel laughs. 'Pip, why do you think Emma and I have never settled down and had kids?'

Emma drapes her arm over my shoulders. 'We love your kids, but they are wild. Sometimes I feel like bringing my ear plugs when I pop round. Dan has a point; you do need a man who is ready for all that and one who accepts your kids are a big part of your life.'

I frown at both of my friends and go on. 'Ask to hold your date's hand. The person with a hand which gives you a magical tingling feeling is the one for you.'

Emma pulls a face. 'I never get a tingling feeling when I hold Phil's hand. What about you and Jeff, Mel?'

We watch something flicker across Mel's dark eyes. 'I got a tingling feeling with Jeff, but it wasn't when I held his hand.'

As Emma shrieks with laughter, I think back to holding Dan's hand. It always sent a train of tingles up my arm. He would always reach out to take my hand in the supermarket or on the high street, making Daisy cringe with embarrassment.

Mel gestures for me to carry on.

'Watch for the invisible thread starting to form between you and your date. This is the only way I can describe how it was when I first met you. It was like we were joined by this invisible thread, which kept pulling us towards each other. Follow the thread, Pip.' I wipe away a tear which has broken free and started to make its way down my cheek.

Emma curls her hand around the street light and swings round. 'With Phil, there is an invisible thread, it pulls me towards his wallet.'

Mel hangs off the iron railing. 'With Jeff, there was an invisible thread and it led me to the plane toilet.'

Emma turns to Mel. 'What are you going to do about him and work then?'

Mel shrugs. 'We're having some time apart. I need to sort out my head and find another job. Although I can't see anyone taking on a disgraced flight attendant.' She sighs. 'My life is a wreck. I joke about Jeff and the toilet but one moment of passion has ruined my career. It was going so well in the skies for me.'

Emma and I glance at each other. We decide to keep our thoughts on Mel's career to ourselves. She's obviously forgotten about the warnings she got for forgetting her emergency procedures before a flight, "accidentally" spilling drinks over rude customers, and arguing with other flight attendants.

I return to reading Dan's next point.

'Don't get back with your weird ex, Anthony.'

Anthony's face materialises in my mind. As childhood sweethearts, Anthony and I spent all our spare time together, scaring our parents witless with talk of marriage at fourteen, and by fifteen naming our future children. Luckily, I came to my senses a few years later.

Emma casts me a look of approval. 'As I said when we first read these instructions, don't go anywhere near Anthony.'

'Haven't seen Anthony for years,' I say, dismissing that thought.

Mel peers over and reads the next instruction. 'Get to know the person who moves mountains and make him a part of your life.

'I don't think Phil has moved any mountains.' Emma fiddles

LUCY MITCHELL

with one of her blonde curls. 'He did get me a gym membership discount though. It wasn't a huge discount. Maybe that's why our relationship went wrong?'

'I think your love of dating sites and other men has had a lot to do with it,' chuckles Mel.

Checking my watch causes me to start walking, dragging my two friends. 'Come on, I should have been home by now. Mum will be freaking out.'

Emma yanks me back. 'Remind us, how did Dan recommend Mikey Stenton?'

I flick to the back of the notebook. 'On the last page he talks about how hard it is for him to do this. I should consider Mikey Stenton from football. Apparently, *he's not the bloke everyone thinks he is. There's more to Mikey Stenton than photos of half-naked women on Instagram, the football club rumours about how many women he's bedded, and the party mad lifestyle,* etc. I have to get past all that and discover the real Mikey.'

Mel places her arm around my shoulders and looks up at the night sky. 'That's a big ask, Dan.'

Emma grins and waggles her manicured finger at me. 'Hang on, Pip, when Dan was alive, you rarely listened to him.'

Standing taller, I give them both a proud little nod. 'Yes, my personal motto was: do the exact opposite of what my other half says.'

Mel nods. 'Remember when he told you not to turn half of the garden into a giant vegetable patch and take down his football net?'

We all giggle like naughty children.

'He was right about me getting impatient with waiting for stuff to grow,' I say. 'After a few weeks, I hated that bloody vegetable patch.'

Mel continues, 'My favourite was when you bought that old, rusty blue car. The one Dan told you not to buy because he said it wouldn't last five minutes. Two days later Emma and I drove past

26

you and Dan on the hard shoulder. That old car had smoke billowing out of the bonnet. His face was a picture.'

Waving the red notebook at the sky, I say, 'Sorry, Dan, I'm still going to do the exact opposite of what you say!'

Emma throws her blonde hair back and shouts, 'There'll be no hairy ballerina for our Pip, Dan!'

'Definitely not!'

CHAPTER 3

PIPPA

*W*e reach my tired old semi-detached house, with its overgrown hedge and squeaky gate. Under the glare of the porch light, I search for my keys inside my handbag of chaos.

Before I can locate them, my blue front door is yanked open. My mother stands before us, hands firmly placed on her sensible corduroy skirt hips, and a facial expression which screams, *psycho.*

'Your eldest daughter has gone out without my permission!' My mother rubs her creased forehead and whispers something about raising feral grandchildren.

My eyes are drawn to the bulging green vein in my mother's neck. In a flash I'm back to being the naughty little girl who's gone against her mother's wishes and eaten mud pies in the garden again.

Emma shifts her weight from stiletto to stiletto and Mel taps out a text on her phone.

Trooping inside, we make our way to what used to be a wooden coat stand but now resembles a mountain of coats, scarfs, bags, denim jackets, and dog leads. 'Just throw your things over the top,' I advise, 'as you know, the hooks are long gone.'

Emma runs her hand over my Laura Ashley duck-egg leaf wallpaper. 'Still can't believe we managed to put this up last year. It looks so good. Do you remember how pissed we got while decorating?'

My mother slams the door behind us in a bid to get our attention.

'We were all watching TV, apart from Daisy. Libby told me her sister was upstairs doing her homework. When I went to check on her, the window was open and, you won't believe this …' My mother doesn't stop to take a breath. Her chestnut eyes flash with anger. 'An emergency fire ladder was in place.'

Groaning, I rest the side of my head against my beautiful wallpaper, which Dan would never have agreed to. The cost of the wallpaper made my eyes water, but I find pretty coloured paper soothes my flustered mind.

'Pippa,' barks my mother, 'Did you know about the fire ladder?'

A memory of Dan races into my mind. He's stood by the kitchen holding the ladder aloft and lecturing us all on the family order down it in the event of a fire. 'The fire ladder is something Dan was using for an emergency. It's been in the cupboard under the stairs for ages.'

My mother's bushy grey eyebrows climb so high up her forehead they greet her grey hairline. 'You left an emergency ladder lying around, in an unlocked cupboard … with a *teenager* loose inside the house?'

Fiddling with my hair bun, I think aloud, 'Should have known something was wrong when Daisy texted me to say she was doing her homework.'

Emma gasps. 'You believed Daisy when she said she was doing her homework? Even I know Daisy never does her homework. Pip, did those cocktails go to your head?'

29

I'm about to answer when a noise from upstairs catches my attention. At the top, I can see Libby sat in a huff, with a grumpy face, and her little chin resting on her knees. A giant pink hair bow is sat precariously on the side of her head amongst her tangled mass of shoulder-length blonde hair. Maria the bulldog is beside her, wearing a sparkly silver wig and what looks like pieces of cut-up socks for paw warmers. 'It's late. You should be in bed, Libs.'

'Maria won't dance with me,' moans Libby, yanking out her hair bow and chucking it downstairs.

'She's an old dog, dancing is not Maria's thing.'

Maria lets out a sigh and trots downstairs.

'Bed!' I give Libby a wink and remove the wig from Maria. I try to take off the paw warmers but Maria growls and trots away.

My mother bustles past me into my brand-new Somerton duck-egg blue kitchen. It was only fitted a few weeks ago and still smells of fresh paint. The sight of the calming blue-green hue of the timber-style cupboards makes family dramas a little easier to work through.

Standing at my shiny sink, my mother crosses her arms. 'At sixteen, you and your sister were not escaping out of your bedroom window via a fire ladder.'

Mel perches on a stool and admires my kitchen. 'Pip was sneaking out, Barbara, but not via a fire ladder.'

The steel-cold look my mother casts at Mel makes me stifle a giggle.

Emma struts confidently in her black stiletto boots across my tiled kitchen floor and comes to a shuddering halt. She stares with an open mouth at my new cupboards and walls. 'Bloody hell, Pip, everything in this house is …'

'Duck-egg blue,' I say, with a dreamy smile.

Daisy's face appears in my mind and causes me to grimace. 'Where is my daughter?'

'Let's all calm down,' says Emma, 'Daisy's a normal teenager. We were all like her at sixteen. She'll be home soon.'

Mel jumps off the stool and heads towards the tray of fairy cakes I made earlier. 'Can I have one of these, Pip?'

'Only one,' I say, with a smile. 'They're going to be turned into pink flamingos tomorrow.' I grab my sketch for the fairy cake icing artwork, which is pinned to the front of the fridge.

'Pip, you're so talented at making fairy cakes,' coos Mel, grabbing the sketch and showing Emma.

Pacing up and down, my mother starts to think aloud. 'I read all sorts in the *Daily Mail* about young girls and strange men from the internet. I just hope Daisy isn't with one of them.'

Emma sends me a big smile over the top of my mother's head. 'Pip, have you told your mum your news?'

'What news?' My mother spins round on the heel of her sensible shoe.

I mouth the word '*No!*' to Emma.

Excitement floods through Emma; her sparkly blue eyes start to dance. 'Barbara, Pip's going to join some dating websites.'

My mother freezes. 'Is this a joke?' Pulling out a tissue from the sleeve of her knitted jumper, she dabs her forehead. 'Pippa, you need to focus on raising your feral children. Dating should be the last thing on your mind.'

'I could do with a bit of adult company,' I murmur, staring down at the tiled flooring.

We all hear a snort from my mother. 'Rubbish. Your children should provide you with all the company you need. Did you catch me dating when your father decided to run off with Denise?'

She has a point. When Helen and I were kids, and Dad walked out, she made sure we still lived in an immaculate house, faintly smelling of bleach, ate nutritional meals, and practiced our piano scales every night.

'Anyway, what would Dan think about you going on a dating website?'

Emma wiggles her hand like a school girl to the teacher. 'He encouraged her, Barbara.'

I flinch as the stainless-steel kitchen light flickers overhead. A shadowy dark expression glides across my mother's face. 'What?'

Reluctantly, I hand my mother the red notebook. Mel gives my arm a reassuring squeeze as my mother collapses into a chair at the kitchen table and flicks through the pages.

'Dan wrote you this?'

Emma plonks herself down opposite, while I edge towards the table.

Fishing another tissue from her sleeve, my mother wipes her glazed brow. 'Oh God, he's telling you not to listen to me. Pippa, you need your mother at this vulnerable time. Please ignore him.'

Sometimes my mother's reaction to things gets too much. I race over to my colourful baking equipment, which cost me a small fortune in Lakeland. The sight of my azure-blue Kenwood mixer makes me feel calm instantly.

When God handed out gifts, he kindly gave me the ability to make pretty fairy cakes.

I discovered my gift after my father ran off with Denise, my mother's badminton partner. While my mother set fire to all my father's possessions and all her badminton gear in the garden and Helen sobbed from the window, I cheered everyone up with a batch of fancy cakes. The little daisy flowers I crafted and stuck on top put a smile on my mother's face and dried up Helen's tears. At school, art and home economics were the only subjects I enjoyed, and I always dreamed of working in a cake shop. This wasn't my mother's favourite subject as she'd spent my childhood telling the neighbours I was going to study law.

My cakes actually taste great and cure all sorts of ailments: anger directed at my philandering father, broken hearts (mainly Daisy's), Justin Bieber concert tickets selling out, lost football matches, dire MRI scan results, the side-effects of chemo, and grief. They also sell out at Macmillan Coffee Mornings, school fayres, and car boot sales.

Baking is my meditation. When I'm surrounded by cake mixture and piping bags, I escape the chaos of family life and the crater-sized hole in our lives that Dan left, and go into my own little world.

Emma is busy pulling silly faces at my mother and Mel is shaking her head with worry.

After a long silence, my mother looks up. 'Dan was sick when he wrote this. Do you think he was in the right frame of mind?'

The sinking sensation from the pub takes hold of me. *Dan wasn't thinking straight when he wrote it.*

Returning to read Dan's notebook, my mother's eyes widen with horror. 'He's recommending you date someone.'

Mel takes out her phone, logs onto *Facebook*, and flashes the photo of Mikey's bare bum on a beach. 'That's the cheeky fella Dan's recommending, Barbara.'

A loud knock at the front door interrupts my mother as she screams at the sight of Mikey's backside.

My stomach tightens as I lock Maria in the living room and walk into the hall, quickly followed by Emma, Mel, and my mother.

The sight on the doorstep makes us all gasp. Daisy, my teenage daughter, is slumped against a dishevelled ballerina, Mikey Stenton.

'Daisy!' I yell, reaching out to help her inside. Daisy's head lolls around on her shoulders like one of Billy's footballs. She lets out a slurry giggle. 'Hello, Mummy.'

'Oh God,' mutters my mother. 'The *Daily Mail* was right. Daisy is with a strange man from the internet.'

'Calm down, Barbara,' soothes Mel. 'We know this strange man.'

'Pippa … umm …' mumbles Mikey, scratching his thick mop of dark brown hair and looking uncomfortable.

Anger bubbles up inside of me. 'She's only sixteen, Mikey, you of all people should know this!'

Mikey Stenton used to give Dan a lift to football training and they would drop Daisy off at Girl Guides en route.

'How can you let a sixteen-year-old girl get drunk like this?'

He rubs his stubble clad chin. 'Look – hang on a minute. She's not my daughter. I thought you knew she was in the pub?'

The memory of the girl with the long black hair in the pub rushes back to me. I should have gone to investigate and not been fooled by her text about homework or distracted back into our dating conversation.

My heart pounds against my ribcage. 'I've a good mind to call the police about this.'

Mikey stares at me. 'Eh? She turned up drunk. I was on Smithy's stag do. I left the party to make sure she got home safely.'

'Rubbish!' I snap, recalling the social events where all the women would gossip about Mikey's colourful love life, his irresponsible behaviour, and the rumours of wild partying.

Before he can say anything else, I slam the door in his face and yell with frustration. Dan made a serious error when he suggested I date him. Why would I consider dating such an irresponsible idiot, dressed like a ballet dancer?

Daisy leans her head against the duck-egg blue wallpaper. Black mascara tramlines race down her face and bright pink lipstick is smeared over her lips. 'It wasn't his fault. I had a drink in my room before I went out.'

'*What?*' We all shout in unison.

'You heard!' Daisy sniggers, falling against Emma.

I turn to Daisy. 'Where did you get the alcohol from?'

She chuckles. 'I drank the wine Aunty Emma brought you back from Marbs.'

Emma fidgets behind us. 'That wine was for your mother, Daisy, not you!'

'And you climbed down that emergency ladder after drinking all that wine?' I shout as blood rushes past my ears and heat radiates out from my cheeks. 'You could have killed yourself!'

Daisy nods, pointing to the closed front door. 'After leaving the Nag's we went to the new wine bar but they wouldn't serve me. Mikey overheard and brought me home.'

My mother is forced to steady herself and grips onto the coat stand. 'Mikey? You mean *that* man is who Dan suggested? The one with the bare ...'

'Bottom, Barbara,' pipes up Mel.

It's the voice coming through the letter box which makes us all jump. 'I think you've got me all wrong, Pippa. An apology from you would be appreciated.'

I yank open the door to see Mikey shifting his six-foot two weight awkwardly from one ballet shoe to the other and fumbling with his pink tutu.

He lifts his head and grins. Two boyish dimples appear either side of his mouth and something flickers across his warm brown eyes. I'm drawn to his pink ballerina costume. 'You look ridiculous. You do know that – don't you?'

Daisy lets out a moan. 'Mum, just say you're sorry.'

Mikey's eyebrows arch with expectation.

'I'm sorry,' I mumble.

To my annoyance, Mikey gives me a wink, flicks his hips, and struts off down the garden path. I shut the door for a second time, with a strange sensation in my chest.

As we help Daisy into the kitchen, my mother leans over. 'I think tonight proves that you need to concentrate on your children, Pippa.'

Emma is stood by the sink and has already poured herself a glass of wine. She raises it. 'Well played, Pip.'

After seating Daisy down at the table, my mother turns to me.

'Stay away from the strange man in the tutu and stop this madness about dating, Pippa.'

I chew on my thumb nail as my mother paces up and down the kitchen.

'What you need to do, Pippa, is take the kids on holiday somewhere,' my mother advises. 'Bond with them again. I guarantee, you won't think about dating once you're home.'

Maybe my mother has a point?

CHAPTER 4

PIPPA

A whistling sound quickly followed by a fierce rattle of the caravan window distracts me from staring at my wordsearch puzzle.

The caravan lurches forward, making me grip onto the sofa. Our little three-bed, deluxe caravan, *with decking*, is being bullied by the wind and rain. Their torment is causing it to move and groan.

My kids are not being pleasant to it either. A football is being angrily kicked against one of the bedroom doors by Billy, making the cups on the draining board rattle. Daisy is moaning out loud from her bedroom, and Libby is in the bathroom, shouting, '*I hate football!*' as she repeatedly turns the taps on and off.

The page from my book of wordsearch puzzles flaps in the draft from the crack in the window. I lost interest in looking for the word *harmonious* ages ago.

I seem to be the only person who likes our tiny caravan, although I will admit there are size issues with it. Living with three older children in a caravan can be likened to vegetables being squashed together inside a tin.

The walls are lined with cheap wood panelling. An old threadbare couch resides in the living room area and the cooker is an 80s relic. Air does not circulate well in the caravan. Due to the terrible weather outside we dare not open any windows, so the fried aroma of Saturday night's fish and chips meal still hangs lifelessly above our heads.

I keep reminding myself I did get carried away with the advert in the local newsagent window titled, *caravan with decking – available to rent.* For some unexplainable reason the words *with decking* conjured up something of luxury.

Daisy stomps into the living area and falls onto the sofa. She stares miserably at her phone. 'Caravan holidays are hell.' Flicking her long black hair out of her face she reveals two piercing green eyes. For a fleeting second, I can see Dan staring back at me.

A stray tear escapes and trickles down my cheek. Quickly, I wipe it away with the corner of my cardigan sleeve. Dan is like an open wound inside me, which I regularly pick at with my mind.

'Why are you making us suffer, Mum?'

I close my puzzle book. 'We managed to do some family stuff yesterday, didn't we?'

Daisy lets out a snort. 'You and Billy nearly drowned in the sea.'

The memory of grabbing hold of Billy's cold, wet body in bone-chilling sea water makes me shiver.

For most of yesterday I sat on the beach, priding myself for taking on my mother's advice and sorting us out a relaxing family caravan holiday. I was also secretly congratulating myself for squeezing into an old bikini, which had been lurking at the back of the wardrobe. To be honest, the bikini did look like a few bits of cloth held together by string and as I pulled it on, I did wonder whether all the fairy cakes eaten over recent weeks would dampen my swimwear dream. To be fair to my old bikini it managed to hold everything in as I sat on the beach towel. There's nothing sweeter than finding a reliable old bikini.

Things started to go wrong in the afternoon when the sun crept behind a dark cloud, bathing the beach in shadows. It was at this moment Daisy came charging across the sand.

'Mum!' She raced towards my towel. 'Billy's in trouble!'

I followed her trembling hand pointing out to sea.

We flicked our heads towards the water. Billy was struggling to get on his bodyboard. The waves kept knocking him back under the water.

'Why has he gone so far out?' I yelled. 'You were supposed to be watching him.'

Daisy raised her phone at me. 'On *Snapchat*. Speaking to … Tom.' She paused and waited for my reaction.

The mention of Tom made me wince. 'You've been told not to contact him,' I growled.

Billy, trying to clamber onto his bodyboard, distracted me. Before Daisy could say anything else, I raced across the sand, my arms and legs burning. Diving into the cold frothing waves and taking a large gulp of air I powered towards Billy. Seconds before his little body slipped under the inky dark surface, I grabbed his arm and hauled him onto his bodyboard. With an ashen face and dark eyes glazed with fear, he leant his head against mine.

'Oh, Billy!' I coughed, spewing out sea water and kicking my legs.

With an angry cry, I forced the board back in the direction of the shore.

'Mummy!' Billy cried, throwing his arms around my neck.

'I've got you, little man.' I started to paddle us both back to shore.

Exhaustion hit me as I shoved Billy onto the beach and then crawled on all fours out of the water.

After coughing up a lung I pulled Billy to me. 'Are you okay?' I asked, wiping a clump of dark hair out of his face.

'Didn't think you both were going to make it,' Daisy muttered, still engrossed in her phone.

I turned to glare at my teenage daughter. Sizzling hot anger rose up inside of me. Why couldn't Daisy have put down her blasted phone down for one minute?

'Give me that phone!' I barked, rising to my feet, and letting Billy go.

I watched her eyes widen with horror. 'Mum, this isn't a nudist beach.'

'What?'

'You're naked!'

My reliable old bikini, the one held together by flimsy string, had bid me farewell while I was saving Billy.

We all trooped back to the caravan, shivering and tear stained.

I bury the memories of our day out at the beach at the back of my mind and try to focus on my breathing, as my sister swears by it.

Libby rushes in from the bathroom. 'I have red spots on my tummy!' My shoulders and neck stiffen. This is the kind of phrase that haunts parents at night, making them wake in a cold sweat.

'You have fleas!' Daisy shouts, lying down on the sofa and placing her black-legging-clad legs on my lap.

Billy skids into the lounge. 'I have spots too!' Once he has our attention, he lifts up his red football shirt to show us his little chest. My eyes are drawn to a complex pattern of angry red spots.

'OMG – we are in a flea-infested caravan.' Daisy covers her gaping mouth with her hand.

I hug my wordsearch book. Perhaps dating again is a mistake? This holiday has so far been a sign my mother is right. I need to concentrate more on the children.

Half an hour later and my worst holiday fears have come true:

two of my kids have chicken pox, the woman on the radio has informed us a huge summer storm is about to batter the UK, and a dull ache in my abdomen signifies the arrival of my period.

To my surprise, Daisy volunteers to go up to the caravan site leisure complex and buy calamine lotion and emergency Tampax. I watch her leap up from the sofa, race into her cabin, grab a denim jacket, and fly out of the door. It's amazing how teenagers can find sudden bursts of energy.

Libby and Billy switch on the minuscule portable TV, while I sit on the sofa and think about whether I've made a silly decision about dating. Maybe I'm not ready?

Reaching for my phone, I read the text conversation my sister, Helen, and I had the night before the caravan holiday. Doubts about dating again had been plaguing me.

Me: How long does a widow wait before she starts dating again?

Helen: Don't do it!

Me: Really?

Helen: Ask yourself whether you want to put yourself through all that relationship stuff again.

Me: *Why?*

Helen: I would rather read a good book and take a hot bath, than go on a date with a man.

Me: Things not great with Rick then?

Helen: Actually, things are great. He's been working away for the last six weeks. Don't rush into anything and make the mistake I made – start a relationship with a complete idiot!

Me: You married Rick the idiot, and then had his five children.

Helen: Thx for reminding me!

How can I even consider seeing other men after fifteen years of marriage to Dan? He was amazing.

Of course, there were times when he annoyed me: the late

nights at the pub, the local team football tours and his refusal to go anywhere without his rusty bike. Mostly, there were times when he was the centre of my world and the only person who I wanted to get old and wrinkly with. Spending the rest of my life with him was going to be my fairy tale.

Dan and I were unlike so many of our married friends; we actually liked each other. Plus, we enjoyed raising our kids. Life with Dan was never dull. He brightened up our days with his huge smile, twinkling green eyes, and his love of life. There were always adventures to go on, places to see and family projects usually starting with me saying, 'No!'

I never thought Dan would die. Even when Mr Rogers told me Dan's tumour had spread to his liver and lungs, I still held firm the belief Dan would survive. Even when Mr Rogers explained to me Dan wouldn't make Christmas, I shrugged it off; Dan would somehow find a way to recover.

'Mum, my spots are itching!' Billy brings me back to earth with a jolt. Daisy still isn't back. Libby is wriggling beside me on the sofa, hot and restless.

I exhale loudly and try to crane my neck out of the caravan window. Surely Daisy must be on her way back? No sign. I slide out my phone and text her; *Where r u?*

Nothing.

I stroke Libby's messy blonde hair and refrain from asking her when she last brushed it. Billy comes over to snuggle in the crook of my arm. They both watch the grainy image on the TV screen. I try to reach Daisy telepathically.

It's hard bringing up three kids by myself. Dan made parenting easy. He was so patient and sensible. Plus, he was fun, and they all worshipped the ground he walked on. The last three years have proved to the kids I'm neither patient nor sensible. My kids are now experienced in dealing with my hormonal mood swings, rash decision-making processes, dreadful cooking, and random holiday destinations. I know what is going through their minds: God took away the wrong parent.

There's still no sign of Daisy. I need to find out where she is. Quickly, I wrap Libby and Ben in coats, and we race out into the rain towards the small complex on the caravan park.

'I don't feel very well,' moans Libby as we bury our heads into our coats to escape the stinging rain.

Agitation at Daisy makes my head start to throb. She was an angelic child up until the age of eleven; polite, charming, and approachable. Then the mood swings, sarcasm, and general dissatisfaction with life kicked in. We have all been mourning the old Daisy ever since.

We arrive at the complex with dripping wet coats and hair. The caravan park's facilities amount to a musty old convenience store, a café with dirty plastic chairs, and a small dark area filled with a collection of arcade machines.

While I'm scanning the convenience store, Billy catches sight of Daisy, leaning against one of the fruit machines. He tugs at my arm and points to her.

'Daisy!' I shriek at the entrance of the arcade, making her jolt in surprise.

She whispers something to the lad stood next to her and saunters towards us.

'I don't want you hanging around the arcades, Daisy.'

She ignores me and chooses to look back over her shoulder at the older boy, with the dark spiky hair and ripped jeans. 'He is so fit,' I hear her murmur.

Daisy's sudden interest in boys always makes my stomach plunge towards the floor. I wish she was a bit more restrained with her affections and pursuit of them. Daisy showers the boys in her class and the sixth form with tweets, *Instagram* photos, and *Snapchat* messages.

Once they show the slightest bit of interest in her, she locks herself onto them like some deadly heat seeking missile. My mother thinks it's a delayed grief reaction to losing her father.

I've had several calls from Daisy's former teacher about her obsession with a boy called Tom Ridge. According to Miss Brown, Daisy refuses to leave Tom alone and at one time during break, threatened another girl, who he had asked out on a date. Miss Brown's acidic tone left me in tears for hours afterwards. I tried to speak to Daisy about the incident. She shrugged her shoulders. 'I wish he would just kiss me and stop playing games with my mind.' Daisy, my daughter, the trainee bunny boiler.

'Have you got the lotion?' I ask, searching her empty hands.

She lets out a sigh. 'No. I was busy.' Daisy is still preoccupied with the lad engrossed with playing on the machine.

I miss being hugged. Right now, dripping wet and standing inside in a run-down caravan complex, with two sick children, a lovesick teenage daughter, and crunching period pains, I could really do with a hug. Dan gave impressive bear hugs. He used to hold me close against his broad chest, stroking my hair while telling me everything was going to be okay. I don't think I can spend the rest of my life without a hug from a man.

Out of the corner of my eye, I catch sight of a little girl running about in a pink ballerina's outfit. The image of Mikey Stenton appears in my mind. For a second, a small smile creeps onto my face. It's quickly replaced by a grimace. The memory of spending all night with a vomiting Daisy, after she'd been brought home by Mikey, is still painfully raw.

We all trudge back to the caravan in the pouring rain. I bought the lotion, some cotton wool, children's paracetamol, and a box of Tampax. The older woman behind the counter gave me a knowing smile, after glancing at my basket, at each of my three children, at the rain battering the window, and then back to me. She knew what I was about to endure inside our caravan. I think my situation made her grateful for having to spend the next four hours at the till of an empty store in a run-down caravan park.

I settle Libby and Billy under blankets on the sofa, after dousing them in lotion and doling out medicine.

Later that afternoon, I decide to bake some of my fairy cakes.

Seeing as Billy and Libby aren't themselves; I reach for my baking utensils. Daisy is lying tear-stained on the sofa. We argued again after I caught her trying to climb out of the caravan window to go see the boy from the arcade. We shouted at each other so much the caravan started to creak.

They're all tucking into chocolate-icing-topped fairy cakes; Daisy is managing a weak smile, Libby is giggling, and Billy is giving me a thumbs up. It's amazing what sort of miracles sugar can perform.

After clearing away the plates I reapply calamine lotion onto Billy and Libby. Then I open a bottle of wine and decide to put my online dating account live. The sooner I throw myself into this new world of online dating the better.

The one saving grace about the caravan was the owner's decision to get wifi, which all the kids were pleased to discover when they arrived. I dread to think what the holiday would have been like without it.

Outside the window, the storm has passed over and the rain has stopped. 'Daisy,' I call out, 'will you take a photo of me?'

Daisy appears tapping something into her phone. 'Huh?'

'Just take a photo of me, sat on the steps of the caravan.' I hand her my phone.

She goes to stand outside, while I position myself, sitting on the front steps. I use a tea towel to wipe my pink sweaty face and turn around to tell Billy and Libby to stop fighting. 'You are both supposed to be unwell.'

'Billy says I'm rubbish at football,' whines Libby. 'He says that's why I don't play it anymore.'

I glare at Billy who is picking his nose and grinning at the same time. 'Don't say that, Billy. You know why Libby won't play football.'

Daisy exhales loudly. 'Mum, I haven't got all day.'

Removing more sweat from my face, I smile at Daisy.

'Mum, don't do a forced smile.' Daisy screws up her face.

'What?' I snap.

'You have the same look on your face when I used to have my class sleepovers. All the mothers would be greeted by you at the door with that silly smile.'

I think back to the first few months after Dan had died. In an attempt to cheer my kids up, I let them invite their entire class to sleep over at our house on three consecutive weekends.

My mother was right about grief sending some people insane.

Opening my front door to hundreds of kids, all clutching pillows and teddy bears, was when reality hit me. The worst part was watching all the parents push their child into my house, give me a friendly wave, and speed off. Helen kindly offered to help out. When I'd told her that during Daisy's sleep over, at four in the morning, they were all still dancing downstairs, she told me, 'Pip, you're nuts!'

Modelling a new smile, I find myself distracted by Libby angrily kicking the football at her little brother and sending him flying across the tiny living area.

Daisy takes a few shots and hands my phone back to me. I send the kids to their cabins and quickly log on to a dating site Emma had suggested.

Writing the bio is proving to be a challenge as I've just spent the last three years grieving, making endless batches of sugary fairy cakes, painting every inch of my house duck-egg blue, and singlehandedly raising three children.

Staring at the photos Daisy has taken, I ignore the little voice in my head which questions whether an image of me looking harassed and flushed, sat on the step of a caravan with Billy and Libby fighting behind me, is best suited for a dating site.

A noise behind makes me jump. I turn around to see all three children staring over my shoulder at the laptop screen.

'What are you doing? Dad wouldn't have done what you're doing!' Daisy snaps, pointing at the app. 'He would have stayed loyal to you.'

A cloud of guilt descends upon me. 'Oh, Daisy, I was …' My voice evaporates at the sight of her horror-stricken face.

'How can you even think about going out with someone else?'

Words queue up on my tongue, but for some reason I cannot get my lips to process them.

'Mum.' Daisy is stood, clenching her hands, and stamping her foot.

Billy grins. 'Are you looking for our new daddy?'

Guilt eats away at me.

'You'll never replace Dad,' screams Daisy.

'But I wasn't doing it to replace Dad, I was doing it for …' My voice fades away.

Daisy glares. 'We don't need a new father.' She storms out of the caravan, slamming the door shut.

I place my face in my hands and listen to the inner demons, advising me to forget about finding someone else. My mother's voice echoes inside my mind: *concentrate on your kids.* It is quickly replaced by Daisy's words, *We don't need a new father.*

A small hand taps me on the shoulder. I look round to see Billy pointing at the laptop screen. 'Can our new daddy play football and be good at it?'

I slam down the laptop lid.

'Abigail in my class,' announces Libby, 'told me her mother is always looking at a dating site, even when her boyfriend's in the same room watching *Netflix*,'

Groaning, I look for something to take their little minds off Mummy finding a new daddy. I offer them more cakes.

Later, the caravan sways again with the wind as they stuff cake into their mouths. In my head, I wrestle with the idea of signing up. It's not about finding the kids a father figure, nor is it something I'm doing out of a moment of madness. This is something for me. It's about getting out, meeting people, and dare I say, having a bit of fun.

I don't want to spend the rest of my life without hugs, sloppy kisses, and adult conversation. Even though my children are old enough to hold an intelligent conversation with, I still yearn to talk to another adult about things other than FIFA sticker books, glittery unicorns, and *Snapchat* drama.

When Libby and Billy finally troop off to bed, Daisy stomps back inside the caravan, drenched to the skin, her hair plastered over her face. She takes one look me and races to her cabin.

Fishing out the red notebook, I read again what Dan had to say about Mikey Stenton. I drift back to all those football club social events where every female in the room gossiped about his colourful love life.

Shaking my head, I conclude Mikey Stenton is irresponsible, wild, and a tart! Definitely not marriage material and he is certainly not a suitable role model for my children.

What was Dan thinking when he wrote this? Chemo had affected his brain at the time of putting this masterpiece together.

There's no way I'm making the mistake my sister made by marrying an idiot. I have to say though, Rick, my brother-in-law, is nowhere near Mikey's idiocy levels.

I blame Mikey's boyish smile and mop of unruly brown hair. Looking the way he does, it's no wonder women across the globe are falling at his feet. In every photo there's some female fluttering her eyelashes at him or clamping her lips over his.

Tucking the notebook back in my handbag, I vow to show Dan and my mother I can find a nice sensible man online, who likes feral children, chaos, and fairy cakes.

I take a deep breath and mutter the words, 'Sorry, Dan, I don't need your advice.'

If he was sat beside me now, Dan would be shaking his head and muttering something about how other men have wives and girlfriends who listen to them, whereas he has a wife who does the complete opposite. A memory of him telling me to go steady with my home-made summer punch at one of our garden barbeques comes back to me. Hours later, he was holding my hair back as I heaved up my burger and summer punch.

Later, I put my online dating profile live.

CHAPTER 5

MIKEY

'Up you get,' growls a deep voice. Two tree-trunk-sized arms drag me out from underneath a table. Clutching my empty wine bottle, I attempt to stand, but soon collide with the hard floor. Through one eye I watch the remains of Smithy's white wedding cake, trays of leftover buffet food, piles of empty paper plates, an army of half-filled plastic cups, saggy balloons, and stacks of chairs pass by me. Weird – I seem to be moving backwards, but without using my rubber-like legs. Watching them drag along the floor in front of me is turning my stomach.

The harsh yellow lighting above is making my one eye blink and water at the same time. Why is only one of my eyes open?

I try to wriggle myself free but bony fingers dig deeper into my armpits, tightening their hold of me. The deep voice barks into my ear. 'Time to go home.'

'Where's the groom?' Trying to lift my head up to shout out to Smithy is proving a challenge. '*Smithy – I'm over here!*'

Letting out a loud belly laugh, the deep voice says, 'Smithy and his wedding party left hours ago.'

'But … no one told me?'

We have come to a halt. Keys are jangling and an old door is creaking. The wine bottle is yanked out of my hand. 'That's because you got pissed, had a fight, made a fool of yourself, and was left under a table.'

My dry tongue sweeps my cracked lips. It quickly locates a puffy lump on the right side. With a trembling hand I reach up and touch my right eye, the one refusing to open. A sharp burst of pain shoots across my face making me wince. If I was a betting man I would say, my right eye and lip took a knock. 'Who was I fighting with?'

'Some bloke who thought you were chatting up his girlfriend,' chuckles the deep voice. 'I have to say; you took a few nasty punches.'

A memory bobs to the surface inside my drink-filled mind. Closing my good eye, I can see the woman stood at the bar. Her red fitted dress accentuates her hourglass figure and she's shaking out her hair, sending bouncy brown curls tumbling down over her shoulders.

I remember my heart breaking into a wild gallop at the sight of the woman. For a second, it was like I'd stepped back in time.

After eight pints, countless shots, and a bottle of wine, my brain informed me the woman at the bar was the person who I'd secretly been hoping to bump into.

On approaching her, I had a drunken light bulb moment. Smithy, the groom, and some of the football lads were people she knew. Of course, she'd be at the evening wedding party. I was adamant it was her.

It is important to note here that if I'd been sober, I would have kept my distance. Talking to this person never runs smoothly for me as I always end up feeling like an idiot. She's the only woman in the world who has this effect on me.

Staggering over, with Dutch courage and a belly full of booze, I tapped the woman on the shoulder and asked whether she wanted to know what I'd been wearing underneath my pink tutu a few weeks ago. Okay, I admit this was not my best chat up line.

But it wasn't her.

What didn't help the unfolding drama was the presence of an ex-girlfriend of mine, Claire. To my dismay, she'd also been invited to Smithy's wedding and insisted on telling the woman's boyfriend to keep an eye on me, as I couldn't be trusted around women.

Claire has never recovered from our two-month relationship ending abruptly. I forgot to mention to her that I was going to California for a month, to stay with an ex-girlfriend.

In my defence, the ex-girlfriend, Sasha, who I was going to stay with, was just that. A girl I'd dated a few years ago. Sasha is dating a handsome surfer dude with bleached blond hair and a golden tan. I'm happy for Sasha and it's great we can now hang out over a beer on the beach and take the piss out of each other.

Claire got the wrong impression about our friendship when she saw my *Facebook* picture, the one with Sasha and me riding a horse together along a beach. Claire exploded into an angry rage over *Facebook* and tagged half the female population of the town into her heart-wrenching post about me being an arsehole.

All my ex-girlfriends from long ago came to support Claire online that night. Smithy said it was quite a spectacle. There were a lot of fabricated stories and some compromising photos shared, including one of a bare bottom on a moonlit beach which one girl claimed was mine. She was adamant I'd cheated on her during a boys' holiday to Thailand after seeing this photo on the lads' *WhatsApp* group chat. It was actually Smithy's backside. He'd cheated on his girlfriend, who is now his wife I might add, and didn't want to ruin his relationship so told everyone it was mine.

After an hour of replying to each comment with *that's not true*, I went to Smithy's house and drowned my sorrows.

My mind flashes up the stern face of the boyfriend at the bar. With balled fists, he had got carried away with Claire's feedback and took offence to me talking about what had been underneath my pink tutu with his beloved. Seconds before his fist connected with my face, I realised his girlfriend was not the person I thought she was.

A blast of chilly night air makes me gasp.

'Now – get out of my club.' With a snigger, the owner of the deep voice launches me high into the air.

Shit! I'm now airborne. I know God has my back. He will do his best to make sure I have a soft landing.

'Argh!'

My left cheek, the one that doesn't hurt, is the first part of me to make contact with the cold remains of a half-eaten tray of curry, left on the pavement.

Face planting the silver tray, I crash land in a glorious shower of tikka masala. A loud splat rings out in my ears before everything goes black.

'Have you got a light?' Someone with black fingerless gloves is shaking me. Lifting my head, I catch sight of a grubby, male face, framed by matted black hair. 'I need a light.'

My nostrils can't cope with the combination of tikka masala and the aroma of someone who hasn't washed for a decade.

'Gonna be sick.' I manage to bat him away seconds before my stomach empties itself.

The man grins. 'You had too much to drink?'

Ignoring my new friend, I stagger to my feet. The deserted high street tilts to one side and my legs buckle. Back down into the tikka masala and my own pool of vomit I go.

My new friend roars with laughter. 'Unlucky!'

Hauling myself to my feet I scowl, and grab hold of a lamp post.

'You do know your face is now covered in … curry and sick.' He chuckles and rubs his crotch. 'All this laughter has made me want a piss.'

Wiping stinging curry juice and sick from my face, I shuffle away down the dark street. My hands check my damp suit jacket. At this point, I'm optimistic that after a wedding, more alcohol than my liver can cope with, a poor attempt at breakdancing, a fight, a few hours sleeping under a buffet table, being thrown out of the club, blacking out on a street pavement and being sick, all my valuables are still with me.

'Shit!'

My inside suit pocket where my wallet lives is empty. Turning back, I blink my good eye several times to see if I can spot the man who asked me for a light. He might have seen my wallet and be proudly waving it, with a huge grin over his grubby face.

A sinking feeling turns my stomach. In the distance a figure is sprinting away up the street. Perhaps the urge for a piss got too much for him or he's off to spend the contents of my wallet?

A wave of relief sweeps over my body as my hand finds my phone deep inside my other pocket. It starts to vibrate. There was no signal in the wedding venue, so my phone is now making up for lost time.

Taking it out, I see my brother, Stan, has been trying to get hold of me. A multitude of text messages greet my good eye. Under the glare of a street lamp, I wait for the words from Stan's text to stop jumping around.

It was Mum's birthday on Thursday and once again there was no sign of you, no card, no gift, and no telephone call.

Leaning against a fence, I run my hands through my sticky hair and instantly regret doing that. My fingers disturb a lump of curried chicken buried deep. I watch it fall onto my jacket shoulder. Flicking it off, I mumble, 'Sorry, Mum,' at my phone screen. Is 3.09 a.m. a good time to apologise?

I don't know why he's pestering me. Knowing Stan, he probably gave Mum a wonderful birthday gift, one she'll still be talking about at Christmas. My heroic brother would have also spent his evening sorting out her garden and made her one of his fruit cakes.

I stopped competing with Stan a long time ago.

There are more texts. Smithy has sent the football lads'

WhatsApp group a photo of me trying to stand on my head on the dance floor. *Mikey was on top form at my wedding.* Wisps of nausea curl up my throat as I recall my attempts at break dancing.

The next photo makes me close down *WhatsApp.* I don't want to see a picture of me stood among the other football lads and their wives and girlfriends. Everyone apart from me is happily married or in a decent relationship. Even Smithy has deserted me.

A peal of laughter rings out across the road. I watch a couple, with arms wrapped tightly around each other, walk along the pavement. She's barefoot and swinging her gold shoes. He's pulling her closer. They must have left a club or a bar.

My chest aches at the sight of their happy faces. Despite popular female opinion on *Facebook*, I do want what that couple have found, quite badly actually.

The thought of returning to my empty flat is unappealing. On my phone, Sophie, the woman who I swore not to see again, sent me a photo at 1.17 a.m. It's making me consider one last trip to her flat.

By the time I reach the seventh floor of the tower block, my head is thumping. I can already hear little Zack wailing.

Sophie finally answers when my hand gets sore from knocking. Through my one eye I take in her smudged make-up, frizzy brown hair, black leather miniskirt, high heels, and purple top. Zack is still crying from his room.

Screwing up her pale face at the sight (and smell of me) she screeches. 'Ugh – you stink!'

'You said I could come round,' I mumble, gripping onto the doorframe.

She opens the door wider and I fall inside.

Lying on her kitchen floor, in between a chocolate wrapper and a discarded Coke bottle, I wait for her to go and sort Zack out. With my hands over my face, I pray she quietens him down soon.

Sophie is still standing over me. Her eyes have glazed over, and I notice she's swaying.

Hauling myself to my feet, I point to Zack's door. 'He's crying, Sophie.'

She shrugs, opens her pink lips, and takes out a long string of pink gum. 'He'll shut up in a bit.' After twirling it around her manicured finger, she posts it into an empty can of cider and struts towards me. 'Wash your face and then we can have some fun. I'll be in bed … waiting.'

I watch her leave the kitchen and go into her bedroom.

The little boy is now screaming. I can't let this go on. 'Sophie, Zack needs you!'

No answer.

'Sophie!'

She's lying spread eagled on the bed, snoring into a pillow. A half-filled bottle of vodka is resting against her head.

Zack's howls tug at my heart. Opening the bedroom door, I stagger in, and go over to his cot. 'Hey, little man,' I say, stroking his damp cheek.

The smell of poo is sobering and strong. After switching on the light, I look down to see a huge wet patch on his mattress and a crusty bottle of old milk.

'For God's sake, Sophie,' I mumble, staring at the mess.

'Sophie!' I call out. 'Zack needs changing!'

No answer. I can't leave him in this state. Poor kid.

Lifting Zack into my arms I manage to lie him down on the plastic mat. He instantly stops crying and giggles at me. Zack is a good kid, with a mass of cherub curls and bright blue eyes. He doesn't deserve a mother like Sophie.

'How long has she left you like this?'

Easing him out of his jumpsuit fills the room with the powerful stench of baby poo.

Oh God, it's seeping out of his white nappy! *Sophie!*

Still no answer.

Vomit rushes into my mouth. 'Excuse me, Zack,' I mutter, turning to grab hold of a bin. He laughs as I heave my guts up.

'Sorry, little man,' I gasp, wiping my mouth with the sleeve of my suit jacket. 'Ouch.' I'd forgotten my swollen lip is now a no-go area.

Zack kicks his legs and chuckles as I rummage around the junk for wipes, clean nappies, and a new baby suit. 'Where's she put the wipes, Zack?'

In the short time I've known little Zack I've learnt (the hard way) that a dry wipe followed by a wet wipe has more success with a messy nappy, than straight in with a wet wipe.

He's grinning at me as I locate a clean nappy. I've also learnt that Zack has a sick sense of humour. He's grinning at me. This means … oh God, he's just weed in my face!

'Cheers, little man,' I say, wiping my face and groaning at the prospect of having to search for another clean nappy.

Once I've crawled on my hands and knees into the kitchen, stashed the nappy of hell into the overflowing bin, I clean Zack up. Sorting out his cot proves tricky. I'm not too steady on my feet so all I can do is turn his mattress over.

With his fresh jumpsuit on I lie Zack back down into his cot. He gazes up at me and I wonder what is going through his eight-month-old head. At a guess, it's probably: *who is this drunken idiot who keeps changing my nappy in the early hours?* Drunken idiot – yes that's right.

My good eye scans the cot, nestled among boxes of Sophie's junk, clothes strewn everywhere, and not a teddy bear in sight. What am I doing here? Is this what my life has amounted to? Caring for someone's kid because she can't be arsed to be a parent?

If truth be told, I only come around here when I'm drunk because my loneliness has gotten too much. I just want to feel someone next to me.

The trouble with Sophie and me is that once she lies with me, we have sex and afterwards I always feel sick and want to get away from her as fast as possible. There are so many things wrong with our relationship and I'm not sure I have the time or the energy to put them right.

After filling a plastic beaker with water and removing the wastepaper basket, I let Zack have a drink. When he's settled, I decide it's time to give him some important life advice. 'Zack,' I mumble, rubbing my throbbing forehead. He laughs and points his chubby finger at me. 'Now, listen carefully to what I have to say. When you're older don't be an idiot like me – okay?'

When I stagger into Sophie's bedroom, she's awake and removing her black, lacy bra. 'You got any cash on you? Zack needs nappies.'

Tripping over a pile of her shoes I face plant the bed. My world goes black.

CHAPTER 6

MIKEY

*M*y hangover is at a critical stage. I'm standing in the frozen meat aisle of the supermarket. The pain radiating out from my temples is making me hunch over my trolley.

After passing out on Sophie's bed, I woke to find her rummaging through my suit pockets looking for my wallet. After informing her it was missing, we argued over Zack. I made the mistake of asking why Zack's father can't buy his own son nappies and Sophie went berserk. Apparently, Gary, his father, does enough. As I'm always giving Sophie money for baby milk, clothes, and nappies, I'm not exactly sure what Gary's *enough* means.

It wasn't the first time Sophie had left Zack in a state. When I first met her on *Tinder* a few months ago, she failed to tell me about Zack. The second time I went around to her flat, he started crying from his room as she was climbing on top of me. She said he's a needy child and it is best to ignore him. I couldn't let him cry. We argued about why she wasn't hurrying to sort out her son and why she hadn't told me about Zack. I ended up calming him down.

There are a number of things guaranteed when I visit Sophie: drunken sex, demands for money, and changing her son's dirty nappies. Sometimes I wonder what would happen to little Zack if I didn't show up.

After I got back to my flat from Sophie's, I discovered my door keys had also vanished during my wedding antics. After breaking in, I bathed my swollen right eye, put an ice pack on it, cursed my empty food cupboards, remembered my wallet was missing in action, cancelled all my bank cards, and found some cash in my bedside jar before heading to the supermarket.

Lurching out of the frozen food aisle, my wet tongue tends to my sore lip. I'm lucky to have my teeth. Lifting my head, I spot her. My body and trolley come to a sudden stop, causing the lady behind to barge into the back of me, removing all the skin from the backs of my ankles. I yelp with pain and stare at Dan's wife Pippa and their three kids who are at the far end.

They meant so much to him. He would always leave football practice on time and never hit the bars like we used to. The ear-to-ear smile on his face told everyone he wanted to be at home with his gorgeous wife and amazing kids.

I'm rooted to the spot. My body has turned to stone. Pippa is busy arguing with Daisy, who I rescued from Smithy's stag party a few weeks ago.

Daisy's wide green eyes looked familiar when she'd entered the pub with her friend. I watched her run to loop her arms around Jason's neck. There was something about the young woman's face which I couldn't ignore. Then I remembered. Those same green eyes would stare at me from the back of my car when I used to give Dan a lift to football training. We would drop Daisy off at Girl Guides and Dan would try to embarrass her as she got out of the car by doing some exaggerated emotional farewell.

'Does Jason know how old she is?' I asked Smithy. Smithy

shrugged. Daisy looked a lot older with dark smoky eye make-up, wild black hair, and a tiny miniskirt.

While Simon in the pub sorted out our drinks order and took the piss out of our outfits, I worked out the year Dan got diagnosed: it was the year I went to Magaluf. With a beer-saturated memory, I ascertained Dan had attended football training during his treatment. We used to discuss it in the car, while Daisy sat in the back. Daisy was not as old as she was making out.

'Just leave Jason to it.' Smithy handed out pints of Doom Bar.

I couldn't leave Jason to it. Jason is a bigger tart than me and often makes important life decisions based on sensations comings from his boxer shorts. 'I don't think we should be leaving anything to Jason.'

It was then I'd clocked Pippa sat at the back with her friends. As she was sat in the pub, I assumed she'd turned into the world's most easy-going mother and was happy for Daisy to join a stag party full of men dressed up as ballerinas.

When Daisy left the pub, with her arm draped across Jason's shoulders, she started slurring her words and I knew something was wrong.

In the wine bar I managed to release her from a drunken Jason which wasn't too hard. I simply put Jason's arm around another admirer and grabbed Daisy's hand. She complained all the way back to Pippa's house, but I ignored her. If Daisy had been my teenage daughter, I wouldn't want to see her in a drunken, or even worse state hanging off Jason's arm.

My eyes settle on Pippa's long brown hair, piled up in a messy bun. Her pale elfin face looks washed out and harassed. The children are stood around her like a small, angry crowd. I can hear them voicing their complaints about a lack of snacks in the house and something about a horrible holiday in a caravan. Pippa's voice drifts down the aisle, shrill and exasperated.

As the volume of their shouts increases, shoppers steer

trollies clear of them, my body freezes. In my sober state, whenever I see Pippa, I go a bit strange. Things are different after I've had a few drinks.

Pippa's boy kicks the trolley and she wearily wipes her brow. Her sharp toned response to the lad for the kick makes me smile.

Quick on the heels of that thought is the one that never fails to invade my head every time I see her: Dan's notebook. It arrived in the post a few days before he died. I read the first page and then buried it at the back of my wardrobe.

Thoughts about Pippa plague me with a perpetual awkwardness. Does she know her husband wrote to me before he died?

I often wonder whether Dan told her what he was doing, writing to one of his friends at his football club, giving him instructions on how to make Pippa fall in love with him.

Pippa shouts at Daisy, telling the sulking teenager to stop wearing so much make-up.

I was shocked by the notebook. Dan mentioned the look I used to give Pippa when I used to collect him for practice. According to Dan, it was an unforgettable stare.

How could I miss Pippa when she looked so sexy with her messy hair and those skin tight yoga leggings? I would be drooling by the time we left.

It was great of Dan to think of me. Even though she's the person I secretly think about a lot, Pippa would never date someone like me. She wouldn't lower her high standards. Pippa Browning is at the top of the Premier League. I, on the other hand, am struggling to get out of division three.

Maybe the cancer treatment made Danny Boy delirious? He was very sick. All sorts of stuff must go through your mind while being in a hospice, pumped with toxic drugs. I still remember reading the first part where he told me to take control of my life and stop being an idiot. At the bottom of the page, he'd told me I could learn a lot from my brother.

Pippa briefly turns around. Her eyes settle on something behind me. For a second, I ignore her odd-looking baggy grey trousers and blue shapeless T-shirt and stare at her face. I'm instantly transported back in time to the club's Christmas dinners. The team and their guests used to hush as Danny Boy walked in with Pippa on his arm, owning an amazing hourglass figure, long flowing brown locks, and exquisite porcelain-like skin.

She always turned heads. They all used to take the piss out of him, about how he managed to marry someone as beautiful as her. As I gaze up the aisle, a pang of sadness is set off inside of me at the sight of her looking tired, frumpy, and agitated.

Her little lad is kicking his football along the aisle and her youngest daughter is stood watching him. Dan would be proud of his children. They are good kids.

As I'm nearly forty and looking after myself is becoming a constant struggle, the chances of me becoming a father are quickly diminishing.

Nope, I can't talk to Pippa.

If she'd been at yesterday's wedding things would have been different. After all that booze I was Mr Confident with the woman at the bar who, in my head, was Pippa. My stomach muscles tighten at the thought of how she would have reacted to me asking her whether she wanted to know what was under my pink tutu on Smithy's stag do.

If I'm honest, in the cold light of day, I don't think she would have wanted to talk to me, anyway. The stag do proved to her what a drunken idiot I am. Dan got me all wrong.

Swinging the trolley around purposefully, I make a sharp U-turn, nearly taking out a couple of pensioners. Relief sweeps over me. I've just saved myself from a potentially awkward moment.

Seeing Pippa always makes me think of Danny Boy. He was such a good bloke. Always had time for the lads at the football club and he was someone you could rely on. Bloody good fun as well, with his infectious laugh, terrible jokes, and love of dares. We all questioned his football skills, which were a bit of a standing joke. Dan didn't care. He loved football. Just being on the pitch made him happy.

Dan was like an older brother to all the football lads; rescuing them from career-damaging fights on football tours, taking them out for a pint when girlfriends had dumped them, and helping them fix broken-down cars. He was a great man, the complete opposite to me.

I remember when Ted, the team manager, told us one night after practice Dan's cancer scan results were not great. He said Dan had made a joke about going to play football in heaven. We were all angry and ended up losing four matches in a row. Why did someone like Dan have to go through all that? He didn't deserve to die.

The rest of my food shop is a Pippa Browning-filled blur. Once I catch sight of her, my brain struggles to regain control and floods my mind with all sorts of things. I shuffle towards the check out.

A bleep and soft vibration of my phone distracts me. I slide my hand inside my jogging bottoms pocket to retrieve it.

When are you coming back?

The thought of returning to Sophie's flat is not an appealing one. I need to stick to my plan and stay away from cash-hungry Sophie.

As I pay for my food, I spot a couple romantically entwined and sharing a kiss while carrying bags of shopping. They look like they're going home to cook dinner together and talk about topical things in the news. I watch them wander off towards the exit. Their laughter drifts back to me.

Pippa has once again taken my mind hostage.

I decline Sophie's offer and promise myself that's the last time I'm ever going to pay her a late-night visit.

CHAPTER 7

MIKEY

*C*lutching a plastic bag, full of the basic life essentials: bacon, fish fingers, two bread rolls, a can of deodorant, toilet roll, and a newspaper with a football supplement, I stagger back to my flat.

Flopping into my leather chair in the living room, my unpacked shopping bag is dumped by the side of me. Pain is radiating out of my swollen face. Getting into a fight was not one of my best decisions. I need to sleep. The second I allow myself to drift off, my phone starts to ring. Groaning, I shove it under a cushion. It keeps ringing.

'Leave me alone!'

In the end I slide it out. 'No, no, no.' It's my eight-year-old niece, Tara. For the billionth time this year – why did my brother give her a phone?

'Uncle Mikey, I'm sad.' Her shrill voice is like a gong banging between my ears. I rub my temples to counteract the pain.

'Why, Tara Twinkle Toes?' I hear her giggle at my pet name for her.

'You haven't been to see me for two weeks.'

I yawn down the phone and she tuts.

'I want to see you, Uncle Mikey. This afternoon.' Tara is being her usual demanding self.

'Daddy wants to go and buy some new garden chairs. As you know, I hate doing stuff like that. Boring!'

I place my hand over the receiver and yell, 'Aghhhh, why does she do this to me? Why can't I say no to her?'

Being a popular relative is tough.

Tara is my only niece. I'm helplessly wrapped around her little finger. We've always got on well; I let her boss me around and feed her chocolate in secret. Tara is great fun. She has her bad moments, just like any other kid, but I simply hand her back to my brother. This is one of the perks of being an uncle.

'I'm tired, Tara Twinkle Toes.' I pray she'll let me off.

'Daddy says you've had too much beer *again!*' shouts Tara, making me lift the phone from my ear.

'Tell your daddy to watch it!'

'Oh pleaaaaaassssse, Uncle Mikey.' Tara has started the whining part of her campaign. This is never a good sign. I know she wouldn't think twice about changing tack and bringing out the fake tears. This would then result in me spending the rest of the day plagued with guilt. 'Tell your dad to drop you off.'

Half an hour later and Stan is dropping off a grinning Tara. Her long blonde hair is adorned with sparkly silver clips and she wears her favourite Justin Bieber T-shirt. In her arms she cradles an iPad, clad in a bright pink glittery cover.

'Bro, you look rough!' Stan gives me a look of concern. 'Have you had that eye checked?'

I cast Tara a mock-stern face. 'I'm injured and I should be in bed.'

Tara giggles and barges past me into the flat.

'How was the wedding?' Stan's face lights up. 'I would love to go to a boozy wedding by myself.'

Stan is a single dad to Tara. Just before her first birthday, Jules, her mother and Stan's wife, told Stan she'd been having an affair with an Australian man from work. He was heading back home to Australia and she wanted to go with him, leaving Stan and Tara behind. It was heart-breaking as Jules confessed to never really loving Stan and not having a connection with Tara. Stan tried to convince her to stay, but Jules left him one night and boarded a plane to Sydney with her new lover. She occasionally sends the odd email and Christmas card to see how they're doing, but there's no sign of her ever coming back.

Stan surprised all of us by stepping up and becoming the greatest dad to Tara. He built his world around her and made sure she was never left wanting anything. He joined all the parent-toddler groups in the town and became a heroic single father. When Tara went to school, he joined the Parent Teacher Association and got involved with fundraising activities, which always seemed to involve me dressing up in a ridiculous fancy dress outfit and being pelted with wet sponges by a load of little kids.

My brother is amazing, I will never be like him.

'Wild.' I grip onto the door frame and fight a wave of nausea.

Stan stuffs his hands into the pockets of his black jeans and studies my bruised face. 'Who hit you?'

I shake my head. 'Someone's boyfriend.'

Stan grins. 'You have no shame.'

'Actually, I thought she was someone else.'

Stan gives his bald head a scratch. 'Same old Mikey. You never change.'

Irritation bubbles up inside of me. 'Honest, bro, it's not what you think.'

'Right, I better get off and buy my garden furniture.'

I grin. 'End of rock 'n' roll for you, bro.'

He rolls his eyes. 'Are you going to come over to Mum's this week?' Stan's smile fades. 'Seeing as you haven't even acknowledged her birthday. If you were my son, I would have disowned you by now.'

Scratching my head, I make a mental note. 'Oh, yeah, sorry. I'll call her. Can you buy her some flowers from the garage and I'll give you the cash?'

Stan frowns. 'Why don't you just go and see her?'

I grimace and Stan shakes his head with disappointment.

After Stan leaves, Tara and I take up our favourite seats in the two old brown leather chairs in the lounge. She sips on lemonade and nibbles on a chocolate bar, fresh from the 'Tara snack stash' in my kitchen cupboard.

'Uncle Mikey, why you don't have a girlfriend or a wife?' Tara sits up straight in her chair, giving me one of her intense stares.

I blow the air out of my cheeks and shrug my shoulders.

Tara rolls her eyes, which makes me smile.

'Nobody loves me, Tara Twinkle Toes.' I cast her my best sad puppy dog face.

She crosses her little legs. 'You really need a girlfriend, Uncle Mikey. My best friend, Samantha, says her mum needs a boyfriend.' I watch as she fires up her iPad.

Craning my neck, I watch my eight-year-old niece scrolling through Stan's *Facebook* account. 'Aren't you too young to be on *Facebook*?'

Tara gives me a sugary sweet smile. 'Dad used my iPad the other night and forgot to log out.'

I fold my arms. 'Naughty.'

She laughs and shows me the screen. My eyes are greeted with a photo of a tanned blonde woman posing in glittering gold swimwear by a row of plant pots and a garden hose.

'Where's Samantha's dad?' I ask, trying to ignore the woman's large bust, packed into a tiny gold bikini top.

'He's abroad.' Tara snatches the iPad away from him. 'Samantha says he's a loser.'

'Oh – are they still together?' I'm secretly hoping Tara will give me another look at Samantha's mother.

'No, they're getting a divorce.' Tara takes a deep breath to give the impression something thought-provoking is coming. 'Look, Uncle Mikey, you're really old and you need a wife. Samantha's mum is really old, and she needs a husband.'

I place my arm behind my head and try to stifle a yawn. 'I'm not dating someone with kids.'

Tara glares at me. 'Why not? What's wrong with someone with *kids*?'

As I give my head a good scratch, Tara pulls a disgusted face. 'Why does your hair smell of horrible curry?'

Ignoring her observation about my hair, I return to her original question. 'I don't think I'd be any good with kids.'

Tara ignores me. 'Samantha spends all her time in her room and only goes downstairs when she wants a new app for her iPad or some sweets. You wouldn't have to do much with this one.'

'Nope, not for me.'

Tara's face darkens and then lights up. 'If you go out with Samantha's mum then you can pick Samantha and me up from school.'

I smile and flick the lever at the side of my chair, so the footrest extends.

'Please, Uncle Mikey, please!' begs Tara, who is now standing up on her chair and bouncing up and down. 'I can be a bridesmaid!' she screams, before erupting into a fit of giggles.

Instinctively, I grab hold of her wrist, stopping her from flying headfirst over the side of the chair. 'Sit on the chair or you're going to fall and hurt yourself.'

Plopping back down, Tara carefully re-clips one of her sparkly hair slides. 'Can we play hide and seek?' Her blue eyes shimmer with excitement.

'I'm tired, Tara Twinkle Toes.' The yawn which escapes from my mouth is so wide my jaw painfully clicks.

A missile cushion hits my head, making me raise my hands in surrender.

Hiding inside my utility cupboard, squashed up against an

ironing board, is good for evading capture and checking the football scores on my phone.

'Where are you, Uncle Mikey?' Tara clip clops into the kitchen. 'This isn't fair, you're supposed to let your favourite niece win.'

'Never!' I shout defiantly. The cupboard door is flung open to reveal Tara standing in front of me, arms folded across her chest and tapping her foot with dissatisfaction.

'That's not a great hiding place, Uncle Mikey.'

I fight against the ironing board and emerge into the kitchen.

'My turn,' she squeals and races off into my bedroom.

Ten minutes later and I'm distracted by Cardiff City's latest goal. Tara hasn't come out of her hiding place. I head towards my wardrobe.

As my arm goes to open the door, she pokes her head out. 'Uncle Mikey, do you know anything about falling in love?'

'What?'

To my horror, she waves Dan's notebook at me. 'Someone called Dan has written you instructions about getting a lady called Pippa to fall in love with you.'

'Give me that back!' I reach my arm across.

Tara crawls out, clutching the notebook. Shaking her head so hard we both watch one of her hair clips fly out and skitter across the floor. She leaps onto my bed and starts to jump.

'These are good instructions,' she shouts. 'The first one says you have to stop being an idiot. Uncle Mikey – are you an idiot?'

My mouth clamps shut, and I glare at her.

Still jumping on my bed, Tara giggles. 'Did you know Pippa has kids?'

'Tara, give me that book back?'

Dancing like crazy on my unmade bed she sings. 'Uncle Mikey is going to make Pippa love him!'

I manage to snatch the notebook out of her hand and stuff it into my underwear drawer. 'Enough!'

The afternoon morphs into early evening. Tara is still with me. I expected Stan to have appeared by now and collected her. He knows how rough I am. This late stay is taking the piss.

My gut tightens. It's unlike him to be late. He's always so punctual and organised.

'What did you say your dad was doing this afternoon?' I ask, leaning out of the window to see whether his blue car is down below.

'Buying garden chairs.' Tara is engrossed in a game on her iPad, which involves moving coloured jewels about a grid.

My stomach groans and reminds me it requires food. 'You hungry?'

'Starving,' screeches Tara, jumping out of her seat and racing into the kitchen.

Together we make bacon sandwiches and eat them from plates on our laps, breaking a load of Stan's rules. He is a stickler for food being eaten with cutlery and at the table.

Tara can't stop giggling at the grease, which keeps trickling down her chin. I keep giving her one of my mock surprise looks. Even when we're eating bacon sandwiches, I still manage to be a popular relative.

It's gone eight. With no sign of my brother, I call his mobile. By nine I've made twenty calls and left numerous messages.

Tara cuddles up to me on one of the chairs. I reassuringly stroke her hair with one hand, while speed dialling Stan with the other. 'Where are you, bro?'

In a dream, a phone is bleeping. Shit! It's ten past one in the morning. Tara is curled up in the crook of my arm and someone is calling me.

'Mum?' I croak, after seeing her photo flash up.

'Michael Stenton?' A stern male voice makes me sit bolt upright in my chair.

'Yes, who is this?' My heart starts to thud.

'I'm Officer Brian Rawlings. I'm here with your mother. Can you come to your mother's house as quickly as you can?'

'What's going on?' I ask as Tara stirs.

'Michael, please come home!' cries my mother from the background.

I pin a note to my flat door in case Stan returns. It reads, *Police with Mum. I'll be there with Tara.*

After packing a sleepy Tara into my car, I drive off into the night.

'Michael Stenton?' A burly looking policeman opens the door. He possesses the frame of a giant and looks like he could carry a hundred small children to safety with just one hand.

I nod and bustle Tara past him. 'Go upstairs and get into Nan's bed.'

As I turn back towards the lounge, a small female officer with a wiry face and crooked nose appears. My mouth runs dry and my hands start to tremble.

'Where's my mum?' I search her face for answers. The officer steps aside and gestures for me to enter the living room.

Racing in, I freeze at the sight of my tear-stained mother, sat in her chair.

'Mikey.' Her voice is croaky and weak. 'Stan …'

The burly policeman is now in the living room. 'Your brother's car was involved in a road traffic accident earlier this afternoon,' he announces.

My shoulders and neck stiffen.

'Is he okay?' I ask, acknowledging both of the police officer's sombre expressions.

The officer takes a large breath of air. I instantly know what he is going to say.

'I'm afraid the driver was pronounced dead at the scene.' His face darkens. We haven't made a formal identification yet, but we have reason to believe it's your brother.'

Time stops. Air lodges inside my throat. I try to say

something. Blood pumps loudly past my ears and the room starts to spin. 'Stan ... dead. No!'

My mother lets out a loud sob and I rush to her side. She rests her head on my shoulder and the sound of her weeping fills the room.

'What happened?' I turn around to face the officers.

'From our initial investigations, the driver lost control of his car. It overturned and collided with a tree. Two dog walkers found it at around eight last night,' explains the female officer.

Mum hangs her head. 'Not my Stan please ... not Stan.'

The burly police officer wipes a layer of sweat from his brow.

My mother presses her sobbing head into my shoulder. I pull her towards me, trying to block out what I've just heard.

'Uncle Mikey, where are you?' A tiny voice from the stairs drifts into the living room.

'Is the little girl his daughter?' asks the female officer, inspecting a hand-held device with some information on it. I nod as tears stream down my face.

'I'm here, Tara,' I croak, gulping back air and wiping my cheeks.

In a flash she appears in the doorway, staring at everyone in the room.

'Why are you all sad?' she asks, clutching Mum's old toy rabbit and stroking one of its long grey ears.

'Is she okay staying with you tonight?' the burly officer enquires. 'We'll send a Family Liaison Officer over here tomorrow.'

I hurry to take Tara out and upstairs to bed. As I tuck her in, she runs her little hand over my face. 'You're crying, Uncle Mikey.'

I kiss her forehead and leave the bedroom. As I bound down the stairs, Mum's sobs fill the air again.

'We will need you to come and formally identify him,'

explains the burly officer, shifting his weight from foot to foot, as I return to the living room.

'Are there any other family members we should contact?' asks the female officer.

'Tara's biological mother, Jules, is in Australia. She left when Tara was one.'

I rub my chest in an attempt to soothe the crushing pain which is emanating from it.

CHAPTER 8

PIPPA

*E*mma, Mel, and I are camped on my extra-large sofa sharing a cheap bottle of Shiraz. We're celebrating the end of my disastrous caravan holiday.

Fresh from work, Emma is wearing an elegant, tailored, navy trouser suit with a silk white vest. Her blonde hair is curled neatly on top of her shoulders. Her new diamond-encrusted bracelet is catching beams of light and sparkling like crazy. Emma explained when she arrived it's a gift from her adoring father, Eric, who has spent a lifetime spoiling his only daughter with designer clothes, posh cars, and expensive holidays. Apparently, he was proud of her for staying focussed on her dating project for three years and achieving her goal with completing her bucket list.

Mel has come from the gym. Her sharp brown bob looks chic tonight and she is dressed in smart navy jeans, a crisp white shirt, a silk neck scarf, and a navy blazer.

In comparison, I'm fresh from a day of washing, ironing, tidying Billy's bedroom, getting drenched at the school gates, and baking cakes. Dressed in my usual attire; tracksuit bottoms and one of Dan's sports T-shirts, my hair hasn't been washed for over a week and is piled up on the top of my head in a greasy bun.

'Our caravan holiday was our first and last,' I announce, recalling the series of disasters occurred both inside and out of the caravan.

'How bad was it with the kids?' asks Emma, scrolling through *Instagram*.

I snort with laughter. 'I had the period from hell, Libby and Billy were covered in chicken pox, Billy nearly drowned, Daisy kept stalking this boy from the arcade, Libby kept puking, I cooked, and ate a lot of cakes, and Billy kicked a football through the bedroom window. Oh, and all three kids caught me on my dating website.'

Emma gasps. 'And how did Daisy react to you on the site? I'm sensing she may have had a few issues; I mean, she was such a daddy's girl.'

I nod. In my head, the memory of a young Daisy appears. We are in the living room and she'd just finished having a tantrum. At the sound of Dan's keys in the door, her tear-stained face quickly brightens. Hitching up her Disney Princess dress she sprints across the living room to welcome her daddy home. She's spent the last hour in her bedroom, putting on her best sparkly princess dress and fancy hairbands. 'Look at you!' Dan exclaims and a triumphant Daisy walks him through the house.

'Not great, I had tears and a lot of shouting. Sixteen is a tough age,' I explain to the girls, before taking a sip of wine. 'Billy and Libby on the other hand seemed pleased about the possibility.'

Mel looks up from her phone. 'I thought sixteen was where you calmed down?'

Emma stares at Mel. 'Melanie Roberts – at sixteen you ran off to the Isle of Wight with that young postman, your mother called the police, and there was talk of your story going on *CrimeWatch*. Pip and I were worried about having to do a reconstruction.'

A smile has found its way onto my face. 'Emma fancied the presenter on *CrimeWatch*.'

Emma hits me with a cushion and turns to Mel. 'No one calms down at sixteen – they get worse!'

'Thanks, Emma.' I groan. I recall the supermarket trip yesterday; Daisy and I had argued in the beauty aisle over the amount of make-up she was wearing for school. She'd sworn at me before snatching a thick black eye liner from the shelf.

My mind drifts. As shoppers had steered their trolleys away from the commotion, I noticed Mikey Stenton at the far end of the aisle. While Daisy proceeded to lecture me on the latest Year 11 fashions, involving false eyelashes, heavy eye liner, and crimson red lipstick, I found myself staring at him. He saw me. I had to turn quickly back to Daisy.

'Guess who I saw yesterday?' I murmur, as the image of Mikey with his trolley, dressed in a black shirt and jogging bottoms, materialises in my mind. Even though he was sporting a black eye and his hair looked like he'd been hooked up to an electricity pylon, the sight of him had brought back the tingling sensation in my chest.

Emma grabs a glossy magazine from the coffee table. 'Who?'

'Mikey Stenton,' I say with a little smile.

Mel and Emma let out a groan in unison.

'You should see his latest *Facebook* profile photo,' says Mel, flashing us his page. 'It was updated last week, while you were away, Pip. I think it was from his holiday in California last year.'

Our eyes linger over his new photo. He's on a sun lounger, wearing a pair of aviator shades and grinning, while a woman with tanned stick insect legs drapes herself over him.

'He thinks he's some kind of celebrity from the seventies,' moans Emma. 'I mean, look at the cheesy smile and big hairy chest. He needs a cigar and a gold medallion.'

Mel squeals with laughter. 'Seventies porn star, more like.'

'What was Dan thinking with his suggestion of me dating a wannabe seventies porn star?'

The longer I stare at Mikey's *Facebook* photo, the worse Dan's recommendation becomes.

Emma points at the photo. 'I bet Mikey comes with an exciting range of sexual diseases too.'

Screwing up my face makes Emma shriek with laughter.

'So, is your dating profile now live?' Mel puts down her phone.

I reach over and grab the iPad. 'It is, but I don't think I've used the best photo and I did struggle with the description.'

Emma and Mel screw up their faces. 'Oh God, Pippa, why did you use that photo?'

'Daisy took it while we were on holiday.'

'I can tell.' Emma places her manicured hand over her forehead. 'Pippa, you look like the woman who lived in a shoe with loads of kids.'

Mel frowns at the photo. 'Why are you so red faced?'

'Billy and Libby wouldn't stop fighting. Air didn't circulate well inside the caravan and no matter how long I had the door open; I couldn't get rid of the smell of cheesy teenage feet and the remnants of a three-day-old takeaway. And Daisy was difficult for the entire time.'

Emma turns to me as a smile slowly spreads across her wide pink lips. 'Where's Dan's notebook?'

'Why?' I grab it out of my handbag and hand it over. 'Remember my personal motto: do the exact opposite of what my other half says.'

Emma raises her eyebrow at me. 'On the beauty front Dan had some good advice.' She sits up straight, clears her throat, and turns to the second page. 'Okay, we can use his instructions for your dating photo. Dan says on the subject of your looks, get a fringe cut into your hair.' Emma studies the top of my head. 'You had one cut in when we were in college resitting our GCSE's. Do you remember?'

Chewing on my thumb nail I nod. 'Anthony and I had split up, so I asked the hairdresser to transform my hair.'

Rising from the sofa I walk over to my new duck-egg blue framed mirror, hung above the wooden mantelpiece. 'A fringe – really?'

Mel comes to stand behind me. She begins to unpick my bun with a disgusted look on her face. 'When did you last wash this, Pip?'

'Last week?'

Grabbing a section, Mel lays it over my forehead. 'He might have a point. It needs to be a blunt fringe.'

Nibbling on my nail I try to imagine myself with a fringe. 'I'm still thinking about a pixie cut.'

Emma sucks in a large breath of air. 'Read what Dan wrote.'

I roll my eyes. 'Dan wasn't right about everything.'

'Book an appointment at the hairdressers,' orders Emma, patting me on the shoulder. She saunters back towards the sofa. 'You might want to consider sorting out your monobrow too.'

Emma runs her fingers down the rest of Dan's instructions. 'Throw away your tracksuit bottoms, Pip. Start wearing dresses again.'

We all head back to the sofa. I watch Mel return to her phone and remember she'd mentioned looking for a job. 'Have you been job hunting today?'

She looks up. Her dark eyes widen. 'Yes, I have an interview tomorrow for a company which sells double glazing. A sales role, but I'm not too sure.'

Emma stares at Mel. 'How have you managed to get that?'

Mel shrugs and goes back to her phone. 'Jeff might have pulled a few strings.'

'What?' Emma and I say, almost together.

'He knows the owner, Ian, and he is willing to overlook what happened in my last role.'

I smile at Mel. 'Are you back with Jeff then?'

Mel casts us both a coy look. 'We might be in contact again.'

'And Cassandra, how is she?' Emma bats Mel's arm with a rolled-up magazine.

'She's fine. She thinks his affair was a one-off and has forgiven him. Jeff and I are just having fun now.'

'Fun?' I raise my eyebrows at Mel.

'Lots of sex but no heavy stuff.'

'Oh.' I look away and hope my future dates don't want to have 'fun' with me.

'He's got a job with another airline, which means he can come see me more often,' continues Mel.

I curl my legs under me. 'What did you mean about not being sure about the interview?'

Mel's face brightens. 'I quite fancy running my own business.'

In view of everything we've been through with Mel and her many life disasters this news makes me grip the arm of my sofa and Emma to squeak.

Mel sits up straighter. 'My inheritance is begging me to do something constructive with it.' She fiddles with the tiny gold necklace around her neck. 'I know Mum won't be impressed with what happened to my budding flight attendant career. Since getting sacked, I've been worried she might shoot me down with lightning bolts.'

'You've still got your inheritance?' Emma asks, her eyes widening with surprise.

Mel's mother left her with a sizeable inheritance when she died.

'The guy I dated with the drug habit never got his hands on it,' says Mel, scratching her neck.

'What about Steve with the casino addiction?' I ask, recalling spending hours sat outside a casino in my car with a tearful Mel.

'He tried and failed. I'm so glad I broke our engagement up.'

'I'm assuming Scott the armed robber never got his thieving hands on it?' Emma asks.

Mel shakes her head. 'No, he was too busy worrying about his court case. You two have no faith in me.'

Emma and I find interesting things on the walls to stare at.

'What are you thinking about doing then?' Emma picks a piece of fluff from the arm of her suit.

Mel shrugs. 'I don't know. Let's see how the interview goes.'

The lounge door opens and in walks Libby, clutching several sheets of paper. 'Mum, I have a letter about parents' evening. It's at the end of term. My teacher says appointments with him fill up quickly so this year he's getting you all to book early.'

I take the letter from Libby, muttering stuff under my breath about who this cheeky teacher thinks he is, forcing unorganised parents like me to commit to a time and date in the future. Libby high fives both Emma and Mel.

'Who is this teacher?' I scratch my head and try to remember a Mr Peterson.

Libby comes to stand by me. 'He's temporary. Mrs Gladson is having her fourth baby at the weekend.'

I take a sharp intake of breath at the news of Mrs Gladson and the imminent birth of her fourth child. When I saw her a few months ago in the school playground, she'd ballooned overnight and had a look of terror etched across her face.

'Mr Peterson is here until parents' evening and then after the holidays we get someone else.'

'What's he like, Libby?' Emma tugs on Libby's pink sparkly top. 'Is he an old coffin dodger of a teacher?'

'What does that mean?' Libby leans over and sticks a finger into one of Emma's blonde curls.

'Old,' replies Mel.

Libby shakes her head. 'Anna's mum thinks he's hot.'

Emma grabs the letter out of my hand. 'Pencil me in too, Pip.'

LUCY MITCHELL

Once I've snatched the letter back from her and signed it, Libby says goodnight and heads back upstairs.

Mel starts to pack up her things. 'Ladies, I better go as I have that interview tomorrow.'

She turns after grabbing her handbag. 'Get your hair cut, that hair bun is ghastly.'

'Goodbye, Melanie,' I chuckle.

Mel grabs the red notebook and waves it at me. 'I know you never listened to your husband when he was alive, but I think you should on this occasion.'

CHAPTER 9

PIPPA

*I*t's been a month since my dating profile went live. The only interest I've had is from a retired professor messaging me to ask whether I would date someone in their late sixties, a young man, who skipped the small talk and sent me a photo of his genitals, and a man who wanted to know whether he could just have casual sex with me as he would like to remain happily married.

Dare I say it, but I'm starting to come round to the idea of Dan being right about online dating.

As it's a teacher training day, I'm making a batch of sugary fairy cakes to keep the kids on my side. After popping the cakes onto a wire rack, I lean against the work surface and scroll through *Facebook* on my phone.

Everyone, it seems, is having fun. Emma has posted a selfie of her and a grinning *Tinder* date from last night. They're both laughing and holding up cocktails to the camera. Phil, the ex-golf captain, is obviously now a distant memory.

A few of the recently divorced mothers from Billy's school have gone on a girls' holiday to Portugal and have posted a photo of their painted toenails on the beach, one of a luxurious white villa, and a photo of them all in pretty swimwear. I let out a sigh. The most fun I'll have today is cleaning the kids' bedrooms, tackling the ironing pile, and taking Daisy to a sleepover later.

Opening my kitchen window, I spot our neighbour, Pauline Jacobs, pruning her rose bush. She lifts her head of tight brown curls and our eyes meet. I wave like a mad woman as I like Pauline. She used to be the head teacher at a private girls' school and always gives me lots of encouragement and advice with the kids.

Pauline quickly averts her attention back to her flowers and frantically starts snipping off dead rose heads. That's unusual. I normally get an acknowledgment from over the hedge; a smile or even a shrill hello.

Billy comes in from the garden. He kicks his football against the wall by my new American fridge. I quickly shut the window as I don't want to give Pauline the impression I'm struggling with my kids. 'Please stop it, Billy.' I grab the milk from the fridge.

He casts me a look of seven-year-old defiance. 'No.'

'If that ball dents my new fridge, Bill, you will be grounded for the rest of eternity – do you hear me?'

Billy shrugs and kicks his ball against my newly painted kitchen wall.

'*Stop!*' I shriek at him. He grins and scrapes back the untidy mound of dark hair on his head. He's been a stranger to a hairbrush for days. 'Bill, go brush your hair.'

He shakes his head, grabs his ball, and races outside.

Daisy saunters into the kitchen. She avoids my gaze and plonks herself down on a chair. There has been an unspoken tension between us since we came back from the caravan. I know Daisy's mood with me is dating related.

'Where's Lib?' I ask, only counting two children.

'She's gone out,' announces Billy, coming back in from the garden and standing by Daisy's chair. He bounces his football on his knee.

The noise of his ball makes my shoulders stiffen. 'I've told you not to do that in here.' He carries on bouncing his ball.

'How can she have gone out by herself? She's only nine,' I ask, staring at both of my children.

Billy kicks the ball towards the back door, making it thwack against the wood panel below the glass.

'Billy!' I turn my attention to my missing child. 'Where is Libby, Daisy?'

Daisy turns around and flicks a pair of long black lashes in my direction. 'Maybe if you weren't so busy on that site …'

I ignore her and take the stairs two at a time. When I knock on Libby's white door, silence greets my ears. I push it open on to find an empty, but freshly made bed. Her bare white walls make me grimace. All her football posters have been taken down and her trophies have been put away.

On her bed is a sheet of paper.

It reads: Mum, I'm sad so I'm running away. See you in a few weeks, Libby.

Oh God, Libby has run away!

'Libby!' I scream, racing out onto the landing.

After checking all the bedrooms, I charge downstairs and into the kitchen. 'Did you know about this?' I thrust Libby's note between Billy and Daisy.

'We might have done,' whispers Daisy, tapping something into her phone.

After grabbing my coat, I bolt outside. 'Libby!' I frantically look up and down the street.

At the far end of the street there's a small hooded figure heading towards the local shop.

From a distance it resembles Libby; a pink coat, blonde hair, and jeans.

I sprint up the street in a cloud of drizzling rain. My hair soon sticks to my forehead and cheeks.

On reaching the shop, my legs are like lead. I burst inside hoping to see Libby.

Someone knocks into me and treads on my plimsoled toe.

'Oh, I'm so sorry,' says a familiar male voice.

I look up to see an unshaven Mikey Stenton staring back at me. His brown chaotic hair reminds me of Billy's. Both of them are in need of a good hairbrush.

My eyes survey his grey crumpled suit and open necked white shirt. He's probably been partying and cavorting with attractive women all night.

'Oh … urm, I've lost my daughter.' I scan the aisles for her.

'The stag do … last month … errr …' he mumbles, hanging his head.

'What?' I cast him an impatient look. His incoherence signals that he's still drunk from dancing with half-naked women. Dark rings loop around his eyes and his skin looks deathly pale. Clearly this man has a lot of fun!

Dan's suggestion about Mikey appears in my mind, heating up my cheeks with embarrassment. How could Dan even consider someone like Mikey Stenton?

'Mummy.' A familiar voice comes from the crisp packet aisle.

'Libby!' I exclaim, leaving Mikey Stanton stood staring at me, while clutching a carton of milk and a loaf of bread.

Libby is eyeing up the crisps with her pink school bag slung over her shoulder and her old toy rabbit dangling out of it.

'Oh, Libby.' I race down the aisle.

'I'm running away, you can't stop me,' Libby snaps, shaking her blonde head.

Grabbing hold of her arm, I hiss, 'You're coming home with me. Libby Browning.'

Libby takes one look at me, yanks her arm free and sprints towards the door.

'Libby!' I yell, dodging a bewildered Mikey Stenton and racing past the check out.

'Have a nice day,' he says as I charge past him.

Stopping dead in my tracks, I turn on my plimsole heel and glare at him. 'Do I look like I'm going to have a nice day?'

He gives me a weak smile. Ignoring it, I sprint out of the shop screaming, '*Libby!*'

After finally catching up with a panting Libby, I stop her from getting on a bus going into town. Grabbing my daughter by the arm, she starts to kick and scream. 'Get off me, Mummy!'

Passers-by are casting me worried expressions.

'How did you escape?'

Libby struggles to break free while I make a mental list of all the ways she could have escaped. Being small for her age she battles with the front door at the best of times and the sound of it shutting would have been heard. Unless she had help?

'I climbed out of my bedroom window. I used Dad's fire ladder.'

'What?' I curse myself for not taking it from Daisy the night she came home drunk.

Libby grins. 'We all use Dad's ladder. Even Billy.'

Throwing my arms in the air, I wail with exasperation, 'For goodness' sake – why do my kids keep using that bloody ladder!'

A man pushing a child in a buggy raises his eyebrows, and an older woman coming out of Poundland shakes her head at me.

Rain starts to pelt the tops of our heads. I'm fighting the urge to scream my head off at Libby. She could have killed herself climbing out of the house. I suck in a lungful of high-street air and the memory of Libby's note comes rushing back to me. As my daughter looks up at me with sad blue eyes and damp hair, I get the feeling the last thing she needs right now is her mother going batshit crazy outside Poundland.

Dan would know what to do. He would be able to sort Libby out. A lump balloons at the back of my throat.

Libby kicks a stone with her trainer. Something is on my daughter's mind.

'What's up, Libby?'

Shrugging, she rests her head against my arm.

Pulling up her hood, I place my hands on her shoulders and hold her gaze. 'Talk to me.'

'I miss Daddy and I miss …'

'What else, Libs?'

Wiping her face she mumbles something under her breath. My heartbeat quickens, I'm sure she said the word *football*.

'Libby, what did you say?'

'Nothing.'

I wrap my arms around her. Her hair smells of the new strawberry shampoo I bought her as a bribe to make her start brushing it. 'Why would you want to run away?'

'I feel sad.'

I stare at her. 'Why?'

'Billy knocked your handbag on the floor this morning,' she sniffs. 'I saw Daddy on that football poster.'

Wiping away a strand of wet blonde hair, I plant a kiss on her rain coated forehead.

'Sorry,' I say, giving her arm a rub. It must be still hard for her seeing Dan's face. I often struggle when I see his photos in the lounge. 'I need to empty my handbag.' My eyes widen in surprise at what just came out of my mouth. This was one of Dan's suggestions.

Libby lets out a sigh and I turn my attention back to her. 'What would make you feel happy?'

She kicks a stone and I find myself longing to see the old goofy happy Libby running about the garden with a football.

'Football used to make you happy.'

Ignoring the subject of football, Libby swings her bag over her shoulder. 'Can I have a sleepover, Mummy?'

'If that's what it takes to stop you being sad then yes you can.'

Pauline Jacobs is sweeping her driveway when we return. I dread to think what she must be thinking as she watches my children come and go as they please, climbing precariously down a ladder at the side of the house.

Once inside, I turn the house upside down in search of the ladder. Billy is unusually protective of anyone going underneath his bed. After a short wrestling match, which I win, I spot the ladder among shoes, trainers, and toys.

Locking the ladder in the shed, I see that Pauline is now sweeping her path.

'Everything okay, Pippa?' Pauline asks, without looking up from her broom.

I force out a sugary smile. 'Couldn't be better, Pauline.'

CHAPTER 10

PIPPA

*W*ith a heavy heart I empty my handbag, putting everything Dan-related in a kitchen drawer, then go to see Libby upstairs. A rap at my front door, followed by the howl of a young child and the scream from a baby, makes me stop in my tracks. Helen, my sister, and her army of small children have made an unplanned visit.

Yanking open the door, I see Helen on my doorstep, with a baby in her arm, a small child clung to her waist, and three children sulking behind her.

'I'm in the middle of a crisis. Rick's changing jobs,' groans Helen. 'It's bad news, Pippa. He's going to be home-based.'

For my sister this is crushing news. Helen and I hug the life out of each other. Her older children troop past us.

'Where are Bill and Libs?' asks Jess, Helen's oldest daughter and the female version of her father Rick: black shiny hair, olive skin, and almond-shaped dark eyes.

'Can we play outside with them?' asks Lewis, jumping up and down in my hallway and nearly bringing down my mountain of coats and bags.

'Bill and Libs!' squawks little Reuben, shaking his mop of red curls as my two thunder down the stairs at the sound of their cousins.

Jess, Lewis, and Reuben squeal with delight. They all race off into the back garden. I remove the small child, Joey, from Helen's side and hand him to Daisy who gives me a filthy look back. Babysitting is not something she enjoys doing at sixteen.

Without saying a word and ignoring Daisy's strict orders to Joey about how he can sit next to her, but not move or breathe, I scoop the baby out of Helen's arms and gesture for her to follow me into the kitchen.

Baby Carla coos and gurgles. Her huge button-like brown eyes grow wider with curiosity as I open the cupboard to reach up for some mugs. She raises her little plump pink hand and tries to grasp mine. I'm reminded of Billy as a baby. It's been years since I carried him about in my arms while Dan entertained Daisy and Libby. Dan and I would take it in turns to look after Billy. On his shift, Dan would stick him in his buggy and head off up the pub. They would return sometime later, Dan with a smile on his face and Billy asleep.

Out of the corner of my eye I notice Helen has slumped into a chair and placed her forehead on the table. Her long auburn hair is spilling over my new John Lewis duck-egg blue place mats.

She briefly lifts her head. 'After ten *idyllic* years of Rick working away from home in the week, he has found himself a new home-based job.'

'Wasn't he happy?' I ask, remembering Rick boasting to Dan about the gyms in the hotels he was put up in during the week.

Helen lets out a wail. 'He's taken the new job because he thinks it will help our marriage.'

'What?'

She nods. 'Rick thinks we need to reignite the passion in our marriage.' Shouts and screams from the garden distract us both.

'We have five kids,' groans Helen staring at her squabbling older children, 'that's quite enough passion in a marriage for one lifetime, thank you very much.'

Stroking the baby's silky brown hair, I find myself thinking aloud. 'A lot of women in your position would be delighted to have their husband at home every day.'

Banging her clenched hand on the table, Helen snaps, 'They're not married to Rick.'

Passing her a cup of peppermint tea I sit opposite her. 'So, what's this about putting more passion in your marriage then?'

Helen casts me a thundery look. 'Rick forgets we have five children and one is just six months old. Also, I've reached a point in my life where I'm happier if he runs me a hot bath, pours me a glass of wine, lights a few candles, and goes downstairs.' She takes a sip of tea. 'I haven't told you all of Rick's news.'

'There's more?'

My sister grimaces. 'I didn't think things could get any worse after he announced his new home-based job, but, as he's going to be at home more he's reforming his old rock band.'

'Okay, well that might keep him busy in the evenings.'

Helen glares at me. 'My husband wants me to act like a young rock band groupie again …' Pausing she looks over her shoulder to check for children and then turns back to whisper, 'in the bedroom.'

'Oh, Helen,' I gasp. 'I'm so sorry.'

Helen casts me a weary look. 'You know how daft I was when I first met him. Well, he wants me to wear his rock band's T-shirt and whisper his lyrics to him over the pillow. Seriously, Pip, falling in love makes you do stupid things which come back to haunt you years later.'

Panic sweeps through me. 'Is this what men want nowadays? Will I have to act out stuff?'

My sister runs her hands through her thick hair. 'Linda, on my Pilates *WhatsApp* group, informed everyone this morning that

Brian, her husband, wants her to dress up as a *stern but sexy* librarian. Apparently he wants to be stood in just his underpants and beg Linda to stamp his library card. Men are sick, Pip. Stay away!'

Scratching my head, I mentally chew over what Rick is expecting Helen to do. 'Won't Rick have actual work to produce while he's doing this new job?'

Closing her eyes and massaging her sweaty forehead, Helen sighs. 'As the kids will be in nursery and school he wants to use his coffee and lunch breaks to bring the passion back to our marriage. Bang go my lunches with the women from the Pilates, coffee dates at the gym, afternoon teas with the ladies from my cookery class, my nude art classes, and my lengthy shopping trips with the joint credit card.'

My sister's social life gets better with every new child.

She pauses and scans my kitchen. 'Pip, what is it with you and this aqua colour?'

'Duck-egg blue, you mean,' I say, gazing longingly at my kitchen cupboards.

Helen returns to her emotional outburst and lets out another wail. 'I never liked Rick's music back in the day, Pip, but as he looked like a sex god on stage I stayed up all night learning it. Now that I'm forty-two I struggle to remember my mobile number.' Banging her clenched fist again on the table, she snaps, 'How the hell am I going to find the time with five kids to study his terrible lyrics?'

I sense it might be a good time to change the subject as my sister's face has turned bright pink and her voice is getting louder. 'Did I tell you I put my dating profile live a few weeks ago?'

'As I told you before your holiday, don't go there.' Helen takes a gulp of her tea.

'Dan wanted me to find someone else,' I mumble, playing with Carla's plump toes.

'Really?' She casts me a look of surprise.

'He wrote me instructions on how to fall in love again,' I say making Carla giggle.

'He did what?' exclaims Helen, choking on her tea.

I rise up from my chair and go to my handbag.

'You are joking aren't you?' she queries, before snatching the notebook from me.

I watch as her eyes scan the first page.

Screams from the garden avert my eyes to the window. All the kids are pointing at Billy standing on top of the garage roof.

I walk quickly to the back door, yank it open and scream, '*Get down!*'

'I don't want to!' Billy walks over to the other side to peer into Pauline's garden.

'*Billy, get down!*' I scream, making baby Carla giggle again. Why do kids not find me scary?

'*No!*' shouts Billy, stamping his foot.

'*Fine!*' I yell. 'If you fall and break your leg, don't come crying to me!'

'I think he would come crying to you as you're his mother,' says Libby, with a cheeky tone to her voice.

I don't know what to do. My kids won't listen to me. If Dan was here, none of them would play up like this. I'm going to do what I do best. Come in, close the door, and carry on talking to Helen, while praying Billy doesn't fall off the garage roof.

'Do you not think you should get Billy down from that roof?' enquires Helen, gazing out of the window.

'He won't listen to me.' I sigh.

'Hang on,' says Helen, rising quickly from her chair.

She yanks open the back door and screams, '*Get down now, Billy Browning!*'

Her voice booms and is almost deafening. Baby Carla starts to cry, which makes me exhale loudly. Billy is climbing down the side of the garage and I can hear him muttering, 'Sorry, Aunt Helen!'

My sister returns and sits back at the table. 'You need to improve your discipline technique,' she says in a quiet voice before closing her eyes and mumbling some stuff under her breath.

'How come my kids laugh at me and listen to you?' I ask, shaking off a cloud of parental failure.

'You come across as their friend. I prefer to act like I'm unhinged. Kids pick up on this stuff. It's good for kids to live with a bit of fear,' says Helen, picking up the notebook.

After a minute of reading she looks up and frowns. 'What is this about you not listening to Emma, Mel, Mum, or me?'

I smile and nod for her to carry on reading.

Helen gasps. 'Pip, do not follow any invisible thread leading to a man. I did that and married Rick.'

I sip more tea.

'Oh my God, he's suggested you get with someone at his football club!' she shrieks, placing a hand over her gaping mouth.

I exhale loudly and go back to tickling Carla's bare feet.

'Mikey Stenton – do I know him?' Helen asks, giving me one of her interrogating looks.

'He carried the coffin at the funeral. Tall and good-looking with brown hair,' I say.

Helen frowns and I watch her forehead crease. She places a finger on her lips, as she tries to recall the coffin bearers at Dan's funeral. 'Nope I can't remember him. What's he like?'

I take in a deep breath. 'International playboy. Single, no kids, and has a *Facebook* album full of photos of him with half-naked women.'

Helen's eyes widen. 'Sounds like the perfect partner for you, Pip,' she says with air of sarcasm.

I throw my hands in the air. 'I can't believe Dan suggested such a ridiculous thing!'

'I dread to think what Rick would advise me to do with regard to falling in love,' Helen groans. 'He'd suggest I hang around the boating lake or go on boating lake dates. This is something he has planned for us when he starts his new home-based job.' She shoots me a fake sugary smile. 'Lucky me!'

'You and Rick on a boating lake date? Really?'

A few miles out of the town is a picturesque boating lake, hemmed in a by a circle of tall trees. You can hire rowing boats and on summer days I've been told it's idyllic. Dan hated anything to do with boats, so he never took me.

Helen places her head back in her hands. 'Avoid these dates at all costs, Pip. They should come with a health warning. When Rick and I were younger and didn't have so many children he would come home from working abroad and take me to the boating lake. I would get carried away with the romantic setting and Rick reciting love poetry ...'

'Love poetry?' I shriek with laughter, trying to imagine Rick, with his thick Yorkshire accent, saying a few beautiful poetic lines.

'I lost all common sense, Pippa. Listen to this, by verse two I would be suggesting we stop for a quiet picnic in a secluded spot ... on that island in the middle of the lake.'

'You suggested that?'

Helen nods. 'Most of my children were conceived on that little island.'

A memory of Dan bursting into the kitchen with a huge grin on his face and pointing to the local newspaper pops up at the back of my mind. He kept pointing at the grainy photo and saying the two, blurry nude figures reminded him of my sister and Rick. 'Do you remember the island being in the newspaper because there were complaints about nudists going there.'

A dark shadow passes over my sister's face. 'No, Pippa, I don't.' After fiddling with her earring she gives me some sisterly advice. 'Don't fall in love because the silly things you end up doing will come back to haunt you and for God's sake – stay away from boating lake dates.'

'When do you have to learn his lyrics by?'

My sister grimaces. 'Next weekend. Why the hell did he have to become home-based?'

CHAPTER 11

PIPPA

*T*he bedside clock reads 9.34 p.m. Sleep is not my friend tonight. Plumping up my pillows, I haul myself up into a sitting position. Inside my head, thoughts and worries are merrily rotating like clothes on the fast cycle of my washing machine.

It hasn't been a good day. Earlier, I plucked up the courage to steal a look at my savings account. The experience wasn't pleasant. When Dan was alive, I never had to worry about stuff like the finances. I simply carried on spending, until he told me otherwise.

When he died, the life insurance paid off the mortgage and left me with a small amount which Dan believed I could live off – if I was careful. Before he died, he planned out the family spending on a handy budget spreadsheet for me.

Grief made me ignore his plans and waste a lot of money. From redecorating the entire house, not just the kitchen, to buying myself the best baking equipment money could buy, I went bonkers with retail therapy. For the first year the kids and I ate out every week, and we went on three holidays abroad.

If Dan was sat in bed beside me now, he'd throw his head

back and laugh at me blaming grief. I enjoyed buying stuff before he got sick.

He would also look around our bedroom and make a comment about my obsession with the colour duck-egg blue. The colour does things to me. Before Dan got sick the entire house was a dull magnolia. He somehow managed to keep a lid on my fascination with duck-egg blue, letting me hand paint an old chest of drawers for our bedroom and buy matching hand and bath towels for our two bathrooms. After his diagnosis he used to lie on the sofa recovering from another round of chemo with a chalky pale face and tired eyes. The painful sight of him was too much and it was then I yearned for comforting duck-egg blue walls. For the past three years, there's been no one to control my obsession with the colour.

Suffice it to say, over three years, the life insurance money has dwindled away.

So, I've therefore spent most of the day sat at the kitchen table, staring gloomily at my bank balance. Things are definitely not so rosy now. We aren't on the breadline or anything, but we need to cut back on stuff.

What hasn't helped is Daisy stomping and threatening to run away if she doesn't get the designer trainers she desperately wants.

Reasons not to date are also stacking up; Daisy still hasn't forgiven me for being on a dating site, my mother believes I should concentrate on my kids, money has become an issue, and my children are running wild. I'm starting to wonder whether the universe is trying to tell me something.

My phone starts to bleep. It's a *Facetime* call from Mel. I accept and am greeted by her grinning face. 'Why are you looking so cheerful?' I ask.

She squeals. 'I've started my own business.'

'What?'

Mel flicks her sharp bob out of her beaming face. 'The

interview at the windows place made me realise I can't work for another company. Lovely guy interviewed me, but by the end I was looking for reasons to escape.' She coughs and places her manicured hand over her glossy lips. 'Anyway, after walking out of the building, I went across the road and saw this little coffee shop.'

'A coffee shop?'

Mel nods. 'Yeah. I went in to grab a drink and I got chatting to the owner. She's selling the business as her partner ran off with a waitress. It's a lovely little place with a quirky vintage vibe. Perfect for snug sofas, lazy mornings drinking coffee, and meeting up with friends. So, I've bought it.'

'What?'

'I'm now the proud owner of a coffee shop.'

Damn that sales company interview! If that bloke had made the job more interesting Mel would have found stability flogging windows and not starting her own business.

'You don't have any experience with running a coffee shop, Mel.' My heart is thudding.

'Pippa, I was a flight attendant for years. It is very similar, and I was great with the general public.'

I try to hide my grimace and ignore the memory of Mel weeping on my sofa after one of her passengers got a nasty groin burn when she'd accidentally tipped coffee into his lap and then she'd argued with his wife.

'I don't know what to say,' I mumble. 'Please tell me Jeff isn't partnering with you.'

Mel laughs. 'No, he can keep flying planes. Guess what?'

Oh God, I feel sick, there's more.

Mel has an odd look about her. 'I need someone to help me out and bake cakes to sell.'

'Where will you find someone to do that?'

Mel rolls her almost black eyes. 'Duh! I'm asking you, Pippa

Browning. You cook delicious muffins so why not let my customers eat them?'

She has rendered me speechless. I can't believe Mel's inviting me to join her chaos.

'Dan said you had to do something with your skill,' she points out.

My stomach twists into a knot. Dan's red book comes rushing into my mind. He did want me to do something with my cakes but I can just imagine the look of horror on his face if I told him I'm going to be working for Mel. Don't get me wrong, I love my best mate dearly, it's just she attracts disaster.

'But … but …' I stammer as a thousand Mel-style worries hit me at once.

Mel beams down the phone at me. 'Come on, Pip, it'll be a laugh. You can earn some money from the sales and you can help out with serving.'

There is no way I can bake cakes for a coffee shop. Mel needs a professional. 'My cakes are *not* that good.'

'Rubbish,' Mel says. 'They're delicious and it's about time you got yourself out of that house. You never know who you might meet in my coffee shop.'

'But I can stand behind the counter and serve?' My brain is slow to process Mel's demands.

'You worked in the school kitchens years ago so this should be a doddle.' Mel is grinning from ear to ear.

Sinking into my pillow, I think back to when Daisy first started primary school and my six-month stint as a school dinner lady. It wasn't a flash job, but it meant I got to spy on Daisy, and I learnt some stuff about food hygiene and preparation.

'Pip, it's time to leave your duck-egg blue house and get back out into the world.'

My mind chews over her offer. I turn to Dan's empty side of the bed and imagine he's lying beside me with his reading glasses on and flicking through a football supplement. Muting Mel for a second, I whisper to Dan's pillow, 'What would you advise?'

Okay, yes initially he would have a look of terror on his face, but Dan would sit up and think it through. He would always try to see the positives with Mel's life messes. I'll always remember Mel calling off an engagement with an abusive boyfriend and finding herself in the local Accident & Emergency nursing a fractured wrist and bloodied lip. Dan and I intervened. We ordered her to live in our guest room for two months and we built her back up with late-night chats, good food, a lot of laughter and reassuring hugs. Even when she started receiving emails from her ex-fiancé threatening to fire bomb our house, Dan came up with some positives; this situation would force us to review our home insurance policy and force him to buy the emergency fire ladder he'd seen on Amazon.

I need to follow Dan's lead. Scratching my head, I order my brain to come up with some plus points. Maybe helping her run the place will mean I can guide her or at least talk sense into her? I do have some food preparation experience too. I do need to get out of the house and earning a little income will help with the money situation. Maybe this could lead to some good old-fashioned romance, like Dan suggested?

'Well?' Mel screeches.

'Okay,' I mutter, digging my fingers into my duvet,

Mel's shrieks are deafening. 'This is going to be fab. Now, get your hair cut! You can't serve my customers with that ghastly bun.'

I put my hands up to my hair and then catch sight of myself in the wardrobe mirror. The phrase 'washed out' springs to mind. Mel has a point about me looking good while serving my cakes in a coffee shop and more importantly, who's going to date me looking like this? Emma has been pointing out for days the greasy long hair look on my dating profile, combined with tired baggy clothes, is probably the reason why I'm seeing little dating traffic.

'Look, I don't mean that about your hair.' Mel casts me a look of concern. 'Are you okay, Pip?'

'Yes, I just realised I need an image overhaul.'

She screams with excitement. 'This is such a good plan. Right, I suggest you book an appointment at *Perfect Image* in town to sort out the monobrow and then a hair salon appointment.'

I force out a smile. 'What happens if it goes wrong and my cakes are a disaster?'

Mel laughs. 'It'll be fine. Oh, before you go, guess who works at the window company?'

I shake my head.

'Mikey Stenton.'

'How do you know that?'

Mel grins. 'When I went for the interview I ran into my friend from the gym. She works there in the finance team. Well, when I said I'd be working in the sales team, she rolled her eyes and told me I'd be working with Mikey Stenton. Can you imagine that?'

I dismiss a strange tingling feeling in my chest. 'Did you see him?'

Mel runs her hand through her bob. 'No.'

My stomach muscles are tightening. 'The man is a party animal.'

Mel nods. 'She said he's a real ladies' man. I think I had a lucky escape. Let's hope he doesn't frequent our coffee shop.'

My heart breaks into a wild gallop. 'Oh my goodness, you mean he works ...'

'Yes, over the road. Pip, he'll have better things to do than come in our coffee shop.'

CHAPTER 12

MIKEY

*T*ara opens my mother's front door with pink-rimmed eyes and tear-stained cheeks. She falls into me as I step inside.

'Hey, what's up, Twinkle Toes?' I bend down to see her face properly. The sight of Tara makes my chest ache. Her little pink mouth droops as she takes a break from chewing her saliva-coated finger.

She shrugs her shoulders. 'I miss Daddy.'

I throw my arms around her. 'I've missed you, Tara Twinkle Toes.' Somehow, I need to deflect her attention from Stan.

She looks up at me with the hint of a smile. 'Have you really, Uncle Mikey?'

My mother shuffles up to us in the hallway. I notice she's using her walking stick. Mum only uses it when she's struggling. The stony expression on her face makes my gut tighten.

'Why don't you go upstairs and tidy your room?' My mother ruffles Tara's hair.

I follow Mum into the kitchen. As we enter, I gasp. There's mess over the work surfaces and child-related havoc strewn across the kitchen table: magazines, toys, an iPad, and an array of scattered colouring pens. Mum's house is usually spotless, regardless of her health.

When Stan and I were growing up she used to drag us out of our beds to help her tidy. Dad died when we were young which meant Mum was on her own. There is a standing family joke that Mum can't sit still if there's something out of place upstairs. Her brain has a 'mess' sensor which picks up an untidy wardrobe or a misplaced shoe.

The shock of the kitchen has turned my legs to jelly.

Mum pulls out a chair and manoeuvres herself into it. She tries to make sense of her messy shoulder-length brown hair but gives up. It's hung limply around her pale face.

'Do you want a cup of tea?' I give her shoulder a squeeze. She rests her head against my forearm and nods.

A pile of cereal-encrusted bowls is stacked in the sink. Buried beneath them are a collection of dirty teacups. My nose picks up on the rotting odour coming from the overflowing bin.

'Everything okay, Mum?' I look back at her, hunched over the table.

She wipes her brow with her apron. 'It's not been a good day, Michael.'

Ditching the idea of a cup of tea I return to sit by her. Since the accident, Mum has become Tara's guardian. Jules sent Mum an email about Stan and asked her to adopt Tara. At the bottom, she said she wouldn't be coming to the funeral. Jules hasn't wanted anything to do with Tara for years, so it isn't surprising. Mum has since taken it upon herself to raise Tara.

'You're doing a great job, Mum.' I lean over and rest my head against hers.

She pulls away and strokes my stubble-clad face. 'How are you doing?'

Blowing out the air from my cheeks, I give my head a good scratch. How am I doing after the death of my brother? I'm not going to give my mother the honest answer, which consists of spending the past month drinking an excessive amount, getting chucked out of three bars for being drunk and disorderly, nearly losing my job, a failed attempt at trying to sleep with a rough-looking woman from Blackpool, and being unable to sleep until dawn most nights.

'Just getting through it, Mum.'

She sweeps my unruly fringe out of my eyes. 'I was worried about you at the funeral.'

Nausea rises from my stomach and shame makes me gag. I turned up drunk to my brother's funeral. The night before had been spent in my local pub drinking myself into oblivion. After I passed out, the landlord, a mate from school, left me asleep in one of the booths. When he came down the next morning, I woke and staggered straight to the funeral. It was not my finest hour. Mum needed me and I let her down.

Her fingers smooth out my brow. 'You can talk to me, you know.'

I fight back an army of tears as she gives my arm a reassuring rub. 'I miss him too. I miss him too, son.'

My eyes survey all the boxes of Stan's stuff, stacked up by the kitchen door. 'You been sorting out his house?'

Mum nods. 'Patricia from up the road has been helping me. Did you not get my message?'

I wince and look away.

The sound of Tara's music upstairs breaks our silence. I meet my mother's watery red eyes. She reaches for a ball of tissue, stuffed up her cardigan sleeve. 'I'm struggling, Mikey.' With a trembling hand, she dabs at her eyes. 'Tara is a handful.'

I place my hand on her arm. 'Hey, come on, it's only been a month.' A lump balloons in my throat. 'Tara's been through a lot.'

Mum shakes her head. 'I know, but I don't feel great. Maybe it's grief or my MS could be playing up.'

My shoulders and neck stiffen at the mention of her MS. 'What do you mean?'

'I'm so weak at the moment. Walking is getting harder and last night I fell in the kitchen.'

My gut clenches. I survey my mother's pale face and spot a purplish mark etched on her cheek. 'Why didn't you call me?'

Mum looks away. 'You have your own life to lead, Mikey. I can't call you every time I fall.'

I want her arms to stop trembling.

'Is Tara helping out?'

A solitary tear trickles down my mother's face. 'Mikey, I don't want her to become my carer.'

'I think it's good for her to help out around the house.'

Mum massages her temples, leaving angry red marks across her forehead. 'I'm not coping, Mikey.'

My heart starts to thud. 'What do you mean?'

Plunging her head into her hands I hear her sob. 'Tara's not sleeping and in the day she's stroppy and emotional.'

Tara's tear-stained face from the doorway reappears in my mind. 'She's going to be like this. I would be surprised if she wasn't like this. When I popped in last weekend, she seemed okay.'

Mum lifts her head out of her hands. 'Michael, you were here for about five minutes and then you left.'

I flick my eyes to the floor and can taste vomit at the back of my throat.

'I'm worried it's not going to work, Mikey. The social worker has been round asking questions about my health. This situation is not fair on Tara or me.'

'Hey – come on now,' I give her arm a reassuring squeeze. She carefully lifts it away.

'I've not been sleeping. Just worrying about Tara. If I can't look after her, she'll have to go into care. I mean, Jules clearly doesn't care about her own daughter.' Tears stream down my mother's face and she buries her head into my shoulder.

'Come on now. Maybe you need a break? Why don't I have Tara for the day and give you a rest?'

She lifts her head and casts me a grave expression. 'I am worried about everything.'

Stan's face flashes through my mind. I have to do something. Mum needs me and if Tara was my little girl, I wouldn't want her going into care. After my dreadful behaviour at the funeral and over the past few weeks, I have to restore Mum's faith in me.

Dan's words in his notebook rush back to me, *mate, you need to stop being an idiot!*

My mind floods with drunken images of the last few weeks. While Mum has been dealing with Tara and battling her MS, I've been slumped in the corners of bars feeling sorry for myself.

I rise from my seat and surprise myself. 'Okay, I'm going to help out with Tara. Mum, you're going to get some rest.'

She grabs my arm. 'Are you sure about this?'

Kneeling down beside her I hold take hold of her trembling hand. 'We have to make this work.'

'But you have work, football training, and your nights out?' Mum casts me a look of concern.

'You and Tara are more important. I can take her out over the weekend and maybe on Monday, I can take her to school and collect her. To make things easier, I'll stay here for a bit. Give you some support.'

Mum's eyes are watery. 'Really? Would you do that for me, Michael?'

I grin. 'How hard can it be helping out with Tara?'

CHAPTER 13

MIKEY

*T*ara insists on holding my hand as we start out on what I'm calling, Uncle Mikey's Weekend of Fun. Both Tara and Mum's mouths fell open in surprise when I made the announcement.

My niece's hand is hot and clammy as we cross the road. I've decided our first port of call will be Perfect Image to get her nails painted. One of the girls who serves behind the football club bar works there and after a quick text, she agreed to do me a favour and paint Tara's nails.

'You okay?' I steer Tara away from a dark muddy puddle.

She nods but doesn't look up.

Tara's long blonde hair is hung like two heavy curtains around her little pale face. She wears an old T-shirt and grey tracksuit bottoms. There's an absence of sparkly clips in her hair, pink lip balm on her lips, and Justin Bieber clothing items. My independent, fashion conscious, and bossy little niece has gone. In her place, is a frightened and insecure little girl.

Last night, Stan appeared in my dream. We were standing at my flat door discussing football tours. Stan had confessed he'd secretly signed up for one and was planning to persuade Mum to have Tara for the weekend. I woke up with wet cheeks and an aching chest.

Stan and I didn't get on as kids: he was always the sensible and mature child, while I was the thrill-seeking lunatic child, Stan delighted our mother with A grades, a first-class university degree, and a job in an accountancy firm. I, on the other hand, nearly drove our mother into an early grave with a string of failed exams, several wild teenage parties at our house, a suspected pregnancy with one of my girlfriends, and a phone call from a Greek police station after I'd been arrested for being drunk and disorderly, while on a lads' holiday.

When Jules left Stan, he became even more of a heroic figure to our mother. She would talk non-stop about Stan taking care of Tara and how proud she was of him.

'I don't feel very well, Uncle Mikey,' mumbles Tara as we draw near the beauty salon. She turns to look at me. Noticing two purple rings circling her droopy eyes, I ask myself whether we should have stayed locked away back in my mother's house, watching TV and eating biscuits.

According to my mother, Tara has been to school twice but has ended up being sent home in floods of tears and been inconsolable. Mum's been taking her to see a trained child bereavement counsellor, who keeps telling her it'll take time for Tara to adjust to her new life.

'Come on, Tara Twinkle Toes.' I squeeze her hand gently. 'You know how you like having your nails painted.'

I can almost see the trace of a smile on her thin mouth. 'What colour are you going to go for?'

She shrugs her shoulders.

'Do you want glittery bits over the top of them?' I remember noticing Sophie's black nails were coated with golden dollar signs.

'Daddy doesn't let me have glittery bits.' Her words hang awkwardly in the air between us.

'Well, you can have them today.' I force myself to smile. We push open the beauty salon door and are met with several heavily made-up grinning faces.

'Hello, Tara.' Sara, the girl from the football club bar, who works at the salon, saunters over. Tara stares at Sara's jewelled nose piercing and silver lipstick.

'Shall we go and have some fun with your nails?' Her metallic lips part to reveal a dazzling row of pearly white teeth.

Tara brightens and nods enthusiastically at Sara. I watch as she reaches up to hold the beautician's hand and walks off to a small table.

I take one of the leather seats by the till. My eyes are firmly fixed upon Tara, who keeps looking out for me.

The sight of Tara giggling with the beautician loosens my shoulders and neck. I sink back into the chair and briefly glance at the person sat next to me. After a frantic double take, I realise I'm face to face with Pippa Browning. The shock makes me sit bolt upright in surprise.

Being in such close proximity to her gives me a weird tingling feeling. We stare at each other and I force out a weak smile.

'Hi,' she speaks with a cool tone to her voice.

My eyes wander over her long brown hair, desperately trying to escape the messy knot on top of her head, her exquisite face. I have to say something and quick. 'You come here often?' My attempt at polite conversation crashes and burns. She rolls her eyes and turns away.

'Pippa Browning.' A blonde beautician is stood beaming at Pippa. I watch Pippa rise and follow her into a little room.

Tara's nails are taking longer than I imagined. I can't understand why it takes so long to stick on paint and glittery bits.

Pippa returns and sits in her seat. I glance at her face and notice an angry red tramline running across her eyebrows. Looking away quickly, I take a gulp of salon air. What on earth has Pippa had done to her forehead?

As she picks up a magazine, I attempt to telepathically connect with Sara. I need to escape before I say something stupid.

'Are you waiting for someone or are you getting a treatment?' Pippa directs the question at me, although her eyes remain firmly fixed on her magazine.

'My niece, she's getting her nails painted.' I gesture towards Tara, swinging her legs and giggling.

'Oh.' Pippa rests the magazine on her lap.

After a brief argument with my brain my mouth decides to say whatever it wants. 'You've had something done to your forehead, haven't you ... it's very red?'

In my defence I don't normally have these communication issues with other women. For some reason Pippa Browning makes me go a little strange.

'I've had eyebrows waxed.' She returns to stare at the fashion article.

A bleeping sound drifts out of her handbag. I watch her bend down to retrieve it.

'Daisy, what do you want?' Pippa gives me a worried glance. 'No, I'm in the beautician's, just look after your brother and sister.'

Lowering myself into my seat I grab a leaflet and try to look as though it's a subject area I'm interested in ... colonic irrigation. Pippa raises her red tramline at me after catching sight of the leaflet. I cast her a nervous smile and bring the leaflet closer to my face.

'Daisy, I've told you to stop using those rude words!' Pippa is barking into her mobile. I want to put my hands over my ears at her shrill voice but don't because it would be rude.

'*Daisy!*' Her voice makes me jump. 'Pack it in!'

I watch her hang up on Daisy and lower her head for a moment.

She lifts it back up and gives me a smile, but her eyes say. 'Daisy's at a difficult age.'

An image of Daisy stood with her arms looped around Jason's neck appears in my mind, quickly followed by the sound bite of her drunken rant as I helped her home.

Apparently, no one knows what it's like to be a teenager.

'Uncle Mikey!' shouts Tara, bounding over. 'Look at my nails.'

'Wow,' I say, rising from the chair. 'Isn't she clever?' I give Sara a wink. Out of the corner of my eye, I catch sight of Pippa watching me.

Tara and I go to leave the salon. I nod quickly to Pippa and she hands me the leaflet I'd left on my seat. 'You forgot this.'

My cheeks go warm as I take it from her. She returns to her magazine.

We walk away from the salon. As Tara grabs my hand and leads us both towards an old-fashioned sweet shop, I look back over my shoulder at the salon window. For a split second, Pippa turns around in her chair and stares at me. Trying to act cool, I flick my hair and dive into the shop, unaware that by doing so I've just agreed to Tara's request for an extra-large packet of sugary sweets.

CHAPTER 14

PIPPA

I expected to emerge from the beauty salon feeling relaxed and pampered. Instead, I burst out of the salon door with a racing heart and my whole body tingling. As I step onto the pavement my clammy hands drop my phone. Picking it up I frantically tap out a message.

OMG, he was in the salon. I message the *WhatsApp* group with Emma and Mel.

Who? Emma replies almost immediately.

Mikey Stenton!

Emma sends a series of kissing emojis and: *with one of his many girlfriends?*

No, with his little niece. Irritation prickles my cheeks. It would have been great to say the international playboy had been in there with one of his female followers.

So what's your issue? Emma follows up her text with a thinking face emoji.

He chatted me up. First line – do you come here often? #gross

Emma's response makes me smile. What do you expect? #internationalloverman?

He was all over the beautician. I recall the wink Mikey gave her.

Eew! Emma's response makes me smile.

He was obsessed with a leaflet on colonic irrigation.

Mel joins in the conversation and sends a series of sick faced emojis.

He looked rough! I text back, recalling Mikey's pale face, the bags nestled underneath his eyes, and his unshaven appearance.

Is he on drugs? Emma's reply makes me stand still in the street.

Oh God – has Dan suggested I date a wild, partying, drug addict?

Walking to the café where the kids are waiting, I catch sight of my new eyebrows in a shop window. I stop and gently run my fingers over them. Persuading me to get them waxed and shaped has been a winning suggestion from Emma. My drowsy and tired eyes have been revitalised.

As I push open the café door, the sound of my children arguing greets my ears.

'Give me back my drink, Billy!' screams Libby.

'No way!' he yells back.

I locate my offspring having a tug of war over a can of fizzy pop. Daisy is stood behind them shouting at someone on her mobile. Taking a deep breath, I make my way over.

Once I get close, I become distracted by the cries of another child having a tantrum.

'*I hate this drink!*' screams the child. The café grows silent. Everyone, including the waitress, turns to look in the direction of the child. I flick my head to see Mikey Stenton trying to calm his angry, red-faced niece. Our eyes meet and I raise one of my waxed eyebrows at him.

He casts me a look of suffering, which I happily ignore. The same look was cast my way when Daisy phoned in the beautician's, threatening to hit both her brother and sister. I knew the things running through his head: her poor parenting skills and nightmare kids.

I head towards my own table of child nightmares. Libby and

Billy both receive one of my new evil stares. This is something Helen could write a book on. She'd emailed me following her last visit. Apparently, she has taken it upon herself to help support me with the kids as she thinks I'm struggling after the garage roof incident. In the lengthy email, she advised me to start mastering a good stare. According to her, a good cold stare will let them know a whole heap of suffering is coming their way if they carry on with their naughty behaviour. Helen advised I should practice daily in the mirror and try to focus on *haunting eyes*. She'd attached several photos of her giving the mirror a few versions of her *haunting eyes*. I sent the email to Emma who thought it was hilarious.

Libby and Billy freeze at the sight of me. My new stare worked. Daisy has hung up and is looking at me. 'Mum, you look so different.'

I smile and touch my new eyebrows. 'Do you like them?'

The sound of the little girl with Mikey hammering her fists onto the table and kicking her feet against the chair distracts us. His down turned mouth makes him look lost and alone.

The second I experience an ounce of pity for him, I remind myself Mikey Stenton is probably getting ready to hand the child back over to her parents so he can go dancing with half-naked women.

Mikey places his head in his hands while his niece rages. I look at his clothes, which look like they haven't been washed or ironed in a long time. This is what happens to someone who has too much fun. They start to lose interest in their appearance.

'Come on, kids, we're going.' I gather my bag and coat.

Daisy shakes her head. 'Mum, I need to stay here and make a phone call.'

The old couple on the table opposite give me a worried glance.

'Daisy, we are leaving now.'

'Mum, you don't understand, I need to make this call,' shouts

Daisy, standing and waving her phone. My eyes flick to Daisy's bare white midriff, poking out of her red cropped top. 'Your stomach is on show,' I hiss, gesturing at her tummy.

'Called style, Mum.' Daisy rolls her eyes. 'You wouldn't understand.'

I gesture for them all to leave. As we pass Mikey, he gives me a smile which I ignore. Once he's child-free, he'll be going out to enjoy himself at some pool party attended by hundreds of scantily clad women, who will no doubt appear on his *Instagram* feed. I suppress the urge to say something about how partying is not the answer to everything in life.

The kids and I head for the car park. Daisy is muttering to herself as she yanks across the seat belt.

'What's wrong, Daisy?' I ask, before swinging the car out of a space.

'I hate my life.' Daisy takes out her phone from the pocket of her black jeans.

'You don't mean that.' I stop the car.

Daisy nods. 'You've taken away my ladder. Now I can't go out and see my mates when I like.'

There's a murmuring in the back of the car from Billy and Libby.

'You should not have been using that ladder.' I start the car engine again and turn onto the main road.

'Can we have it back?' Billy asks, with a serious expression on his little face.

Luckily, the lights are still red when I turn around to my children. 'No, you're not using an emergency ladder to get out of the house whenever you want.' I turn my attention back to the road. 'Pauline next door must be thinking all sorts.'

Daisy nods. 'I bet all the kids at her old school were constantly sneaking out to get pissed.'

I glare at Daisy. 'Libby and Billy, ignore what your sister just said.'

As we pull up outside *Claire's Glossy Locks* hair salon, I take a deep breath and prepare myself for a hair overhaul.

Inside, the salon has a trendy minimalist decor: brilliant white walls, polished black floor tiles, and sleek black leather chairs. Dance music blares out from a speaker and Daisy is making strange dance shapes. At the back is the waiting area: a black leather sofa and a small table covered with magazines. We wait for Claire to finish colouring a young woman's hair.

I flick through several articles on short cuts in the collection of hair magazines. Libby plays on an app on her phone, Billy reads his football sticker book, and Daisy stares at the articles over my shoulder. 'Mum, don't get all your hair cut off.'

Studying an article about the benefits of a shorter haircut in your thirties and at the same time imagining myself with hair shorter than Billy's, I reply, 'It's my hair, Daisy.'

Daisy snorts. 'It won't suit you. Please don't look like my art teacher. Not cool, Mum.'

'I don't care, Daisy, it's time for me to start a new life,' I say with a grin. My chest swells at the thought of a transformed Pippa Browning leaving the salon and sporting a new pixie style haircut.

'Please, Mum, I'm begging you.' Daisy, clasps her hands together in a prayer like pose.

'I need a change.' I leaf through another magazine.

'Pippa Browning,' asks Claire. I rise and order the kids to stay seated.

Daisy casts me a pained expression. 'Mum, please don't do this.'

I smile and head over to the chair. Claire, the young and pretty hairdresser, inspects my hair. As she attempts to loosen the greasy knot on top of my head, I notice her arms are sun kissed golden brown, her hair long, shiny, and black. She's wearing a simple navy vest top, which hugs her minuscule figure perfectly, and cut-off faded jeans. Even Claire's feet look exciting, adorned with toe rings, encased in pink flip flops, and sporting an ankle bracelet. I compare all this to my own faded striped top, baggy cotton trousers, and old plimsolls.

Before I have time to get depressed about how I look, a gown is thrown over me and fastened at the back.

'Pippa, what are we doing today?' Claire's eyes flick to the greasy hair, covering my back and shoulders. The sight of it has sent her sculptured black eyebrows into a sharp arch.

'Pixie cut.' I make wriggly worm-like movements with my fingers around my face.

Claire takes a deep breath and frowns. 'Are you sure you want to go short?' Her voice wavers.

'Yes.' I fold my arms underneath the gown and beam with pride. I'll make my own decisions about my hair. I won't listen to advice from Dan.

'Mum, please don't do this!' Daisy shouts from across the hair salon. I turn my eyes to Claire and smile.

Claire looks towards the kids and smiles. 'Are they yours?'

'Yes, they're all mine,' I reply, turning back to look at myself in the mirror.

Combing through my hair, Claire gives me her thoughts. 'If I was you, I would go for something which rests on your shoulders. Get rid of the heavy length and maybe put a fringe in.'

I catch sight of the red notebook, sticking out of my handbag. Dan's words echo inside my mind: *don't get your hair cut off!* Doubt starts to consume me. Maybe he had a point?

'Mum, listen to me,' shouts Daisy. 'You'll regret it. On Google it says old hair grows slow so it will take years to grow back.'

Claire smiles. 'Look, it will be shorter but not as drastic. You would really suit a blunt cut fringe.'

I chew over her words. Dan said a fringe would suit me.

'Let's get your hair washed and then you can make a decision.'

The warm water trickles over my head. I visualise myself with a cut shorter than Billy's hair. I imagine what it would look like.

In the magazine article I read before Claire had summoned me, a shorter hairstyle apparently forces you to get creative with make-up and accessories. You have to overhaul your wardrobe as what suited long hair won't look good with short hair. A wave of tiredness washes over me at the thought of doing all this.

I return to the chair in front of the mirror. Claire starts to comb through my damp hair.

'Well then, Pippa, what's it to be?' Claire asks.

I take a deep breath. The world needs a new Pippa Browning. Out with the old and in with the new. 'Let's go pixie cut. Very short.'

'Noooooooooooo!' shouts Daisy, staring at her phone.

I scowl at my daughter.

'Tom Ridge,' blurts out Daisy, flashing her phone at me. 'He's got a girlfriend.' She lets out a piercing howl and everyone in the salon turns to stare at her.

Claire's eyes widen in surprise.

'She's got a little crush on Tom Ridge,' I say to Claire as Daisy breaks into a series of noisy sobs.

Claire takes in a deep breath and casts Daisy a worrying look. 'That doesn't look like a little crush.' She turns back to me. 'Do you still want the pixie cut, Pippa?'

The urge to radically change my life vanishes. All I want to do is rush home and talk to Daisy about Tom Ridge. Common sense kicks in. I don't possess the inner strength or energy to deal with a new short haircut, establish a new make-up routine, buy a new wardrobe, and deal with a teenage daughter struggling with her emotions. I can barely function with brushing my hair in the mornings.

'Let's just go shoulder length and add the fringe.' I nod at Claire, who breaks into a huge grin.

Daisy shuffles back to her chair and allows Libby to cuddle her.

'Looks like you have your hands full,' Claire smiles, while snipping my wet hair.

I let out a nervous laugh. 'Yes I have.'

When she finishes blow drying my new shoulder-length hair, I stare in amazement at how shiny and bouncy it looks. The cute curl to the ends makes me smile and the new fringe frames my face.

'Thank you, Claire,' I gush, stepping out of the chair and letting her unfasten my gown.

'Wow, Mum, you look cool.' Billy races over to give me a cuddle.

As we leave the hairdressers, I catch Daisy's arm. 'Are you okay?' I ask, sensing the need for some mother and teenage daughter time.

'He's playing games again. I get it,' replies Daisy flicking her black hair out of her eyes.

Seconds before I erupt with frustration at Daisy, I catch sight of myself in the butcher's window. I stop and stare at the woman in the reflection. She looks fancy and chic. Dan was right, the fringe did suit me.

My eyes linger over my shabby and tired clothes. If I switch to the supermarket's own brand of wine, buy Daisy a cheaper pair of trainers, and work a few shifts a week for Mel, we could work through this.

'Kids.' I bring them all to a halt. 'I need some new clothes.'

CHAPTER 15

PIPPA

On the way home, the kids and I check out Mel's new coffee shop. She's sent me a text with the address and directions where to park.

As we enter the newly named *Mel's Coffee Shop,* I notice the tan-coloured leather sofas, an array of little tables covered with red polka-dot tablecloths, wooden dressers full of colourful china, and huge vases filled with pretty flowers. My heart quickens at the thought of working in a place like this.

Billy and Libby sit at a little table near the window and Daisy goes to sulk on a table at the far end. 'You okay, Daisy?' I ask.

She wipes a tear from her cheek. 'It was going to happen at some point. I knew Maisie had the hots for him.'

Squeezing her shoulder, I plant a little kiss on the top of her head. 'Come on. Let's put an end to the Tom Ridge situation. I know it hurts, but he wasn't doing you much good.'

Daisy nods and puts down her phone. 'You're right, Mum.'

Mel is stood by the counter talking to Emma and when she sees me, her face breaks into a huge smile. 'Oh my goodness, Pip, look at you!'

They both rush over, screeching and waving their hands.

'That is some makeover. Your hair is amazing!' gushes Emma. 'The ghastly bun is gone.'

Mel touches my hair. 'It's so shiny and bouncy. You really suit the fringe. Dan was right.'

A beaming smile spreads across my face. 'I'm glad I listened to you both.'

Emma shakes her head. 'All Dan's doing.'

Looking around the pretty little coffee shop and to my surprise it gives me a burst of excitement.

'This is a fabulous place, Mel.'

She lets out a little squeal. 'I would come to a place like this. You know, hang out with friends and relax.'

We all nod with knowing looks. This was the sort of place we would come to sip coffee, catch up with each other's lives, and scoff delicious cakes.

I watch Mel beam from ear to ear at the sight of the new elaborate silver coffee machine behind the counter.

My excitement evaporates as I see the empty cake counter. The public will get a chance to eat my cakes. Fear turns my legs to jelly. I still don't think my cakes are good enough for this. Stifling a sinking feeling I turn to my friends.

'So, when do you want me to start?' I run my hand over the gorgeous red polka-dot tablecloth and touch the little white vase holding a colourful bouquet of flowers.

Mel loops her arm through mine and steers me behind the counter. She takes me into the back with its large kitchen area. 'This is where you can create your magic cakes.'

My mouth falls open at the sight of the large wooden table taking centre stage in the middle of the room. Surrounding it are two gleaming ovens, a brand-new stainless-steel sink, a huge fridge-freezer, and an array of utensils hanging off the cream walls. 'I can bake in here?'

Mel nods. 'We open officially at the end of the month, so it would be great to have the first batch of cakes for then. Are you going to do some shifts behind the counter too? We can agree on what I need to pay you.'

I run my hand through my new hair and attempt to suppress a wave of baking anxiety. 'Are you sure you want my cakes, Mel?'

'What?'

'Well,' I mumble, 'I've spent the last three years looking after kids and before that I ...'

'Pip, it's time for you to do something with those fabulous cakes and as Dan said, you need to find yourself.'

Emma butts in. 'You can't stay at home painting everything that moves duck-egg blue.'

I stammer, 'But ... I ... have no idea ... how to use the ... coffee machine.'

We walk back out to the counter. Mel goes to stand in front of it and says, 'I'll train you.'

Emma places her arms around us. 'This is the start of something special, ladies.'

Mel is buzzing with excitement and hopping from one leg to the other, I can't remember seeing her this happy. 'Look at you, Mel,' I gush, 'you look like a new woman.'

Letting her eyes wander around her coffee shop, Mel nods. 'Mum would be proud.'

Gesturing for me to take a chair, Mel plonks herself down. 'I know it's a lot to take in, but I think together we can do something wonderful, Pip. Let's have a coffee. What do the kids want?'

Huddled around a table, the three of us sip delicious cups of freshly made coffee. The kids stay at the far end of the coffee shop on their phones and iPads.

'So, are you going to take a new photo for your dating profile?' asks Emma, placing her cup down on its saucer.

I take a deep breath. 'Yes, even though I'm still not totally convinced about the idea of dating.'

Mel reaches out to give my shoulder a rub. 'Pip, you'll be fine.

Seriously, you look amazing. This transformation of yours will definitely get you some dating traffic.'

Emma shoots up out of her seat. 'Right, no time like the present. Are those new clothes in your bag?'

I nod. 'Three tops and a pair of jeans.'

'Okay, go change in the toilets and we'll take some photos here.'

'What? Now?'

Mel hands me my bag of clothes. 'Yes, now, Pip.'

I come out of the toilets wearing a white and red striped top and my new fitted dark blue jeans. Emma grins as I go to stand by the table. She grabs her phone and asks me to sit down at one of the little tables.

'You look so different, Pip,' coos Mel. 'The next stage is getting you into a dress.'

'Make-up,' advises Emma. 'We need some make-up on your lovely face. Not a lot, but I'm thinking a bit of mascara and some lip gloss.'

Mel thrusts me her mascara. 'Go on, put some on.'

Using Emma's compact mirror, I apply a coat of mascara to my newly tinted lashes and smear on a coat of glossy pink lip balm.

Emma takes a number of profile shots, and as she says, 'Looking like I'm in the mood for some romance.'

We gather round Emma's phone to decide which picture I should use. 'I look so different,' I murmur, struggling to recognise the glamorous woman in the photos.

'You look very French,' says Mel, placing her hands on her hips. 'Chic and sophisticated.'

Before I have time to think, Emma has grabbed my phone and is busy uploading the best one onto to my online profile and updating my bio. 'I'm saying you work in a funky little coffee shop and bake prize-winning fairy cakes.'

'But they're not prize winning,' I say.

Emma shakes her head. 'Trust me, they will be, and men don't pick up the details on these things.'

Mel places her arm over my shoulders. 'Pip, next month will be the start of your new life. Are you excited?'

I survey the coffee shop and imagine friends meeting up for a coffee, a cake, and a chat. The place has a wonderful homely feel to it and those comfy sofas would be perfect for new mums to park their buggy next to and relax. My eyes trail over my new clothes and my hand reaches up to feel my new shorter, glossier hair. A warm tingling shoots across my chest.

'Yes, I am.'

CHAPTER 16

MIKEY

'Tara, turn the music down!' I bark as my head throbs with pain. Tara cranks up the volume on her iPad.

'*No!*' she shouts, defiantly, leaping off the sofa with excitement.

It's been two weeks since I agreed to help Mum with Tara. I think it's safe to say I'm a shadow of my former self. Tara and I have spent so much time together, my bachelor life is a distant memory.

Some days I'm so tired I can barely keep my eyes open by late afternoon. When I'm not helping Mum with the housework, the washing, and the cleaning, I'm playing board games with Tara, colouring in complicated drawings, and reading endless stories to her. Going to work has become a place where I can have a rest.

'Michael ... it's all right if she wants to play her music.' Mum smiles at Tara. 'It's nice to see our girl happy. You've done so well with her.'

To our surprise, Tara has crept out of her grief-encased shell. Since I've started doing the childcare, her tears have dried up, and she's managed a full week at school.

Tara rushes over to my mother. 'Nan, can I go get some lemonade please?'

I've learnt, the hard way, over the last fortnight, too much sugar leads to a hyper and hard to control Tara. 'No more fizzy drinks.' I give Tara a nod.

'Whhhhyyyy?' moans Tara.

I know I'm losing my popular relative shine.

Tare walks out of the living room and into the kitchen. A wave of tiredness envelops me. I'm not sure I have the energy to follow her. Last night she woke up numerous times shouting for Stan.

Her voice from the kitchen travels through into the living room. 'This lemonade is yummy.'

I take a deep breath and try to stay calm.

Tara charges back into the living room. 'Nan, will you play with me?' she cries, grabbing a board game and racing over to Mum.

'Go upstairs, Tara. Come on, Nan's tired.' Mum's been complaining a lot lately about being weaker and in the early hours of the morning, after settling Tara, I found her lying twisted on the bathroom floor, in a pool of urine. She'd tried to go to the toilet by herself. Guilt wrapped itself around me as she made a joke about what she would have done if I hadn't stayed the night. I asked her whether she'd fallen since Stan had died and when she'd been looking after Tara. Mum looked up at me with watery eyes and confessed to it being a regular occurrence.

Once I'd cleaned her up and helped her back to bed, Tara wandered into Mum's bedroom demanding to be read a story. I nearly cried with exhaustion.

'Nan,' moans Tara, tugging on Mum's arm. 'Play with me.'

My patience is wearing thin. 'Tara – *upstairs!*'

'*No!*' Tara stamps her foot. Her cheeks are red and inflamed.

I lay back in my chair, close my eyes, and count to ten. When I open them, Tara has become distracted with my mother's photos.

'Nan, you have lots of photos of Daddy.' She gently touches each one.

There are so many: Stan at his graduation, Stan up a hill, with baby Tara strapped to his front, Stan on his bike with a young Tara sat in a child seat at the back, Stan with Tara sat on his shoulders and Stan on a beach with Tara who was dressed in a sparkly unicorn swimming costume.

My mother smiles and wipes her eyes. 'Yes, I do.'

I scan the room for photos of me. The only one she has resides behind the brass candle holder on the mantlepiece. Lying in the sea on an inflatable dolphin, I look like a grinning idiot in Magaluf. I'm wearing dark shades to disguise the fact I'd drunk too much the night before. An unknown female arm is massaging my bare chest. My mother has cut the owner of the arm out.

Shame crawls over me, turning my stomach. A few years ago, I would have laughed with Stan at our mother's army of *proud son* photos, in comparison to my single, half cropped, beach bum photo. I chew on my thumb until I can taste blood in my mouth.

My eyes flick to Tara, still gazing at all the photos of Stan. Doubt sets up camp inside my mind. This young girl does not need a beach bum like me spending so much time with her. Perhaps I should leave and let Mum take over? My hands are becoming hot and clammy.

Rising from my chair, I start to pace the living room. It's not been easy over the past few weeks struggling with Tara and coming to terms with my mother's deteriorating health. Tara has been hard work in the daytime and inconsolable at tonight. The photo of me in Magaluf drags my attention back to it, leaving an indelible imprint on my mind. Tara needs someone sensible, mature, and not a Magaluf beach idiot.

'Uncle Mikey,' says Tara, 'will you do some colouring with me?'

'Not now,' I mumble, sitting back down and crossing my arms.

I can't drag my eyes away from the photo my mother has of me. A painful reminder of my old, carefree, and pleasurable life, where I didn't have to worry about a thing. I happily blocked out my mother's Multiple Sclerosis diagnosis, ignored the signs her condition was worsening, broke all serious commitments with people I loved, let Stan down on numerous occasions with helping out with Tara, cared for no one, and did what I wanted.

The air inside the living room evaporates. Scratching my neck turns into clawing at my shirt collar. Mounting pressure inside my head quickens my breathing.

'Are you okay?' My mother casts me a look of concern.

I grab my car keys. 'I need to go out, Tara, you stay here with Nan.'

'No, please … no … please no, Uncle Mikey.' Tara holds onto my arm. 'Please don't leave me!'

I disentangle her arms from mine. 'Tara, I need some time on my own.'

'*No!*' she screams, tears coming from nowhere and pouring down her face.

Guilt makes my head throb and nausea collects at the bottom of my gut.

I have to escape. Ignoring her cries, I stride out of my mother's house and dive into my car.

My hand grips the steering wheel as I head for Sophie's flat. Images of Tara's little tear-stained face persist in popping up inside my mind. I need some time out.

Even though Sophie has been texting me, I've not replied or gone to her flat since Stan died.

As soon as the traffic lights change, I accelerate, and then turn sharply into the street which leads to her flat. After dumping the car, I walk purposefully towards her flat. All the shit in my life needs to be blocked out. I want to get back to being the grinning idiot in the beach photo.

Sophie answers the door after my fourth rap. She leans against the doorframe, holding a bottle of cider and staring at me. Her brown hair has been straightened and hangs poker straight, framing her pale face, which is covered in a thick layer of foundation.

'Uh hello, stranger.' She raises a pencil-thin eyebrow. 'Did you not get my texts?'

'Been busy – can I come in?' I lean in to kiss her on the cheek.

She steps back and bats me away. 'You don't respond to my texts. You don't return my calls and without warning, you turn up on my doorstep.'

I exhale loudly. 'Look can I come in or not?'

Sophie rolls her mascara-clad eyes and steps aside. I barge past into her cramped kitchen diner.

Tara's crying face appears in my mind. I do my best to block it out by grabbing Sophie by the arm and pulling her towards me.

'Where have you been?' she scowls. 'You look like shit!'

I let her break away to get me a bottle of beer from the work surface. When she presents it to me, I snatch it out of her hand, flick open the metal lid and drink greedily.

'I have a boyfriend now, you know,' she says.

I shrug and take another drink. Sophie's love life has never really concerned me.

She drains her bottle. 'What do you want then?' She holds my gaze.

I begin to kiss her neck. 'You.'

'Listen, Mikey …' she pushes me away. 'I'm really skint.'

'What … again?'

She averts her dark eyes to the floor. 'I don't have any money. Zack needs a new coat.'

'I've given you enough money.'

She starts to unbutton her shirt, revealing two shapely breasts, packed into a black lacy bra.

Arousal takes over. I step towards her.

'I need some money.' She brushes herself against me.

'All right.' I reach in my back pocket for my wallet. The sound of Zack crying in his cot makes me hesitate. The image of Tara begging me not to leave flashes inside my mind.

Fumbling about with my wallet, I tell myself I'm not ready to be grown up or to stop being an idiot. I don't want to have to face uncomfortable things like dealing with my niece and sick mother. I have to preserve my carefree old life.

Sophie snatches my wallet and smiles. She takes out several notes. My stomach fills up with shame. This is wrong. I rub my face. Everything is so muddled.

'Please go sort Zack out,' I say as Sophie runs her hands over my hips.

She shakes her head. 'He's tired and needs an afternoon nap.'

I'm pulled by the hand into the bedroom. We collapse onto her bed and I watch her climb on top of me. Her hands frantically pulling at my jeans. I notice the look of determination on her face.

She glances at her bedside clock.

'Why do you keep looking at the clock. Are you going out?'

A smirk appears on her face. 'A few of us are going to the club later.'

I take hold of her hands. 'With my money? I thought you said he needs a new coat?'

Zack is letting out loud pitiful sobs. I can't do this. Tara's face comes tearing into my mind, dampening my arousal. She has no one apart from me and my mother. Her world imploded the day my brother died. As much as I kid myself, my mother's deteriorating health can't withstand caring for an energetic eight-year-old all day and night. Stan wouldn't have wanted me to leave Tara in such a distraught and broken state.

'I have to go home.' I push a half-naked Sophie away. 'Sort your son out.'

'What?' Sophie screeches, pulling the sheet around her. 'Ignore him.'

I make my way out of her bedroom. Nausea and disgust knot together in my gut as I walk out of her flat. I don't look back.

Yanking on my seat belt, I hit the steering wheel with frustration. 'Damn it!'

It takes ten minutes to get back to my mother's house. From inside the narrow hallway, I can hear Tara sobbing. She's stood by the side of Mum's chair, her blonde head resting on her Nan's shoulder. As I enter, she lifts her tear-stained face, making my heart ache.

'I couldn't leave you for long, Tara Twinkle Toes.' I smile. Her little face lights up as she races towards me, throwing her arms around my waist. A warm sensation floods through my chest. I crouch to her level and wipe a matted clump of blonde hair from her sweaty forehead and stroke her damp cheeks. 'How about a Disney film?'

Tara finally falls asleep on my shoulder, while Mum and I watch the rest of the movie.

'Proud of you tonight, Michael.' Mum reaches over to give me a tap on the knee.

I look up in surprise. 'Really?'

She nods. 'I don't think you realise how much Tara has come to depend on you over the last few weeks.'

I stroke Tara's golden hair. 'It's not easy, but I enjoy being with her.'

Mum smiles. 'When you offered to help me, I thought it would be a day or so. I never thought you'd be here every day, taking her to school and going on adventures with her.'

I lean back, placing my spare arm behind my head. I enjoy seeing my mother's face etched with what looks like pride for me.

'I've decided to join a new MS support group.' Mum casts me a furtive look.

Chewing on my lip, I imagine Mum sitting in a room full of strangers. 'Are you sure about this?'

She lets out a little laugh at my shocked expression. 'I can mix with others, Michael. Stan suggested it to me, before the accident. He said this group has a good social side.'

Guilt once again becomes a friend to me. Stan had been there for Mum. While I was dancing with half-naked women in bars, drinking the nights away with the football lads and taking unsavoury women back to my flat, Stan was taking Mum out on day trips, cooking her meals after he finished work, sorting out her disability allowance, and spending time with her. It's no surprise that he'd suggested support groups to her. He did all that and singlehandedly raised Tara. I'm starting to realise how much of a legend my brother was.

'But how would you get there?' I ask, picturing my boss's reaction at work when I inform him I need more time off to taxi my mother.

A faint smile spreads across my mother's face. 'I have a friend who'll give me a lift.'

I start to relax; Mum does have a few supportive friends; Patricia from up the road and Beryl, who she went to school with. It's nice to think they'll help her out.

Mum casts me a look of concern. 'I do worry about you sleeping on that camp bed so much.'

'Think my body has got used to it.'

Mum turns to me. 'Did I tell you we have a buyer for Stan's house?'

I shake my head. 'No, that's good.'

'Patricia has been a godsend dealing with all of Stan's affairs.'

Guilt finds me again. I should be the one helping out my mum.

After I help Mum to her bedroom and make sure she's okay, I return downstairs and carry Tara up to bed. She lays down with her toy rabbit tucked under her arm.

Before leaving her room, I stare down at the little girl, fast asleep in front of me. She stirs and opens her eyes.

'Uncle Mikey,' she whispers, with a warm smile.

Instinctively, I bend down and place a delicate kiss on her forehead. 'Goodnight, Tara Twinkle Toes.'

CHAPTER 17

MIKEY

*L*ying on the makeshift camp bed in Mum's spare room I stretch out. My mind is awash with leaving Sophie's and coming back for Tara. It has to be one of the best things I've ever done. Seeing Tara smile again, watching her Disney film, made me feel like a hero and not an idiot. This is new emotional territory for me.

A shaft of silver moonlight lights up the opened navy-blue sports bag on the floor next to my bed, stuffed full of clothes, underwear, a toothbrush, shaving stuff, and my PlayStation. Sticking out of a roll of boxer shorts is the notebook Dan wrote me. I scratch my head. How the hell did that get in my bag?

I reach out to grab it. After turning on the light, I open it.

> *Mikey,*
> *By the time you read this I will be in heaven, scoring endless goals for God in the new Heaven Football League.*
> *I know this sounds crazy, but I think you should consider dating Pippa.*
> *Before you go off on one and tell me I've lost my mind, read what I have to say.*

Pippa is so precious to me, but I don't want her to spend the rest of her life in mourning.

She needs to find someone who'll put that smile back on her face, the one my brain tumour sadly took away.

Mikey, let's be honest, you've always fancied my wife. On those nights you used to come and collect me for football training, I saw the way you looked at her. Mate, it was an unforgettable stare. Everyone at the football club used to take the piss out of you as they said you went silent when Pippa and I walked in. I'm okay with this.

You're a great bloke and over the years I'm glad I've got to know the real Mikey Stenton. You've rescued me on more than one occasion, and I couldn't think of anyone better to make my Pippa happy.

The issue we have is that you need to sort your life out.

I've written you some instructions on how to make my wife fall in love with you.

I know you don't need much help with falling in love as she's had a place in your heart for years.

But first, here's some life advice for you:

Stop being an idiot! Pippa is not going to fall in love with an idiot.

Learn a thing or two from Stan. Your brother hasn't had it easy raising his kid alone, but he's done it admirably. Learn from him!

Put an end to the constant partying and nights out.

Take responsibility for your actions.

Start thinking of others.

I can almost hear Dan's booming voice in my ears. With a trembling hand, I turn over the page.

How to make Pippa fall in love with you ...

Do something for the community. She likes local heroes.

Support and encourage her to follow her dreams. Pippa has so many talents and skills, which she has kept hidden away while raising the kids and looking after me. She just lacks a bit of confidence.

Get my kids on your side. Mate, you're great with kids. I've seen you with your niece. My kids will like you.

Make her smile every day.

Treat her with respect.

There are a few more pages where Dan has advised me on what to wear on dates, where to take her, and what wine she likes. Then there's another message.

Mate,

I know there's a great bloke inside of you. Shall I tell you why I know this? A few years ago, we went to Magaluf on a football tour. Remember the one? I was having a hard time at home: kids were young and demanding and Pippa wasn't happy with me for working away a lot.

On the tour we got talking to those girls from Lancaster. I got friendly with that girl, Rosie – the one with the massive chest and red hair. She wanted me to go back to her hotel. Mate, I was tempted. It would have been so easy for me to go to her room. So many of the lads were up to no good. Pippa would never have known, but you stopped me. You took me aside and told me not to risk losing what I had at home. You asked why I'd want to destroy something so precious. Remember our heated chat by the pool? I wanted to punch you.

I'm so grateful to you for stopping me. You rescued me. This is why I know you're a great bloke, Mikey. Under all that bravado is a decent man. Someone I'm proud to know.

This is why I want you to sort your life out and consider dating my Pippa.

With the back of my hand, I wipe my damp cheek. Closing my eyes, I can see Dan sat in a white plastic chair by the pool, telling me all the reasons why he should go back to Rosie's hotel room. I remember something deep inside of me urging me to stop him. At one point I think I said, 'you have a beautiful wife and three great kids at home, mate, don't ruin everything with Rosie. Trust me, you'll feel like shit tomorrow.'

We came close to a fight as Dan couldn't understand why I was being so protective of Pippa and the kids.

Placing the notebook back in my bag, I lie back on my bed. It's nice to know Dan had such faith in me but I still don't think I'm worthy of Pippa's attention.

I can't have been asleep for long when Tara's sobs drift into the bedroom. Hauling myself up, I ignore my aching back and heavy lead-like legs.

'I want Daddy.' Tara is by my side as soon as I enter her room. She presses her hot head into my shoulder.

'I'm here, Tara, don't cry.' Wrapping my arms around her, I rock her gently.

She leaves a damp patch on my T-shirt. 'I don't feel very well,' she whispers, wiping away a tear.

'Let's go and get some medicine, you're a bit warm.' I lead her by the hand downstairs.

There are a handful of stars dotted across the sky, blinking through the gap in the living room curtains. Then the sound of Tara vomiting all over the carpet fills the air.

Her eyes are brimming with tears as she stands in her pink sparkly pyjamas, staring down at the yellow sick on the carpet.

'Let me find you a bowl.'

A wave of tiredness washes over me as I clean up the vomit. Tara sits on the sofa, swinging her legs and waving the empty sick bowl around her head.

Once I finish, I open the window to get rid of the smell. I go back into the kitchen to find some medicine. As I rummage through the first aid box, more vomiting sounds drift into the kitchen. Tara screams. She's missed the sick bowl and a fresh pile of yellow lumpy sick is splattered across Mum's carpet.

An hour later and we are both sat on the sofa. She has been sick several times, and it's easier to sit and watch a Disney movie with her than go upstairs to bed.

There's no way she can go to school. My shoulders have stiffened, and nausea is making my stomach turn. I'm anxious about ringing Ian, my boss. Last week I fell behind with my sales projects and there was a complaint about poor service from one of my clients. The last thing he's going to want to hear is me phoning in sick.

The irritating monotone bleep from my phone alarm wakes me. With heavy eyelids, I sit up. Both Tara and I are curled up on the sofa. A strong aroma of vomit still hangs in the air. The credits to the film are running up the TV screen.

Mum appears, walking unaided. Before I have a chance to ask whether she's feeling better she picks up on the sick. 'Oh no, is our girl not well?'

I stroke sleeping Tara's hair. 'She stopped throwing up at around three.' Before heading off to the bathroom, I give my beard a satisfying scratch. The bright light makes me groan. I don't recognise the man staring back at me. His skin possesses a grey tinge, there are puffy pink bags lining his eyes, and a thick wiry beard coats his chin.

After a cold shower and a coffee, I wake Tara. She stirs and begins to cry. 'I don't feel well, Uncle Mikey.'

'It's okay, I'm going to stay with you today.'

'I don't want to go to school.' She rubs her tummy.

Sitting on the sofa beside her I put my arm around her little shoulders. 'Tara, come on, don't cry.'

'What about work, Michael?' asks Mum.

I look up and force out a positive smile. 'It'll be okay.'

CHAPTER 18

PIPPA

*M*aria, the bulldog, is howling downstairs. When God was handing out pet patience, Maria was not at the front of the queue.

I'm busy showering and washing my hair after a stressful school run. Strong jets of hot water are soothing my aching head.

We all woke late, which I've tried to blame on the kids, but it's actually my fault. Mel and Emma turned up last night. We had a mini celebration about Mel's new business. It soon got messy after we opened a bottle of rum and Mel handed me my outfit for Monday's grand opening.

Mel and I are both going to be wearing red-and-white polka-dot fitted dresses, which match the tablecloths. Several rum and cokes later, Mel and I were modelling our outfits up and down the living room. Emma was cheering us on from the sofa and taking embarrassing pics for *Facebook*.

To be honest, I'm glad Mel approached the idea of me wearing a dress on Monday after a few shots, as if she'd done it when I was sober; I would have refused.

Mel also made a point of showing us Mikey's *Facebook* feed. One of the football lads had tagged a photo of him last year, stood on the pitch, with a cigarette hanging out of his mouth. The post said something about Mikey needing to get his lazy arse back to training.

'He's probably partying abroad,' I said, before draining another rum and coke.

Emma put her arms around me. 'Stay away from the hairy ballerina!'

Before the school run had even started, I was nursing a thick head and no amount of toothpaste could get rid of my wild dog breath.

As we left for school, I caught Daisy texting Tom Ridge a video clip of her own love rap. Wearing a cap worn back to front, Daisy rapped into the camera about Tom realising he's made a mistake with this year ten girl called Maisie and confessing he's actually in love with Daisy. I can't help but think the name of his new girlfriend plays into Daisy's rap writing skills.

After lecturing Daisy on yet again stalking Tom Ridge, I caught Libby stuffing my laptop into her school bag. She claimed a brilliant idea for her school project had come to her in the night and in order to get a gold star for it, she needed my laptop.

While all this was going on, Billy kicked his football along the hallway and knocked over my favourite vase.

Everyone climbed into the car, tear-stained and fed up.

My hair is now dry and doesn't need much styling. I'm loving my new look.

Maria and I've decided to go for a nice walk, forget about shouting at the kids, and try to get rid of my hangover. It's also a chance for me to wear the new casual clothes I bought the other day; a pair of jeans and a striped white-and-navy top.

Underneath a cloudless and brilliant blue sky, Maria and I make our way towards the park. With the kids at school, the vast green carpet of grass looks peaceful and inviting. Maria is gently tugging on her lead. Golden rays of warm sun are caressing my face. We've stepped onto the winding path which passes the children's park and I can see a familiar figure and a child.

Mikey Stenton stops pushing his niece on the swing and turns in my direction. Shrieks of laughter from his niece fill the air. All I can wonder is why the child isn't in school. This is yet another example of him being irresponsible. I can't believe he's taken a child out of school to play on the swings.

Maria's eyes are fixed on Mikey. She can smell his nervousness. My dog is obsessed with humans who don't like dogs. She'll pick up anyone in a mile radius who's displaying the slightest sign of nervousness. She'll become obsessed with that person and refuse to leave them alone. I've often compared this behaviour to Daisy's approach to crushes.

Before I can think, Maria bolts away from me. I lose the grip of the lead and watch in horror as Maria heads towards Mikey.

'Nooooooo!' I sprint towards Mikey, screaming and waving my arms.

Once I reach them, Maria is weaving excitedly in and out of Mikey's legs. She soon gets bored and resorts to jumping up at him.

'*Maria!*' I take back the lead.

'I don't like dogs.' Mikey raises his hands in defence and backs away from Maria.

I grab Maria by the collar. 'She knows. I'm sorry.'

He casts me a worried look.

Maria strains on her lead and gazes longingly at Mikey.

His attention turns towards me. For a second, neither of us speak. My eyes run over his red T-shirt, his toned arms, and faded blue jeans. The crop of stubble on his chin and the dark rings circling his eyes suggests he's been having fun again.

He scans my new hair, skinny jeans, and striped top.

My cheeks grow warm and I nervously twirl a strand of hair around my finger.

His niece shouts, breaking our awkward silence.

I glance over at Tara. 'Is she not in school today?'

'Oh … she's not … been … well,' he mumbles as Tara squeals with laughter while shooting down the slide.

I cast him a puzzled look. There's nothing wrong with his niece and she needs to be in school.

He shifts his weight uncomfortably from one foot to another.

'Uncle Mikey,' cries Tara, from the top of the slide.

He flicks his attention back to me. I see something flash across his warm brown eyes.

'I better go,' I say, before hurrying away, rubbing the top of my chest and making a mental note to buy some indigestion tablets when I'm next in the supermarket.

Once Maria and I have walked out of view, I text Emma and Mel.

OMG guess who I met in the park?

Mikey Stenton? Emma's reply is instant.

How did u know? I text back.

Just a hunch, she replies with a smiley emoji.

I walk back to the house unable to get his annoying face out of my head. In an attempt to forget about him, I make a start on tidying Libby's bedroom.

My phone bleeps the minute I stop screaming after discovering Libby's secret pet field mouse. The poor creature has been cleverly rehomed in a cardboard box with holes in and stuffed at the back of her wardrobe. When I look inside the box, the mouse makes a bid for freedom, into the dirty washing basket which has collapsed from all the clothes stuffed inside it.

After catching the mouse in a large saucepan from downstairs and setting it free in the garden, without Maria seeing, I place my hand against our tree and suck in lungfuls of air. Being a single parent is tough. Pauline Jacobs gives me an awkward look from her rose bushes as I put the saucepan down and wipe the sweat from my brow. My exhausted heart starts to calm down as I reach for my phone.

The beep is a notification from my dating app. A man has sent me a message. My heart breaks into another gallop.

Chris, aged 37, and a fitness instructor. From his photo, he looks reasonable: sea-blue eyes, a rugged face, and short blond hair. His stocky physique does not appeal to me, but I reassure myself with the hope of Chris having other attractive features.

Over a coffee and one of my fairy cakes, which I've awarded myself in view of all the stress I've endured, I debate whether to reply to him.

Apparently, on his exercise-free days he finds himself at the cinema, walking his dog, Rex, and socialising in town. On my exercise-free days, I chase field mice around Libby's bedroom, shout at all my kids on the school run, and stuff my face with fairy cakes.

I send Emma and Mel a screenshot of Chris and his profile.

Emma calls within seconds. 'OMG, Pippa, he's so fit!' she screams.

I stare at the phone. 'Are you being serious?'

In my head I quickly dismiss the outcome of my mind's comparison of Chris's and Mikey Stenton's looks – Chris comes second.

Emma giggles. 'Oh, come on, Pip, he is one hot dude, plus he's a fitness instructor. A date with him would knock you into shape.'

My eyes linger over Chris's profile. 'He doesn't have kids.'

'Pippa Browning, give him a try. Get out there. You'll love it.' Emma picks up on my disinterested vibes.

The reality of finding someone else hits me. My stomach knots itself as I come to terms with being forced to think about a dreaded first date. I cringe at the thought of kissing someone other than Dan and even worse sleeping with someone. I'm still struggling to say aloud the word *sex*.

'*Pippa!*' shouts Emma. 'Online dating is great!'

'Online dating is shit,' murmurs a male voice.

145

I stare at the phone. 'Are you in the car with someone?'

'Yes, my assistant, John. He's just been dumped by his girlfriend so ignore his views on dating. We're off to a client lunch meeting.' Emma has a job at a PR agency and to me all she seems to do is attend posh lunches. 'Message Chris, please.'

'What? Communicate with him?' I gasp, forgetting John is listening to our conversation.

Emma shrieks with laughter. 'Yes, Pip.'

Hanging up I notice my armpits are damp.

In a panic I send a quick text to Helen for her opinions on Chris. She responds quickly. Don't tell Rick but I'm secretly enjoying our rock star groupie bedroom events. He's making me feel eighteen again. When he stands on our bed in his underpants, strumming his electric guitar, I go a bit strange. This is just a phase. I'll find him annoying again next week. Stay away from dating!

My mouth falls open with surprise at my sister's text. I can't believe she's enjoying going along with Rick's bedroom fantasy.

Over a cup of soothing tea, I read Dan's notebook. He didn't know what he was doing when he wrote these instructions and more importantly, I rarely listened to Dan when we were married, and he wasn't sick. My eyes find a framed photo on the wall. It's of Mel, Emma, and me outside a tent, clad in cowboy hats, leopard print skirts, *Girls on Tour,* shirts. It was a few months after Billy had been born and Dan did his best to talk me out of it. First, he told me new mums should be taking it easy and then he confessed the thought of being left alone for a night with a newborn and two small children terrified him. I laughed at him and then went to the music festival.

With a flick of my fringe I turn to talk to a photo of his grinning face hung on the wall. 'Dan,' I say, closing his notebook. 'I *can* find happiness with a complete stranger.'

With trembling hands, I log onto my profile and reply to Chris's message.

Hi, Chris, thanks for your message. How are you?

I then keep myself busy by making a batch of princess fairy cakes. Since our discussion outside Poundland, Libby has had several sleepovers. After each one she's told me she's still feeling sad, so I've kept organising them. Daisy thinks I should have stopped after the first one as she thinks Libby is 'taking the piss.' Tonight's sleepover is princess themed, and I've made a huge batch of cakes adorned with tiny crowns.

Chris messages me back as I'm repairing one of the tiny silver crowns which has started to look wonky. The ping makes me jump and I squash the crown.

I'm good – what are you doing?

This is so nerve-wracking. What the hell do I say to him? I need to think about my reply.

Libby races into the kitchen and admires the cakes. 'Cool!'

Standing by her, I unpick a blonde knot in her hair. 'What time are your friends being dropped off?'

'Five. I have to go sort out my bedroom.' She tries to make a dash for the door, but an image of the field mouse makes me grab her arm.

'Why was there a mouse in your wardrobe?'

She groans. 'Oh, Mum, you found George?'

I roll my eyes. 'Yes, I found George and set him free.'

Libby glares at me. 'He was excited about meeting my friends.'

It's early evening. I still haven't replied to Chris's message. The princess themed sleepover is going downhill fast. Libby has fallen out with all her friends and is now sitting alone in her bedroom.

Huddled in the corner of the living room I'm trying to make polite, but interesting conversation with a bunch of moody nine-year-olds.

'Why isn't Libby coming down?' One girl with mad frizzy hair stands up.

Another little girl in a bright pink fairy dress stands on her chair to make an announcement. 'This is the worst party I've been to!'

Another notification pings on my dating app. It's Chris.

Hey, Pippa, how's your evening?

Messaging him will give me something to do. All of Libby's friends are now dancing to one of my party playlists and knowing Libby's stubbornness, I could be down here for hours. Hopefully, Chris and I can strike up a long and engaging conversation.

My daughter's sleepover party isn't going well.

Oh, okay.

My immediate reaction to his message consisting of two little words is one of disappointment. I remind myself he doesn't have kids so he's not going to engage in my sleepover conversation.

What are you up to?

Just been to the gym. Tough work out.

One of Libby's friends trips on the rug, sending her plastic cup of cola all over the fabric sofa. Rising from my chair, I place my phone in my jeans pocket and set to work on cleaning up the mess. Daisy comes up behind me as I rummage around in the kitchen cupboard for a miracle furniture spray. 'You okay, Daisy?'

'Why is Libs upstairs?'

I spot the can of spray and get to my feet. 'Argued with her friends.'

Daisy nods, clutching her phone. It lights up with a text and my eyes catch sight of the words, *love you x*.

A pink blush spreads quickly over her face. 'I have a boyfriend.'

'Oh,' I say, crossing my fingers behind my back and silently praying it's not Tom Ridge. I don't think relationships should start after twelve months of stalking and several complaints to the school.

'His name's Josh.'

Relief floods through me. Hurrah! We are out of the stalker phase. 'Great, Daisy. How did you meet him?'

'He wouldn't talk to me, so I locked him in the science lab until he agreed to go out with me.'

She grins and saunters out.

The urge to talk to someone right now is strong. Without thinking I take out my phone and message Chris.

Think my teenage daughter might be a bunny boiler.

Why the hell did I send that? Oh my goodness, he must want to run for the hills. Who would want to date a woman who suspects her teenage daughter is a trainee Glenn Close?

Libby eventually comes downstairs and the sight of her makes her friends squeal. Hurrying into the living room I come to a shuddering halt. Libby is stood in the centre of the living room, Dan's old pub football shirt is over her princess dress, a football is tucked under her arm, and her lovely, shoulder-length blonde hair … has been chopped off.

With a smirk, she runs her hand through her own attempt at her father's gelled quiff. 'Mummy, I'm happy again.'

Everything goes blurry for me as Libby gushes. 'I read Daddy's notebook. He wanted me to play football, so that's what I'm going to do. The bathroom's a bit messy.'

Emotion rises inside of me. Tears spill from my eyes. 'But I thought football made you sad?'

Libby admires her short hair in the mirror. 'It made me think of Daddy. But, not playing it was making me sad too.'

Even though I'm struggling to take my eyes off her badly cropped hair, I rush over and pull her into an embrace. Libby's friends are staring at us with open mouths.

Several painful hours later. I'm getting into bed and my phone pings.

Chris.

Fancy going out for something to eat?

CHAPTER 19

MIKEY

I'm stood in the playground waiting for Tara to finish school. It's her first day back since the tummy bug. Earlier, I'd watched her run excitedly across the playground to her friends. The sight had sent me into work with a beaming smile.

Dotted around are a few parents, plus a handful of grandparents. Behind me, I can hear a couple of mothers talking in hushed voices. Someone mentions Tara's name and then mine. I don't have the energy to turn around to listen to what they're talking about. Last night, Mum took a tumble in the hallway and I spent a long, arduous evening at the hospital with her and a fractious Tara.

The incident resulted in me having a sleepless night. It's becoming increasingly clear Mum can't look after Tara full-time.

A woman who looks like Pippa Browning walks across the playground with a toddler running behind her. It reminds me of bumping into her the other day at the park. There was something about her new haircut which made it hard for me to drag my eyes away. I noticed she was wearing a touch of make-up and there was no sign of her washed-out look. Once she'd walked away, I found myself wishing I'd struck up a conversation with her.

The image of Pippa fades as the teacher opens the school doors and beckons for me to talk to her. As I walk towards her my heart bangs against my rib cage.

Tara's teacher, Mrs Golding, is an older woman with a kind face and warm brown eyes. She leads me into a corridor adorned with children's colourful paintings of pirate boats. We enter a small empty classroom where she closes the door and gestures for me to sit on a little plastic chair.

I sit and fumble with my jacket zip. Is she going to tell me Tara's struggling at school and she thinks she should be taken into care? Nerves get the better of me. I start to talk fast about the regular visits to Tara's bereavement counsellor, how it's not ideal, our current living arrangement, but we're doing the best for Tara.

The air in the classroom evaporates. I claw at my collar, imagining Mrs Golding telling the social worker that Tara should go and live with someone else.

The photo of me in Magaluf rushes into my mind. I carry on talking as Mrs Golding flicks through a paper folder. Looking after Tara has been hard and there are times when I'm so exhausted I can hardly stand, but the benefits have been huge. With a wavering voice, I tell Mrs Golding how Tara makes me laugh and how she's bright as a button. I add that I look forward to collecting her from school, how she talks non-stop all the way home, how she beats me at PlayStation, how we've just started watching *Star Wars,* and seeing her charge across the playground towards me is one of the highlights of my day.

Noticing Mrs Golding is smiling at me, I stop talking.

'I'm pleased to say we've seen a significant improvement in Tara at school. Over the last few weeks, she's stopped crying in lessons, and we've seen a happier Tara coming into school.'

I stare in surprise at her.

'I've passed on my feedback to the social worker supporting you.'

Mrs Golding hands me a blue exercise book. 'This is something Tara wrote in class today. I think it might help you.'

With a trembling hand, I take the book and read the page of Tara's handwriting.

The title of the passage reads, *My Uncle Mikey & My Nana*. Below, Tara has written out a list of the reasons why she loves us. They make her laugh, let her watch *Star Wars*, let her get her nails painted, and tell silly jokes. Nana plays Monopoly and Uncle Mikey reads the best stories.

I look down at the hand-drawn picture. If I ignore the out-of-shape face outline, a dark cloud underneath the stick man's chin which is my beard, and the stick woman's amazing perm, I would say it was me and Mum.

'You're doing a good job,' says Mrs Golding. 'Still a long way to go, but I think Tara is on the right track.'

I run my hands through my hair and blow the air out of my cheeks. Despite the worry that I'm making this parenting thing up as I go along, there has to be something I'm doing right.

'I can't imagine what you're going through but whatever you're doing at the moment, keep going,' encourages Mrs Golding. She then takes me through Tara's schoolwork and the handwriting practice I've been doing with her has worked as Mrs Golding comments on how much neater her exercise books look.

When I collect her from the school hall, she's sat on the blue PE mats, and her face breaks into a wide smile as I walk towards her. She flings herself at me, nearly knocking us both over.

As we walk through the school car park to my car, Tara is greeted by her friend, Samantha, a girl with long brown pigtails and red glasses. Samantha's mother introduces herself to me as Steph. I smile briefly before remembering Steph was the woman in the gold bikini.

I guide Tara towards my car.

'Mikey, isn't it?' asks Steph, as I yank open the car door for Tara.

I loosen my tie and turn to her. 'Yes.'

Steph strokes her long blonde hair. 'Samantha's told me about what's happened. Listen, if you ever want me to have Tara for a few hours, just give me a call. Here's my mobile number.' She hands me a scrap of paper.

'Thanks.'

'If you ever fancy a coffee, let me know?' She flicks back her fringe. 'I know how hard it is being on your own.'

I thank Steph and get into the car. Tara grins at me from the back seat.

'What's so funny, Tara Twinkle Toes?' I look at her in the mirror.

She dissolves into a fit of giggles. 'Samantha's mum fancies you.'

As I pull out of the school gates I forget about Steph and fill my mind with snippets from the conversation I had with Tara's teacher. A little smile takes over my face. I've somehow helped to turn Tara around. With a smile plastered across my face, I give her a wink and sit up straighter in my seat. It is a great feeling to be finally doing something good.

Stan would be proud of me.

CHAPTER 20

MIKEY

*J*angling keys in the front door signal Mum has returned from her first MS support meeting. An unfamiliar male voice drifts into the kitchen. I immediately put down my bottle of beer and stride out into the hallway.

What the hell is going on? My mother is being helped into the house by a tall, older man with a thick patch of grey hair.

'Mum, what's going on?' I exclaim, rushing to help her.

The man steps back and I give him a cold stare.

'Where are Patricia and Beryl?'

'I'm fine.' Mum beams, steadying herself on the doorframe. 'Come on, Keith, let me make you a cup of tea.'

I stare in bewilderment as Mum and the stranger, Keith, move past me. They go into the kitchen, talking in hushed voices.

As I enter, Keith is stood by the cupboard, taking out two mugs. He's wearing a smart brown tweed jacket and beige trousers. My mother is sat in the corner at the table. She's smiling at Keith with lips coated in freshly painted pink lipstick.

'Here, let me do that,' I say, taking the mugs from Keith.

Mum chuckles. 'Michael, please let Keith make tea, he's done it before.'

Blood drains away from my face. Spinning round, I notice Mum is grinning. Has Keith been here before?

'Michael, this is my good friend, Keith. We've been friends for a long time. Keith helped me find the support group.'

I reluctantly outstretch my hand. 'Nice to meet you, Keith.'

'You too, Michael.' Keith coughs and clears his throat. 'Excuse me, I need to go fetch something from my car.'

As the front door opens and closes, I hurry over to my mother. 'Anything to tell me?'

She beams. 'Keith's been good to me.'

'You're wearing gold eyeshadow,' I can't stop staring at Mum's made-up face. She's not worn make-up for years. Her once messy hair is styled and sleek.

'So, why haven't you told me about him?'

Mum laughs. 'Michael, I've seen you more times in the last few months than I have since you left home at eighteen.'

'Did Stan met Keith?' Why am I feeling hot and uncomfortable?

To my dismay she nods her head. 'Stan talked to Keith while sorting out my garden. He invited Keith and I to a couple of his barbecues.'

'But I never knew about Keith.' I wipe a layer of sweat from my forehead. 'Why has no one told me about Keith?'

'You were always busy with football and your social commitments.' Mum squeezes my hand as guilt wraps itself around me.

'He's a nice man and he makes me forget about everything. When I am with him I feel young and carefree. I'm sure you two will get along fine.'

'You only had to call me and I would have come round.' Chewing the inside of my cheek I find myself on the defensive.

She tucks a strand of hair behind her ear. 'I did, Michael,

every week. You were always too busy with your friends or girlfriends.'

I take a deep breath and bid a silent farewell to my shitty old life.

Tara and I make home-made veggie pizzas before settling down to do her school spellings at the kitchen table.

Mum and Keith remain in the kitchen. I tear off pieces of pizza and try to stifle the feelings of guilt. I've spent too many years being a crap son, partying, socialising, and not spending enough time with my mother.

Once I'm happy Tara has learnt all her spellings and can recite them without giggling or getting distracted, I check my dating app. There are new notifications waiting for me.

When Stan died, all plans of dating went out of the window. If I'm honest, I still don't feel like dating, but I'm curious about what my app wants to show me. Tara is engrossed in her TV programme about a dance group.

I click into the app and see there are several messages from interested women. Ignoring the messages, I click through what the site refers to as *new additions.*

I almost miss her. My eyes widen in surprise as I catch sight of Pippa Browning's face staring back at me. Pippa Browning is on my phone screen. Is there no escape from this woman? After three years of avoiding her, I don't seem able to stop bumping into her.

She does look sexy in that photo though.

Tara squeals with laughter making me lift my head. I find myself causally glancing back at Pippa's photo and smiling at her sassy new hairstyle.

CHAPTER 21

PIPPA

'Check out my latest Tinder acquaintance.' Emma thrusts her phone in front of my face. 'Guitar-playing Poldark!' Tapping the screen with her long pink nail, Emma grins.

I gasp at the striking black-haired man staring into the camera. 'He's handsome.'

Emma sighs. 'He's so sexy and an added bonus is that he claims he has *nimble guitar playing fingers*.'

'I didn't know you were into guitar music?'

Mel places three mugs of tea on the coffee table before flopping down onto Emma's black leather beanbag. 'She isn't, Pip, she's keen to test out his musician's fingers.'

Emma flings a leopard print cushion at Mel. 'I'm addicted to dating.'

Something Dan wrote in his notebook about Emma being addicted to dating sites gives me a silent nudge.

Mel laughs and turns to me. 'Daisy update please!'

Taking out my grapefruit lip balm I smear on a good layer. 'Before I came here, I dropped her at her new boyfriend's house.'

Emma's perfect eyebrows shoot up her forehead. 'She has a boyfriend?'

I nod. 'He lives in a lovely house in Llanhennock with a posh garden and a sweeping gravel driveway.'

'This is not the one who complained to the teacher about her?' Mel asks.

I savour a mouthful of Mel's tea and ignore my anxious mind.

'No, this is someone called Josh.' My neck has started itching. Even though Daisy has showed me numerous photos of Josh on his bike and kicking his karate punch bag, I can't get rid of an uncomfortable feeling. There's something not quite right about him but I can't put my finger on it.

Emma crosses her long, tanned legs. 'Well at least she's grown out of the stalking phase.'

I grimace and look away. Daisy's voice echoes in my head. It's times like this I wish Dan had written me instructions for how to navigate the teenage years.

'And the *Libby hair* situation?' Emma giggles, sliding out her phone and flashing the pic of Libby I sent them. Libby is beaming into the camera with an ear-to-ear smile and looking like an urchin child with wispy, short, unkempt hair.

'What did the parents think of you ending the sleepover?' asks Mel.

I recall the filthy looks from some of Libby's schoolfriends' parents as they arrived to collect their child. The sleepover had ended abruptly after Libby decided to return to her football in the garden while her friends stood and watched from the kitchen window. A few of the girls asked me to phone their mums as they wanted to go home so I had a series of awkward conversations with Libby, trying to persuade her to come inside and be with her friends. Libby refused.

'A few hated me for ruining their night off.' I sighed. 'But most understood.'

Emma chuckles. 'You can understand their irritation though?'

'It wasn't my finest parental moment. I should have been stronger with Libby and made her entertain her friends.

However, the old football-mad Libby is back,' I say, feeling a little burst of happiness shoot across my chest. 'Although we're not sure what Claire's going to do with what hair she has left. I'm collecting her after this and we're going straight there.'

Mel leans over and gives me a cuddle. 'We love her; she's created her own Dan quiff. I still can't believe she went upstairs at her own party and cut all her hair off.'

'Libby is a legend. So, how's Chris?' Emma asks.

'I have a date on Saturday night and I don't think the clothes I bought the other day are any good.'

Emma frowns from her cream leather sofa. 'What do you mean?'

'I think I went too casual. Jeans and a nautical-looking top.'

'On a first date?' Emma stares at me with huge eyes.

'We're going to the posh pizza place in town.'

Emma leaps up from the sofa and gestures for Mel and me to follow her.

We watch her open the wardrobe revealing an array of smart dresses and skirts.

'I can't wear one of them,' I exclaim, gazing at the beautiful designer clothes.

Emma smoothes out the sleeves on her silk shirt and starts to flick through the garments. 'Some of these clothes are gathering dust hanging here. So, you might as well dive in.'

I reach out and start inspecting. She'd always had good taste in clothes. Even when we were at school her school uniform always looked stylish and fashionable.

Mel strokes a green wrap around silk dress. 'Pip, this would look amazing on you.'

Emma smiles. 'I bought it for a work's night out, but ended up changing my mind and wearing another. It's brand new. Look, it still has the labels.' She shows me the beige label.

'I like it.' I press it up against my body.

Emma giggles. 'You'll look hot, Pippa.'

Mel places her hands on her hips. 'Try it on!'

I slip on the dress and fasten it. As I raise my head to look at my reflection in the mirror I gasp. A fancy woman modelling a sassy haircut and a divine green dress smiles back at me.

As I step out of the bathroom to face Emma and Mel, huge grins spread across their faces.

'Oh wow, Pippa – look at you!' Mel jumps up and down.

I turn to survey myself in the bedroom mirror. 'Do you think I look fat in it?'

'I think you look like a real woman. With curves and bumps. I'm actually quite envious,' says Mel.

I glance back at Emma. 'Can I borrow it?'

'Yes.' Emma inspecting her bronzed legs.

I look down at my feet. 'What about shoes?'

'Black heels,' says Emma. 'We're the same size so grab a pair from my shoe rack.'

'Wow, I have an outfit and a first date,' I say. 'This is it, my first real date.'

We sit on Emma's blue satin king-size bed. Curling her feet up, Mel grins at me. 'So, how are you feeling about your date?'

I shrug my shoulders. 'If I'm honest, I'm not getting any urges when I stare at Chris's photo.'

'Urges?' Mel queries, raising a sculptured eyebrow at me.

'I don't feel anything physically, you know, inside.' Placing my hand over my chest I note how there is a silence inside of me when I talk about Chris.

Emma twirls a strand of blonde hair around her finger. 'It might be different when you see him in the flesh. When I first saw Phil on *Tinder*, my heart slowed down instead of speeding up. There was no shiver of excitement when I looked at his profile picture.'

Mel sends Emma a puzzled look. 'So, why did you start talking to him?'

Emma flicks her mass of blonde curls. 'Don't know.'

Turning her attention back to me, Mel places her manicured hand on my arm. 'Pip, this is just the first date. Remember, Chris might not be the one. Are you having any urges for anyone else?'

'No,' I murmur, scratching my nose. This is a blatant lie. Every time I see Mikey Stenton or hear his name in conversation, it feels like my organs are having a party. An image of him stood in the park comes rushing back to me. I quickly bury it at the back of my mind. He's a bad boy and a male tart.

'When I first met Dan, there were urges. I fancied the pants off him and wanted to do things to him.'

Mel laughs. 'I know what you mean. On that flight to Malaga, when Jeff summoned me on the tannoy to the front of the plane, I had urges too.'

'LOL!' Laughs Emma.

'How is Jeff?' I ask.

Mel takes a deep breath. 'I've been too busy getting the coffee shop ready. For the first time in my life I've been putting myself first.'

Instinctively I throw my arms around her. 'Well done. This is what Emma and I have been wanting to see for years.'

'Yeah, nice one, Mel,' says Emma, squeezing her shoulder.

I leave Emma's house and go to pick Libby up from my mother's.

'She's outside with a football,' says my mother, ushering me inside. 'Pippa, I'm really worried about that child.'

From across the living room I can see out of the back window. Libby is shooting a ball against the garage. 'She seems fine to me,' I say, noticing the wide smile on Libby's face.

'She cut all her hair off, Pippa,' barks my mother, making the green vein in her neck bulge. 'Aren't you concerned?'

Shaking my head, I wipe away a tear of happiness which has trickled down my face, watching my daughter. 'Mum, it was a shock seeing her hair, but I've got my daughter back and that's a hundred times more important.'

'Pippa, this is worrying. Your children are feral. If they're not escaping down ladders to go underage drinking, they're cutting all their hair off at parties.'

I wince. When my mother describes my children like this, it does sound worrying.

I nod and my mother shakes her head. She points to Libby out in the garden heading the ball into the air. 'You need to stop all thoughts about dating and concentrate on your children.'

A cloud of parental guilt hits me. That night Libby cut all her hair off was when Chris started messaging me.

CHAPTER 22

MIKEY

*T*ara and I are walking to school. Ian, my boss, has let me work from home. To my surprise, he's been supportive about the Tara situation. When we reach the school gates, Tara stops and gives me a hug.

'Are you okay, Tara Twinkle Toes?' I ruffle her blonde hair.

She looks up at me with those blue sparkly eyes I've come to love even more. 'You'll pick me up at home time?'

'Of course.' I kneel in front of her and check her school bag. We don't always remember to pack her lunch and water bottle and I've had to leave work and drop her some dinner money off which my boss is getting tired of.

Tara chews on the zip of her coat collar. 'You won't forget about me?'

'Never,' I say softly. 'Now off you go, you'll be late. Be a good girl.'

I watch her run off and head for a cluster of children in the playground.

'Mikey?' A voice behind makes me whirl round. Steph is standing smiling at me. She rearranges her dark sunglasses on top of her head. 'You haven't called me for a coffee?'

I run my hand through my hair. 'It's been a bit hectic.'

'Do you fancy one now?' She gestures towards town.

Half of me wants to decline her invitation. I need to get back and answer a few emails. The other half wants to say yes as I've been longing to talk to someone else other than Tara and Mum. Smithy and Jason aren't really interested in my texts about Tara which isn't surprising.

'Yes. Great.' I let her lead the way and ignore a few of the mothers raising an eyebrow in our direction.

We find a quiet café in town. Steph orders the coffee, while I choose a seat by the window.

I watch her carry the tray of espresso towards the table.

'So, how's it going?' Her strong perfume, in such close proximity, leaves me needing a breath of fresh air.

'It's not been easy.' Swirling the dark liquid around my cup. 'The broken nights of sleep, the school homework, the hospital visits with Mum, taking Tara to parties, and the school runs.'

Steph nods. 'Samantha's been giving me a running commentary. She's been very concerned.'

I try not to stare at Steph's gigantic bust, which she seems intent on lifting onto the table and making it difficult for me to avoid. Her top must be two sizes too small for her.

'Do you go out much?' Steph asks, giving me an intense stare.

I shake my head. 'Tara is so up and down at the moment and my mum has MS so things are tricky.'

Steph's face brightens. 'How about we all go out for a pizza or something? The girls can come too.'

The thought of doing something different other than being sat inside Mum's house is appealing, and I still have the memory of Steph, squeezed into her gold bikini, filed away at the back of my mind.

'Great, Tara and I would love that, thanks.'

Steph's brown eyes grow wider. 'How about this weekend?'

I drain my espresso. 'That would be good. Tara and I will have to check our hectic social calendars.'

'I used to have Tara round all the time. Stan used to drop her off and collect her.' She runs a tanned hand through her hair. 'He was a good man raising her by himself.' She stops, realising what she's just said.

The trouble with grief is that you never know when it's going to creep up on you. On hearing Steph mention Stan's name, a cold sweat breaks out on my neck. Within seconds his face appears in my mind. He's laughing at one of my rude jokes.

The café goes blurry as I push away from the table and leap out of my chair, much to Steph's surprise. After flying out of the doors, I stagger onto the pavement, bending over, and sucking in lungfuls of air. As I rub my heaving chest, I realise Steph is by my side, methodically rubbing my back. 'I'm so sorry,' she whispers.

'It's okay.' I lift my head up. Steph opens up her arms, offering me a hug. I step into it and feel her gigantic bosom pressed up against my chest.

We pull away and Steph smiles. 'Sorry …' she says, rearranging her white top. 'You looked like you needed a hug.'

We say goodbye on the corner and I walk back to my mother's house. Steph's text reaches my phone as soon as I put the key in the door. It reads, *Pizza on Saturday evening, bring Tara too x*

Tara rushes over to me when I pick her up from school. As we walk home, she keeps grinning and tugging on my hand.

'What's up with you, Tara Twinkle Toes?'

'I saw you talking to Samantha's mum before the bell went.'

'Oh, yeah, she wants us all to go out for a pizza sometime.'

Tara squeals with delight. 'Cool!'

We reach the high street and sensing I'm in a good mood, Tara leads me into the sweet shop. I try to resist, but she casts me her sweetest face and I can only surrender.

Tara scoots inside, weaving in and out of the throng of school children and parents. I step inside and head over to the coconut mushrooms. Without looking where I'm going, I bump into someone.

Stepping back in surprise I exclaim, 'I'm so sorry.' As I raise my hands in surrender, I find myself gazing into the eyes of Pippa Browning.

'Hello!' She beams, with a hint of a blush on her cheeks. Her eyelashes look thicker and darker. My eyes settle on her pink glossy lips and her smile robs me of breath. Whatever this woman has done to herself, the transformation has been amazing.

'Hi … sorry about knocking into you.' I find myself wanting to lean into her.

She flicks her fringe out of her eyes and it makes my stomach flip. 'Are you getting some sweets?' She gestures towards the counter and the snake-like queue of children.

My brain gives up all control over my mouth. 'Yes, I love a couple of coconut mushrooms, what about you?'

She smiles, sweeps her hair away from her face, filling my chest with a fluttering sensation. 'I'm a sucker for a sherbet dip.'

As my eyes grow wide, I notice she's turning away with pink cheeks.

'Uncle Mikey!' shouts Tara, from the back of the queue, frantically waving at me.

I cough before pointing at Tara and saying, 'I'm being summoned.'

'Yes, mine are done now,' Pippa replies as her three make their way towards the door, clutching bags full of sweets.

'Okay then,' I say, running a sweaty hand through my hair. 'See you around.'

She smiles and I dissolve. 'Yes, see you, Mikey.'

I'm glued to watching her leave.

'Can you carry my sweets for me?' asks Tara, handing me her bag.

As I come to my senses, I find myself telepathically trying to encourage Pippa to turn back. Just when I think all hope is lost, she glances back at me over her shoulder.

CHAPTER 23

MIKEY

*I*t's Saturday night. Tara and I are going out with Steph and Samantha for a pizza. Steph let me choose the venue, so I plumped for the posh pizza place on the high street.

We're walking up to town and Tara is wearing her favourite Justin Bieber T-shirt and glittery jeans. The sight of her outfit brought a massive smile to my face when she ran into the living room. It's been weeks since she has shown any interest in clothes. Seeing the return of the old Tara has made me so happy.

Shaving off my beard earlier brought a huge smile to Mum's face. She told me I'd been looking like a homeless man for months and it was nice to a new Michael emerging.

My phone vibrates. Without Tara noticing I slide it out of my pocket and groan. Another photo of Sophie and her naked breasts. The eighth one this week. She refuses to believe we are over.

I look up and catch sight of Steph and Samantha standing at the top near the bookshop. As they get closer, I can see Steph modelling a tight red dress and black stilettos.

Tara squeals as we approach. Steph reaches out and touches

my arm. 'Shall we go inside?' she asks, pointing to the pizza place. I nod and we follow her in.

The kids rush over to a circular table by the window. They don't wait to be seated and this brings an instant scowl to the face of the waitress. Customers are meant to wait before being seated. Luckily her irritation fizzles out, and she swaps her look of annoyance for a bright smile to greet us.

Steph sits opposite me with her back to the window. Tara stays close and chooses to sandwich herself between me and Samantha.

As we're presented with our menus, Samantha breaks into an angry tantrum. 'I don't like any of this food. I don't want to eat here, Mummy.'

Steph makes no attempt to quieten Samantha down. While Samantha rages, Tara leans in and whispers. 'I'm not hungry either, Uncle Mikey.'

The waitress appears. Steph and I order our food while Tara asks for some lemonade and Steph requests a bread roll for Samantha.

Steph launches into telling me all about her last holiday to Turkey, which was an eye-opening experience for her as it was the first time she'd been away as a single woman and she was nervous about meeting men. I try to act interested in Steph's holiday experience, but I'm drawn to someone stood outside the window.

An attractive brunette in a green silk dress, is stood outside the restaurant. She's idly playing with her hair.

Steph is telling me how she met a man from Blackpool on the first day by the pool. I'm nodding at her while secretly stealing glances at the woman outside. According to Steph, the nice man from Blackpool couldn't stop paying her compliments about her gold bikini. My interest in the conversation has evaporated.

To my dismay, a man has joined the brunette outside. He's

stretched his hand to shake hers. After exchanging pleasantries, he places his hand in the small of her back and guides her inside.

With my eyes fixed on the door, I gulp back more of my bottled beer. The wearer of the green dress is Pippa Browning. As she glides into the restaurant, I choke on my drink. Her beauty robs me of breath. She looks absolutely stunning. The green dress hugs her hourglass figure perfectly, accentuating her womanly hips.

Steph mops up my beer spillage with a napkin. 'Do you know her?' she asks, gesturing to Pippa.

I shake my head, willing myself to think of something to get Steph talking again. 'So, did you meet anyone else on your holiday?'

Her heavily made-up face lights up. She leans forward to tell me about her strange experience with the German man who insisted on lying on the sun bed next to hers and bringing back a selection of cold meats every time he went to the all-day buffet. Steph would have preferred him to bring her a cocktail back, but she wasn't going to turn away his plate of cold meats. I return to sneaking a look at Pippa's companion.

Two things strike me: the guy works out a lot and he likes Pippa, given away by how close he's sat to her.

The waitress arrives and places a large spicy pizza in front of me. As she leaves, I glance over at Pippa's table and catch her eye. I hold the gaze for longer than necessary and she rewards me with a sexy flick of her fringe. A light-headed feeling takes hold and, in a bid to control myself, I stuff my gigantic pizza into my mouth.

Pippa turns to listen to her companion talk and Steph tells me about the Swiss man she met on the third night who asked for her hand in marriage after watching her dance in her gold bikini, on top of one of the hotel tables.

Pippa's food arrives as I finish my pizza. Steph switches the conversation from holidays to Samantha's latest dance competition. After ten long minutes of listening to Steph describe Samantha's dance routine in detail, I watch Pippa get up from the table. She clutches her abdomen and scurries off. Before I can think straight, I'm rising from the table and telling Steph I need the gents.

The toilets are on the next floor and away from the prying eyes of our respective tables. I casually hang about outside, checking my phone. The door to the ladies' toilet swings open and there she is, standing in front of me. Pippa. I've never seen her looking so beautiful.

My eyes sweep her dress and then pick up on the angry dark stain coating the front. She moves her shiny brown hair away from her face. She's trying to act cool. 'I had a bit of an accident with some food at the table,' she says, quickly. 'I'm a messy eater.'

Words fail me as I'm mesmerised by her twirling a strand of hair around her finger. Her face embodies perfection.

'I'm a messy drinker,' I confess, pointing at the beer splatters on my shirt.

She smiles and hurries back to her table, leaving me against a pillar with an army of butterflies in my chest.

We leave before Pippa and her date. Sneaking a glance or two while Steph pays the bill, ensures I catch Pippa's eye. In that brief moment, I desperately want to run to her table, whisk her away, and kiss her like crazy. Steph's hand on my shoulder brings me back to reality.

'Let's go back to mine,' Steph purrs. 'The kids can play upstairs and we can entertain ourselves.'

Her house sits on the edge of a large sprawling new housing estate. We're all ushered into a gleaming white and black lounge. The children are sent upstairs.

She gestures for me to sit with her on the sofa. We talk about the latest school trip to the local theme park and how Samantha has asked for a pet goldfish for her birthday.

Steph keeps smiling at me. When our conversation about the

goldfish comes to a natural end, we both go silent. To my surprise, Steph reaches over and clamps her dark red lips onto mine. She sucks the air out of my mouth and presses her large body against mine. I sink into the sofa, wondering whether I'll ever breathe again.

When she finally releases her sucker lips, I lay gasping on a cushion.

'The kids are upstairs, tiger,' she whispers, caressing my neck with her manicured red nail.

I've found myself in new territory. For the first time in my life, I'm frantically thinking of excuses to leave a woman's house.

'Got to go,' I stammer, searching for the door.

She kisses me again, sucking the air out of me like a giant hoover.

Her hands are everywhere. I tap her away as she starts unbuttoning my trousers. 'I'm tired.' Sitting up, I wipe a layer of sweat from my brow.

With a look of dissatisfaction, Steph moves aside. 'I don't normally get this reaction. The men I met on holiday were very keen to get to know me.'

I give her a weak smile and she starts edging closer. 'I find you very attractive, Michael. Can I call you, Michael? I have condoms.' She giggles. 'In the supermarket I got a bit carried away.'

For a split second I find myself at a crossroads. I can either take the well-trodden path of sleeping with someone like Steph, who I don't really fancy, but I do it anyway, just to block out my shitty life. The sex won't be meaningful and afterwards I'll end up hating myself.

Or, I can take a new direction. Rising from the sofa, I shake my head. 'Sorry, Steph, I just want to be friends. Thanks for a lovely evening.'

Tara and I make a quick exit.

CHAPTER 24

PIPPA

*C*hris and I are stood outside the taxi rank. It's been a nice evening, although tipping spaghetti bolognese down myself halfway through was not one of the highlights.

Chris seems a decent guy. Quite the gentleman, holding open doors for me and constantly asking whether I'm okay. He's talked a lot about how he enjoys being a fitness instructor and flexed his thick muscle-bound arms at me a few times.

In a prosecco-fuelled moment of madness I told him *at length* about my children. Looking back, I don't think this was one of my best moves. When I told him about Daisy's approach to dating, he squirmed uncomfortably in his seat. The story about her coming home drunk, resulted me getting a polite smile. The story about Libby running away using the emergency fire ladder and cutting her hair off made him wipe his sweaty forehead. When I told him about Billy's issue with glass windows and footballs, Chris quietly said he hated football.

We're going our separate ways, once the taxis appear. I'm secretly glad about this as I've not experienced any urges for Chris. If we went on a boating lake date, I wouldn't be looking for a secluded spot to have a passionate picnic. If Helen knew I was thinking this, she'd start lecturing me.

The black cab slides up to us. Chris turns to face me and smiles. 'Thanks for a lovely evening,' he whispers, before reaching out to touch my cheek.

Oh my God, he wants to kiss me. My entire body has stiffened.

His cold lips lock onto mine with such force, I take a step back in shock. Quickly, he looks away and starts to cough.

That isn't how you kiss. Dan's kisses were warm, soft, and inviting. He never clamped his lips onto mine. I don't have the energy or inclination to spend my time teaching Chris how to kiss me.

'Are you okay?' he asks, looking concerned.

'Tickly cough,' I say, placing my hand over my chest and realising I've not actually coughed once.

He leans in again to kiss me. Once again, I'm caught in an icy grip with his lips. I try to run my fingers through his hair, but they get tangled in the spiky bits at the front.

The blank look we give each other says it all. We both know we'll not be seeing each other again.

After saying goodbye, I leap into a taxi feeling relieved.

Sinking into the comfy leather seat, I watch the city flash by. My mind drifts back to the restaurant and Mikey. Why did he keep looking over if he was out with his girlfriend?

Almost bumping into him outside the toilets was a surprise after the spaghetti bolognese incident. Even though Mikey, in my head, is a wild, irresponsible male tart, he did look attractive tonight, in his fitted navy-blue shirt and dark jeans. He's shaved his beard and has brushed his chaotic hair.

Emma is asleep on the sofa when I sneak inside the living room.

The kids weren't thrilled when I announced that I was meeting an old school friend in town and Aunty Emma was going to be sitting for them. Aunty Emma has a very different approach with children. Basically, she takes no nonsense, no cheek, or back chat, and sends them to their rooms with a cold glare.

'How did it go?' Emma asks, with a groggy voice.

'His kissing was horrid.' I screw up my face with a look of disgust. 'I also got the feeling he wasn't into kids.'

'You told him about your kids?' Emma smooths out her beige skirt.

I shake my head. 'It didn't feel right to leave such an important part of my life out.'

Emma casts me a look of concern. 'I think you should wait until the second or third date before you tell him about your kids.'

I sit down and fiddle with my handbag. 'I saw Mikey Stenton.'

'In the restaurant?'

Nodding, I place my hand over my chest. My heart is like a wild horse. 'I was cleaning myself up after chucking half of my dinner down my dress. He was there outside the toilets.'

Emma rises from the sofa. 'You keep bumping into him, that means something.'

'It means nothing,' I say, playfully swiping her arm and shoving all the images of Mikey looking sexy outside the toilets inside a box at the back of my head.

CHAPTER 25

PIPPA

The grand opening of Mel's Coffee Shop has finally arrived. Yesterday was spent in the kitchen baking batches of cakes and arguing with Daisy about going for a sleepover at Josh's house. I'm sticking to my guns and saying no.

It's breakfast time in the Browning household. I swan into the kitchen wearing my red and white polka dot dress. The last hour has been spent doing my hair and putting on some make-up.

Billy's spoon falls from his hand and clatters into his cereal bowl, sending milk everywhere. Libby's mouth could house a family of flies it's so wide, and Daisy is gripping onto the table.

'Do I look okay?' I ask, giving them all a twirl.

Daisy shakes her head. 'Mum – who made you wear a dress?'

'Mel,' I say, flicking on the coffee machine and ignoring Daisy's look of concern.

Libby returns to eating her cereal. 'Remember it's parent's evening.'

I groan and set a reminder on my phone. 'Who's your teacher?'

Libby rolls her eyes. 'Mr Peterson. He's leaving at the end of the week. You'll get to see my project.'

Admiring her new gelled quiff, I run my hands over the top of it. 'Libby, how much gel did you use on this?' Her hair is rock hard.

She puts her hand over her mouth and giggles. 'Like Daddy's hair.' We all chuckle and recall the amounts of hair wax Dan used to go through.

'You've been keeping your project secret,' I say, taking out a carton of fruit juice from the fridge. Libby normally expects me to get involved with all her homework, but this project has been kept under wraps, which is worrying. She flicks her eyes to the cereal box, and I turn my attention to pouring myself a glass of cranberry juice.

Billy shoots up from the table. In his hand he's clutching a leaflet. 'Libs and I want to do this.' We all follow his gaze to the application form for the local children's mixed football practice. All ages welcome. Libby squeals with excitement to confirm her approval.

I give it a quick read. Dan's instructions come rushing back to me. This was what he would have wanted.

'It's every Saturday morning, Bill and Libs.'

'Yes – can we do it?' He jumps up and down before going to hug Libby.

To my surprise, they both rush out of the room and come back clutching Dan's notebooks. 'Daddy wanted us to play more football.'

The sight of them both holding aloft their notebooks, combined with their happy little elfin faces, melts my heart. I plant a kiss on each of their foreheads. 'Okay, you can do it.'

In unison they both wipe off my kiss with an embarrassed look.

'Kids, I need to get to my new job. Are you okay to walk them, Daisy?'

∞∞∞

Mel and I jump up and down when I arrive. 'I'm so excited,' screeches Mel.

Wrapping my arms around my friend, I say, 'You have surprised me with this new venture.'

'What do you mean?' Mel asks, as I pull her closer.

'You're happy, confident, and back to the Mel I used to know. I did doubt you at first, but I have to say, buying this coffee shop was a brilliant decision.'

Mel pulls back and places her hands on my shoulders. 'Thanks for being a great best friend, Pip. I've lost count of the number of times you've rescued me over the years.'

Tears sting my eyes. 'That's what best mates do, rescue each other. You and Emma have done just that for me since Dan died. I'll be forever grateful.'

'Do you think we will still be rescuing each other when we are in our nineties?' Mel asks with a smile.

'Definitely,' I grin.

We both admire our dresses and then get to work making sure we're ready.

I place my selection of chocolate owl cakes in their display boxes. Mel comes over and gasps. 'Bloody hell, Pip, look at those!'

Our first ever customer is a male version of my mother. An older man, wearing a harassed facial expression and sporting a bulging green vein in his neck. His square forehead is coated in a layer of sweat and he talks fast. Mel sorts out his flat white order and I smile sweetly at him.

Before long, there's a queue of tired-looking office people waiting for coffee and a handful of customers sat on the leather sofas. I stop and let myself enjoy the moment. The whoosh of the espresso machine, the clink of the cups, the frothing of the milk, and the chatter of the customers is filling me up inside with a new kind of joy. This is a hundred times better than sitting in my living room wondering what to paint duck-egg blue next and spending a fortune online.

Pride is also stretching my smile even further across my face. I've managed to get myself a job, a new hairstyle, and somehow, I've managed to get Libby loving football again. Dan would be happy to see this new me.

Whirling round after handing a cake to a young woman, I come face to face with Mikey Stenton. He's standing in the queue giving me a puzzled look. My eyes wander over the creases in his shirt and his pale demeanour. Obviously, he's still leading a wild lifestyle.

Before I can ask him for his order, two older women rush up to him and throw their arms around his shoulders. They're telling him how good it is to see him and they both hope he's doing okay. I glance at Mel and make an exasperated face. This is so typical of him.

When I turn back to him, a cute boyish smile spreads across his face. 'Do you work here?'

Heat starts to blossom over my neck. His stare is almost hypnotic. 'Yes, I do. What can I get you?'

He glances up at the drinks menu and then steps closer to the counter. 'Can I have a latte, please, Pippa, and one of those … cakes … wow … who baked them?'

'I did,' I say as a warm blush blossoms over my cheeks. I turn on my heel and accidentally knock over the pile of trays stacked next to me. He watches me pick them all up.

Mel makes his order and I pass it over with a trembling hand.

After he leaves, Mel leans into me. 'Do you fancy him?'

I glare at her, before wiping down the counter. 'No, I don't, Melanie! You saw him with all those women.'

Mel grins and goes back to making an order of three flat whites and a peppermint tea. 'Did I tell you he's deleted his *Facebook* account?'

'What?' I squirt spray over the counter and wipe harder.

'Yep, what do you think that means?' Mel rinses out a cup.

I chew my lip, cover the counter for a second time in spray, and start to wipe. 'Obviously been caught doing something he shouldn't.' I'm putting my back into getting this counter clean.

Mel nods. 'He's probably having an affair or something.'

I'm now giving the counter what only can be described as an aggressive wipe. 'Mel, I'm so glad I've decided to go against Dan's wishes with Mikey.'

'How dirty was that counter, Pip?'

My first batch of cakes don't last long. Mel and I have been inundated with requests for more cakes. Everyone has commented on how delicious they are, and my cake confidence levels are soaring.

'Pip, we need more cakes,' gushes Mel, pointing to the empty trays. 'I can't believe how well they've sold.'

CHAPTER 26

PIPPA

I never thought working in a coffee shop could be so exhilarating. Leaving the coffee shop I take a quick glance of myself in my compact mirror. My eyes are shining and my cheeks have a pink glow. I feel energised and so unlike the Pippa six months ago who shuffled around the house wondering what to paint next. I am also bursting with pride for Mel. She's done so well, and her life has taken a new direction. No more chaos or disasters.

As I drive to the school for Libby's parent's evening, all I can think about is Mikey Stenton's boyish smile and Mel's comment. Swinging the car into the school car park I chuckle to myself. How could she think I fancy him? Why would I find an irresponsible and wild tart of a man attractive?

Mr Peterson, Libby's teacher, is a striking six-foot two, rugby playing man, with hands the size of dinner plates. As he tells me how lovely it is to meet me, I can't help but stare at his muscular chest through his crisp white shirt. His eyes roam my red and white polka dress and black stiletto heels.

We sit on little plastic chairs. I have to drag my attention away from his bulging thighs, encased in tight grey trousers. As he talks, all I can think about is how fabulous it would be to go on a boating lake date with this handsome specimen. We wouldn't get far out before I would be suggesting a quiet picnic in a secluded spot.

Mr Peterson has given me my first physical urge. Well, actually, that's not entirely true as I've been getting urges every time I see Mikey Stenton, but they don't count.

I regain my composure and try to focus on what he's telling me about my daughter's educational development. His lips look very kissable. He passes me Libby's project and our fingers touch for the briefest of seconds.

I wipe my brow and try to get a grip of myself. This is Libby's teacher I'm talking to. For all he knows, I'm a smart, sophisticated woman with a bright daughter who is going to wow us both with her project on rocket science or something intelligent.

'Libby has chosen an interesting topic to research.' He chuckles.

I let out a nervous laugh and read the title of the PowerPoint presentation Libby has crafted. *My Mummy Has Started Online Dating.*

'Oh God,' I murmur.

With a trembling hand, I turn over the slide to see a lengthy list of online dating sites. My goodness, there are more than twenty. This must give the impression I'm busy in my spare time and desperate for a man.

'She's certainly done her research,' I say, quickly turning to the next slide which is a long list of ideas for dates, according to a nine-year-old. The top being, *hang out at the top of the climbing frame in the park.*

I wrap up the parent session quite quickly. From what little of Libby's presentation I've seen, her research skills are amazing and when I get home, I'll be having words about using my laptop.

As we stand at the door, Mr Peterson brushes against my arm.

I stand and find myself gazing into his large blue eyes. 'I'm leaving on Friday,' he murmurs. 'It will be my last day.'

'I know,' I whisper, imagining his trunk like arms rowing me around a lake.

He wets his lips. 'This isn't very professional of me and I don't normally do this sort of thing, but as I'm leaving the profession … would you let me take you on a date?'

I nearly topple over with shock. Gripping onto the table behind me, I force out a squeak. 'Yes.'

We exchange phone numbers and he promises to text me.

CHAPTER 27

MIKEY

The person who I've been dreaming about for years now works in the coffee shop across the road from my office. I've got to pinch myself every morning when she greets me with the most beautiful smile.

My daily amount of coffee has increased and so too has my cake intake. Every day, I'm forced to think up new excuses to go to the coffee shop. My colleagues can't believe how many hot drinks and cakes with animal faces on I'm consuming at my desk.

Things got awkward in the queue for coffee yesterday when Fiona asked me out for a drink just as Pippa turned to serve us. Pippa raised her eyebrows at me and turned away, which stung a little.

Before Stan died, I'd been chasing Fiona's attentions. She's an attractive girl, with long dark hair, and an eye-catching voluptuous figure. We share the same sense of humour and for several months, she gave me nothing but knock backs. Now, my feelings for her have evaporated.

I'm stood in the queue. There are three people ahead of me. Today Pippa is in a flowery dress and I'm struggling to take my eyes off her. From where I'm standing, I can hear her talking to Mel, who is busy at the coffee machine frothing milk.

'He's taking me to the cinema tomorrow night,' says Pippa, handing a tray containing a little red tea pot and several cups to an older woman. 'I'm actually excited.'

My stomach tightens, and a deflated feeling passes over me. This isn't the sort of thing I wanted to hear her say.

I crane my neck to hear more.

'As Dan said, I need someone who knows the kids,' Pippa informs Mel, glancing back at her friend. 'Mr Peterson, I mean Tom, teaches both Libby and Billy.'

'Perfect,' replies Mel. 'He looks scrumptious.'

I bring my hand up and anxiously chew on my nail. This is terrible. Pippa is going to the cinema with a handsome teacher who knows her kids.

Pippa spots me in the queue. I hold her gaze and receive a wonderful smile. My whole body has become enveloped in a warm, tingling feeling.

'Hello, Michael, your usual?' Pippa beams at me.

I nod and force myself not to look at her low-cut dress. Instead, I focus on a dull painting of a bridge on the wall a little to the left of her.

'How are you today?' She places her hand on her hip and flicks her sexy fringe.

'Good. Are you doing anything nice tomorrow night?' The words surprise my brain and fly out of my mouth. What the hell am I doing? Oh God, Pippa is going to think I'm a weirdo.

An awkward silence follows. We both look down and find things on the stone floor to study.

Mel comes over. 'Why? Are you asking Pip out?'

I loosen my tie and wipe my sweaty forehead. This isn't going to be easy. 'No, just wanted to know how she's going to be spending her Friday evening?'

Pippa lets out a nervous giggle. 'I have a cinema date.'

'That's lovely,' I say, picking up my coffee. 'Have a nice time and ...' My voice falters as half of my brain screams at me to keep walking and the other yells at me to find out which film she is seeing. 'Which film will that be?'

Mel is now giving me an odd look.

A blush has covered Pippa's face and neck. She straightens her dress and takes a deep breath. 'I think he said a spy thriller.'

As I leave the coffee shop, a plan materialises in my mind. I reach into my pocket, take out my phone, and ask Fiona whether she wants to go to the cinema. Mum and Keith said they would be in tomorrow night, so they can look after Tara. Keith enjoys playing board games with her so Mum will get some peace.

My phone bleeps. It's another text from Sophie. She wants to know when she's going to see me again. Apparently, little Zack is missing me. I've text her several times to say that it's over, but the message clearly hasn't got through. I tap out, *sorry, I won't be coming round anymore. Really enjoyed what we had but it's time to move on.*

To my delight, Fiona texts back to say that even though she's a little confused about my rejection yesterday, she'd love to go to the cinema with me.

While Ian, my boss, lectures us all on a new marketing campaign, I do some film research. There's only one showing of a spy thriller tomorrow night and it starts at seven thirty. This means Fiona and I need to be at the cinema complex for seven so I can make sure I bump into Pippa.

∞∞∞

Fiona and I are stood by the side of the dual carriageway. It's raining and several van drivers have already driven too close, coating us in muddy water. My car has decided to break down on the way to the cinema.

Fiona keeps telling me she's cold and hungry, but I've had other things on my mind. A breakdown truck is pulling up onto the hard shoulder. I doubt we can make the start of the film, but I'm going to stay hopeful.

CHAPTER 28

PIPPA

*T*om Peterson is coming to the house to pick me up. Little does he know, but upstairs Mel, Emma, and Helen are all desperate to catch a glimpse of this mystery man. They've promised not to make a sound or be seen at the window.

Emma has let me borrow a blue silk wrap around dress and a pair of nude heels. Mel has done my eyeshadow for me, which looks great.

Helen is upstairs making Emma and Mel laugh with her account of rock star groupie love making. I can hear her say, 'It's so good, I've learnt lyrics to three of Rick's dreadful songs,'

I should be feeling on top of the world, but my period is due. If I stand sideways in the mirror, a stranger might wrongly assume I have some pregnancy news to share. My breasts ache and my body feels like lead. My day has been spent snapping at the kids, being short with Mel, and sending stroppy texts to my mother about her refusal to babysit anymore. She claims my kids are out of control.

After shoving a couple of Evening Primrose capsules down my throat and some painkillers for my headache, I start to feel better. It's going to be okay, I tell myself in the bathroom mirror.

As long as I watch what I say and try to control my hormones, the date should be fine.

The annoying thing about my hormones is that when my period is due, I'm like a monster to be around, but my horny thoughts go into overdrive. I just hope I can keep a lid on everything.

'He's at the door,' I whisper up the stairs.

A few giggles travel back down. 'We've seen him walk up the path,' shouts Emma. 'If you don't like him, give him my mobile number.'

Tom's huge, muscular body takes up the entire door frame. My heart has started to gallop. Tonight, he's wearing a smart pink shirt and navy-blue jeans. His short and spiky dark hair compliments his rugged face.

'Pippa.' He leans in to place a delicate kiss on my cheek. His lips feel soft and warm.

Before I can say anything, I am led out of the house and down the garden path. I glance behind and look up at the bedroom window. Helen, Emma, and Mel have their thumbs raised with what look like huge smiles of encouragement plastered across their faces.

Although, in view of the stinking mood I've been in all day, they're probably smiles of relief.

We arrive at the cinema after a car journey which was painfully long and frustrating. Tom drove his car like he was on a go-kart track. On several occasions, I found myself gripping the passenger door and muttering stuff under my breath about his heavy right foot.

His tiny leather sports car seat wasn't made for my large bottom and there was a strong odour of sweat and old socks. Tom told me, as we pulled away, his dirty washing was in a basket in the back and he was planning to drop it off at his mother's. As he swung his car into a parking space at the cinema all my sizzling feelings for him had evaporated.

But, settling ourselves in our cinema seats I find I've forgiven him for driving like a maniac and sticking his dirty washing in the back of the car. The sight of his smart shirt, straining across his muscular chest, is making me want to run my hand across it. He strokes my cheek and leans towards me. 'Can I kiss you?' His request, wrapped in a sexy deep whisper, sends shivers down my spine.

Neither of us notice the lights dimming. Tom knows how to kiss. I'm leaning back into my seat and enjoying being locked in a passionate embrace. His huge dinner plate hands are running up and down my thighs. My head is awash with all sorts of saucy thoughts.

To my annoyance, a couple have arrived late and have decided to sit in the row in front of us.

I know this because their whispered argument disturbs my sweaty kiss with Tom.

'I hate spy thrillers,' hisses the woman. 'The film's already started. We don't know what's going on.'

A familiar voice drifts my way. 'Don't worry, we can catch up.'

'Plus, I'm cold, wet, and fed up.'

'You'll warm up.'

It's Mikey Stenton. Oh God! What is he doing here and why has he turned up late? I push Tom off me to sit up in my seat to get a better look. Knowing what I do about Mikey, they've probably been having wild sex beforehand and lost track of the time.

'My dress is wet, Mikey,' hisses the woman.

I let out a yelp of shock at what she's just said. What the hell have they been doing if her dress is wet? Probably having sex outside or they've been on a boating lake date. Oh God, Dan, why did you suggest I date this sex machine?

'I want to go home,' says the woman.

Mikey's head leans towards her. 'Calm down. You'll enjoy it.'

Tom has turned his attention to the film, and I find myself staring at the back of Mikey's head.

Whoever he's with has turned her face away from him and folded her arms tightly across her chest.

'Mikey, I'm going home,' she says, getting to her feet. 'To be honest, I don't why you invited me.'

Tom taps on the seat and asks them to keep the noise down.

'Sit down, Fiona,' whispers Mikey.

I roll my eyes. Fiona was the attractive woman in the queue, the one who asked him out the other day. The first week in my new job has been enlightening, as far as getting to see the real Mikey Stenton. When women aren't throwing their arms around him, they're begging him to take them out. Now I have this example to add to my collection. Seriously, why would anyone find him attractive?

I push Tom's wandering hands away and give the subject of Mikey Stenton some more thought.

Yes, I admit, he's drop dead gorgeous, he has the funny banter to make me laugh and there's something unexplainable which draws my attention to him, but I'm constantly reminded of his irresponsible and hedonistic ways.

Tom tries to kiss me again, but I push him away. Too busy thinking about Mikey.

There is no way in this world a nice, sensible woman like me could date someone like him. I would be constantly surrounded by women wanting to chuck themselves at him.

Fiona has marched out of the cinema, leaving Mikey still in his seat, which is infuriating to watch. He should be chasing after her and making sure she's okay. I bet his poor date is stood snivelling in the foyer, with her muddy dress, desperate for him to come out and give her a lift home.

I uncross and cross my legs. Tom places his hand on my thigh. I tap it away.

In the bright light of the screen, Mikey turns around to grin at me, which is annoying. Who the hell does he think he is?

His handsome outline leaves an imprint on my brain. In a flash, I'm imagining Mikey rowing me around a boating lake. His sexy brown eyes are urging me to search the shoreline for a secluded spot so we can have a passionate picnic.

I gasp and rub my temples. My hormones are making me muddled.

Every time Tom tries to kiss me, Mikey noisily sucks on his drink straw, chomps on his popcorn, or clears his throat. It's both annoying and funny, as the film is incredibly dull.

Once the film finishes and the light goes on, Tom starts searching the seats for his wallet, which he claims fell out during the film.

'Fancy seeing you here,' Mikey says, as I stand and wait for Tom.

I give him a snooty look. 'Where's Fiona?'

'She's not happy with me. Probably gone home in a taxi.'

I roll my eyes and huff at him. 'You could have given her a lift.'

He makes a slurping noise with his drink. 'I wanted to watch the film.'

To my horror, he gives me a wink and walks out of the theatre.

'Who was that?' asks Tom, red faced and on his hands and knees, still looking for his wallet.

'Coffee shop customer,' I say. 'I really need the toilet, Tom.' After three children, my bladder is a shadow of its former self.

'Please help me look for my wallet?'

I cross my legs, but it's no use. 'Sorry, but I'm desperate for the loo. Please can you move out of the way?'

His giant frame, which I initially found sexy, is now an irritant as it's blocking the aisle and if he's not careful, I might wee myself.

Tom exhales a little too loudly and I can feel my agitation

levels rising. His giant foot knocks a cup and it tips over, coating my feet and ankles in lemonade.

All horny thoughts about Tom disappear as I storm past him and march away with dripping wet feet.

He's waiting for me after I emerge from the toilets, with clean feet and an empty bladder.

'Can I drive you home, Pippa?'

I hold my tongue about his driving, even though he narrowly avoids a crash with a gigantic lorry and takes a corner so fast, my life whizzes before my eyes. The smell from his dirty underwear makes me gag, but I keep my mouth shut.

As we park outside my door, I know Tom and I won't be seeing each other again. I don't think I can endure another car ride for starters, and I can't date a man who still expects his mother to do his washing.

He kisses me on the mouth. I close my eyes and find myself wondering whether Mikey Stenton kisses like this. I gasp. My hormones are to blame for these silly thoughts. In a fit of frustration with myself, I pull away from Tom and get out of the car.

Helen is waiting for me when I enter the house. She shuffles out into the hall, wrapped in my sofa throw. 'Well, how was it with Mr Gorgeous?'

I shake my head and kick off my heels. 'Not great.'

'That's a shame. Pippa, he's stunning to look at.'

After collapsing onto the sofa, I place my hands over my face. 'Mikey Stenton was in the cinema.'

Helen comes to sit down on the chair opposite. 'The one Dan said you should date?'

I nod. 'He tried his best to distract me from Tom.'

Helen reaches out and takes my hand in hers. 'As I said the other week, you end up getting carried away and before long you're in the bushes on that island.' She studies my face. 'Do you fancy him?'

'NO!' I screech. 'He's an irresponsible tart!'

'Let me get you a cup of tea, you look all hot and bothered,' she says with a glint her eyes.

Argh! Why won't anyone believe I do *not* fancy Mikey bloody Stenton?

CHAPTER 29

MIKEY

*M*y boss, Ian, and I are standing in the coffee shop queue. I suggested to him earlier that we have our planning meeting somewhere different to the office. To my surprise, he agreed.

Pippa is serving and once again, she looks super fit. Her hair is tousled, and her pink rose bud lips are coated in lip gloss.

As I stare at her, the memory from Friday night in the cinema comes rushing back. The thought of her being kissed by someone else had been pure torture. It was new territory for me.

'How's Tara?' Ian asks, looking interested.

'On Saturday she fell out of a tree and I thought she'd broken her arm. We spent five hours in the accident and emergency department getting it x-rayed and examined.'

'Nasty. Is she okay?'

I nod. 'Luckily it wasn't broken, and we were sent home with some painkillers.'

Tara's accident and the spell in A&E gave me lots of time to think about things while sat in a plastic chair with Tara curled up beside me.

I came to the conclusion it's time I give Pippa the impression

I'm the sort of bloke she might one day consider taking to the cinema.

Pippa greets us with a smile which turns my entire body to jelly. I have to grip onto the counter and pray Ian orders first.

He asks for a flat white and I grin like an idiot at her. 'The same, please.'

She whirls round to give Mel our order. Ian starts checking something he wrote on his notepad and I try to stop staring at Pippa.

As Mel passes our drinks to Pippa, my phone bleeps. With clammy, trembling hands, I reach inside my trouser pocket and slide out my phone.

'Did you enjoy the film, Michael?'

Her soft voice makes a goofy look spread across my face and loosens my grip on my phone. It clatters to the floor.

Pippa and I both bend down to grab my phone, which has fallen between the gap in the counter. Our heads clash for a second but I don't feel the pain because I'm too busy thinking about how beautiful she is close up. She reaches it first and spots the unsavoury photo Sophie has just sent me.

Pippa drops the phone with a cry of horror at Sophie's breasts and straightens quickly.

My plan about improving Pippa's image of me has crashed and burned.

I shove the phone in my pocket and curse Sophie a hundred times for not getting the message about our relationship being over. Why does she have to keep sending me pictures of her body parts?

'Ex-girlfriend,' I mumble as Pippa glares at me from behind the counter. 'Won't leave me alone.'

Pippa nods and turns her attention to the next customer.

Feeling like shit, I grab my coffee and shuffle away to a table where Ian will proceed to bore the socks off me about planning.

Ian talks in a lifeless monotone voice. He also doesn't pick up on when the other person is not interested in what he has to say.

I can't stop stealing glances at Pippa. She's stood talking to Mel and they both keep looking over in my direction with concerned looks on their faces.

Ian clears his throat and I turn my attention back to planning ideas.

Our meeting lasts for a few hours. In that time, I've managed to hold Pippa's gaze twice and overheard countless people compliment her cakes. To my amazement, I've caught her looking at me when Mel has been talking.

Ian has left his lunch over the road so he's heading back to the office. 'You coming back?'

I check my watch and shrug. 'Think I might grab something here.'

Ian leaves me sat alone at the coffee table.

Pippa comes over, clears our cups away, and wipes down the red tablecloth. She remains silent but gives me the faint hint of a smile.

As she leaves, someone comes into the coffee shop and heads for my table. I look up to see Stan's best mate, Andy.

'Mikey,' he says, outstretching his hand. He's a tall guy with a thatch of black hair at the front of his head. His pale skin hates the sun, so for as long as I've known him, he has been a deathly shade of white. 'I thought it was you. How are you?'

I shake Andy's hand and offer him a seat.

'Can I get you a coffee?' Andy asks.

He returns to the table carrying a tray with two coffees and a plate containing two monkey faced fairy cakes. 'I couldn't resist,' Andy says, gesturing towards the cakes.

'Soft git,' I say, with a smile.

Andy plonks himself down and grins at the big ears and the iced smiley face. 'Flossy would love these.'

'She still doing her *YouTube* channel?' Andy's sister, Flossy, is a famous baking vlogger and thousands watch her create wild and wonderful cakes.

He nods and lets out a little sigh. 'She's so famous now we can't walk down the street together without someone noticing us.'

'So, Andy, what brings you here?' He works away a lot so it's unusual to see him out locally.

'Got a new job in town,' he explains, undoing his tie and unbuttoning his blue shirt collar.

Stan and Andy had been friends since school and Andy lived on the same housing estate as us. When Jules left Stan, Andy would make a habit of calling in on his way home from work to see how my brother was doing. He's one of life's good guys.

'I miss Stan,' he says, watching his black coffee swirl in his cup below. 'Life's not the same without him.'

A Stan-shaped lump rises at the back of my throat.

'Some new family has moved into his house. I drive past every day, thinking I'll see the daft bugger washing his car for the tenth time that week.'

I smile. Stan was obsessed with washing his beloved car.

'I expected to see Jules at the funeral,' says Andy, before sipping on his coffee.

My shoulders and neck stiffen at the mention of her name. 'She emailed Mum to say she has a new life now.'

Andy's dark eyebrows come together in a thick black line. 'Tara's her daughter. Does she have no feelings at all?'

I shake my head. 'Jules says she has no connection to Tara. She wants Mum to legally adopt her.'

'But ...' Andy's voice fades away.

I nod. 'Yeah, Mum's not well and she's not getting any better.'

'So, what's going to happen to Tara?'

I sit up straight in my chair. 'I've been looking after her. It's been a life-changing experience, caring for someone else.'

Andy eyes widen with surprise. 'You?'

I chuckle. 'I know it's hard to get your head around, but it's true. Been living with Mum, taking Tara to school, collecting her, and cooking us meals. I've even survived a sickness bug.' Pausing, I wipe my brow. 'Tara has turned me into an adult.'

Andy reaches over and pats me on the back. 'Well, done, mate. Stan would be so proud.'

A warm glow shoots up my spine.

Andy and I talk some more about Stan before he is reminded of a meeting he's supposed to be attending. 'Right, I better dash. Mikey, it's been great seeing you again.'

I stand and go to shake his hand. 'You too, Andy. We should go for a beer sometime.'

The couple on the table next to us are tucking into two piglet faced cakes. Andy is distracted. 'I need to tell Flossy about this place. She needs to meet whoever's baking these cakes.'

Dan's notebook materialises in my mind. After serving a group of mothers with babies clinging to their hips, Pippa comes over to clear away the coffee cups. 'Have you finished?'

I smile and rise from my seat.

'Was that a work friend?' she asks, with a quizzical expression.

I shake my head. 'My brother's best mate.'

Pippa's sculptured eyebrows arch. 'You have a brother? Is he like you?'

Stan's grinning face appears in my mind. 'Yes, but ...'

Her large almond-shaped brown eyes give me a sudden urge to tell her everything. 'My brother, Stan, was killed in a car crash a few months ago.'

Her mouth falls open. 'I'm so sorry, Mikey.' She sinks into Andy's seat so I sit back down.

'I know what it's like to lose someone. How are you doing?' she asks, softly.

I shrug my shoulders. 'Good and bad days.'

Pippa gives me a knowing nod. 'Your little niece ...' Her voice fades away.

'Yes … Tara was his daughter.'

'Oh God,' murmurs Pippa, instinctively reaching out to give my hand a squeeze. 'How is she doing?' Her warm fingers wrap around mine and then in a flash she yanks her hand away as though I've somehow given her an electric shock. She composes herself first and runs a hand through her hair.

'She's not been great, but we're making progress.'

'How's Tara's mum doing?'

Picking up my coffee cup, I gently cradle it. 'Jules left Stan when Tara was a baby. He raised her himself.'

Pippa's eyes widen. 'So, who's looking after Tara?'

Tracing the rim of the cup with my finger, I summon the strength to tell her. 'Me.'

'You?' Her voice is tinged with surprise.

'Mum has MS so I'm looking after the both of them.'

'Oh, Mikey … that's awful. I … umm … really want to give you a hug!' exclaims Pippa, standing up and holding out her arms to me. It takes her a few seconds to register what she's offering.

By the time I've talked myself into hugging someone as beautiful as Pippa Browning, she sits back down in her seat. I watch a blush blossom over her cheeks.

She turns away and avoids my gaze. I sense she's cursing herself for offering me a hug. The thought of potentially blowing my chances for a second time in one day with the world's most attractive woman, is too much. I find myself saying, 'I would like a hug.'

I stand up and open up my arms. In a second, she rises out of her seat and she's in my arms.

CHAPTER 30

PIPPA

*M*el and I are tidying up after shutting the doors to the coffee shop for another day. While sweeping the floor, all I can think about is Mikey and his revelation at lunchtime. If what he said is true, about looking after his mum and Tara, those are not the actions of an irresponsible man.

'You're quiet,' says Mel, wiping the counter.

I stop sweeping and rest my chin on the top of the brush handle. 'Mikey told me earlier about how his brother died in a car crash a few months ago.'

Mel stops squirting spray and looks up. 'What? I didn't know, how awful.'

I nod. 'He's caring for his brother's little girl.' The face of the blonde-haired girl in the park shouting on top of the slide appears in my mind.

After putting the cloth away, Mel comes to stand by me. 'You like him, don't you?'

My eyes widen with surprise. 'I don't *like* him,' I snap. The weird tingling sensation is taking over my chest. 'He has women sending him photos of their breasts.'

Mel points a manicured finger at me. 'I saw you hug him earlier.'

The broom clatters to the floor as my defences start to rise. 'He told me about his brother dying and before I could stop myself, I was getting emotional too. It was just a ...'

My voice fades as I recall the delicious feeling I got when he wrapped his arms around me and pulled me close.

Mel casts me a strange look. 'That was no friendly hug. You were both wrapped up tight in each other's arms. It had sexual chemistry written all over it.'

'It was, I promise you, that's all it was.'

'Jeff and I hugged like that before the toilet incident.'

A banging on the door makes us both look round to see Emma waving. Mel hurries over to let her in.

'Evening, ladies,' Emma says, planting air kisses over our cheeks. 'How are we doing?'

Mel comes over to me and drapes her arm across my shoulders. 'Pip has a thing for Mikey Stenton.'

Emma laughs and slides onto a tall stool by the counter. 'Helen texted this morning to say she thinks you fancy him too.'

I stare in horror at Emma. 'She never?'

Emma takes out her phone. 'Let me read you this. Em, I think my sister fancies Mikey Stenton. You should have seen her after she came home from the cinema. He was all she talked about.'

A chuckle escapes from Mel's glossy lips. 'Pip, just be honest. He's a handsome guy.'

'I don't fancy Mikey Stenton,' I snap, picking up the broom and putting a hand on my red-hot cheek.

Emma swivels on her stool to face me. 'You're blushing now, Pip. Oh my God, you fancy the hairy ballerina!'

'For goodness' sake,' I screech, 'Mikey Stenton is not my type.'

Mel grins. 'Yeah, whatever, Pip.'

Emma turns to Mel. 'Seen much of Jeff?'

Relief sweeps over me as the conversation moves onto Mel's love life.

Mel collapses into a chair and takes a huge lungful of air. 'I can't keep this a secret any longer. I'm pregnant.'

My heart grinds to a halt. I should have known trouble would find Mel. Emma slips off her chair with surprise and clatters to the floor. She picks herself up and comes to join us at the table. 'What?'

Mel traces an imaginary circle on the table with her finger. 'I'm going to keep the baby although I can't see me being a mummy at all.' She continues, 'Not sure what Jeff will say or Cassandra for that matter. He has five children with her already.'

'Five?' Emma and I stare at her aghast.

'He did joke with me, before the ummmm … toilet incident, that he was very fertile.'

'So, this will be his sixth kid?' Emma asks Mel, who nods.

'He told me he only ever wanted one.'

I sit down next to Mel and take her hand. 'How long have you known?'

She wipes her watery eyes with the cuff of her shirt. 'I assumed my periods had stopped due to the stress of losing my job and opening this place.'

'How far gone are you?'

Mel hides her face with her hands. 'Three months.'

Emma gasps.

I massage my temples. 'Are you sure about wanting to keep the baby?'

Nodding, Mel dabs at a stray tear which has escaped and trickled down her face. 'Life never turns out how I planned.'

I lean my head on her shoulder. 'Yep, I agree.'

Emma applies a thick layer of lip gloss. 'Does Jeff know?'

Mel shakes her head and lets out a frustrated wail. 'Just as I thought everything was falling into place.'

I pull her close. 'Maybe it's doing just that? You can be this cool coffee shop owner and a mummy too.'

'I'm not maternal,' groans Mel. 'Can you see me looking after a baby? I don't make the best decisions for myself, so I dread to think about me caring for my child.'

Emma plays with one of her blonde curls. 'Just make sure Pip and I are godmothers.'

Giving Mel a kiss on the cheek I whisper, 'we'll be here for you.' Even though Mel is the best mate who gives both Emma and I sleepless nights, we will never stop looking out for her.

My phone pings from the counter. I recognise the bleep from the dating app. Reaching over I grab it and read what it says.

'I have a new admirer,' I announce. 'Liam, late twenties, and he's a nurse.'

Emma peers over my shoulder and gasps as his profile picture comes up. Liam has huge brown eyes, short tufty chestnut-coloured hair, and a chiselled jaw.

'Mel, check out this guy,' whispers Emma, nudging her.

'He'll definitely take your mind off Mikey Stenton.' Mel gives me a wink.

I exhale loudly. 'How many times? I don't fancy Mikey Stenton.'

'Liar,' says Mel. 'Emma, you should have seen her hugging him at lunch.'

Emma's blue sparkly eyes narrow. 'You hugged the hairy ballerina?'

Frustration bubbles up inside of me. 'Look, I'm going to message Liam and show you both I'm not harbouring any secret feelings for Mikey Stenton.'

Feeling confident, I send Liam a message and ask him how his day is going.

Emma whispers something to Mel and they giggle at me. I turn away and mentally promise to prove a point to my two best friends.

'Emma, Pip's cakes are a sell out,' says Mel, pointing to the empty counter. 'We now have regulars coming in for her cakes and a lady today asked Pip whether she did Christening cakes as a side line.'

My chest swells with pride and I sit up straighter in my chair. I didn't think they'd be such a hit.

Emma rests her head on my shoulder. 'We love you, Pip, and your wonderful cakes.'

Mel reaches over and squeezes my arm. 'We're only teasing about Mikey Stenton.'

'No, we're not!' squeals Emma.

I roll my eyes before rising to get my coat.

∞∞∞

As I make my way up to the front door, I hear Daisy upstairs shrieking with laughter. Libby greets me at the door. 'Daisy's in her bedroom with Tom Ridge.'

'What?' I climb the stairs two at a time. What the hell happened to Josh and what has she done to lure Tom Ridge into her bedroom?

I knock on her door. Daisy opens it looking flushed and smoothing down her wild black hair. 'Yes?'

My eyes are drawn to her skimpy pink vest and skintight jeans. 'Libs says you have Tom Ridge in there?'

Daisy grins and glances back over her shoulder. 'Yes, I have.'

'He made all those complaints against you,' I hiss, imagining being summoned once again up to school.

She nods. 'He was just messing around. We're back together – aren't we, sweetie?'

Frowning at my daughter's pet name for Tom, I ask, 'What about your boyfriend, Josh?'

Daisy's smile evaporates. Her eyes widen and she places a finger over her lips.

A voice from inside her room asks, 'Josh?'

Daisy freezes. Her ring-clad fingers dig into the wood of the door.

'You never told me Josh Harding was your boyfriend? I can't believe you'd date him after what he did to me last year.'

Before Daisy and I can say another word, Tom opens the door and barges past us. He stomps down the stairs, exits the house, and slams the door.

Daisy lets out a terrifying howl. *'All my hard work has been wasted!'* She slams her bedroom door in my face.

Placing and arranging the cheap fish fingers on a baking tray helps to soothe my agitated mind. I dread to think what she meant when she spoke of *work* to get Tom Ridge to go out with her again. Daisy has switched on her radio and a loud bass is making the house vibrate.

A ping from my phone distracts me from going upstairs to yell at her. Liam has replied to my message. In his profile picture he has a "Mikey Stenton" look about him. Oh God – why am I thinking about Mikey Stenton? Emma and Mel's joking echoes in my mind. I have to show them I don't fancy the hairy ballerina.

Determined to show them I'm not in love with a man who has women throwing themselves at him and sending him photos of their bodies, I strike up a conversation with Liam. His messages are flirtatious and funny. A few hours later and my irritation with my two friends has subsided.

While waiting for Liam to reply to one of my messages, I text Helen and let her know who I'm in contact with. Her reply is almost instant.

Can't talk as Rick has livened up the rock star groupie thing. He's going to inform me his band are leaving town, as it's the end of their imaginary world tour. I have to get emotional before reciting four of his verses, including chorus. I then have to ask him to give me a farewell gift I'll struggle to stop thinking about for years to come. Must dash. H x

After chuckling at Helen's text, I tell the kids I'm having an early night and spend the evening messaging Liam from my bed. It's nearly one o'clock in the morning when I tell him I must get some rest.

He sends a message back with a link to the new bar in town; apparently it has a karaoke booth. At the bottom he asks whether I'll be free tomorrow night. Dan's red notebook appears in my mind and so do the instructions about not singing on a first date.

'You've been wrong about other stuff, Dan,' I picture Mikey in the coffee shop queue with women asking him out, Mikey's *Facebook* feed, and the photo on his phone. 'It's time for me to make my own mind up.'

CHAPTER 31

MIKEY

A few of us from the office have gone out after work. Tara's at Samantha's for a sleepover. This, I suspect, is a cunning move by Steph to have a reason to talk to me tomorrow morning when I go to collect her.

Somehow, I've managed to get myself sandwiched between Fiona and Karen from finance. We're in a trendy pub near the office. Fiona hasn't spoken to me properly since our disastrous date and Karen still hasn't forgiven me for not progressing things after our one-night stand two years ago after a Christmas party.

I had good reasons for not taking things further with Karen; her ex-husband is in prison for armed robbery and after Karen and I had sex, she confessed to falling in love with me. I couldn't understand why as the sex wasn't great. I'd been drinking heavily and for most of it her face was blurry. When I tried to leave ten minutes later, she repeated her strong feelings for me and said her ex-husband would be over the moon to hear she'd found someone. I couldn't get away fast enough.

Ian is handing out the drinks he bought at the bar. He passes me a bottle of beer, and Fiona her glass of wine. Fiona takes a sip of her wine and turns to look at me. 'Why didn't you take me home the other night?'

I shift uncomfortably in my chair and ignore Karen rolling her eyes at Fiona.

Fiona crosses her legs. She's a little frosty with me. 'Shall we go and have a chat?' She gestures to the other side of the bar where there are a few empty booths.

I reluctantly get up. Maybe a quiet chat with Fiona will help clear up any bad feelings.

Karen places her hand on Fiona's arm. 'I wouldn't go there, if I was you. He'll break your heart, like he did mine.'

Fiona leans into Karen. 'I can handle him.'

She slides in next to me and I can feel the toe of her shoe stroking my trouser leg. 'I wanted to ask you whether we could start again?'

I can feel her hand on my thigh. 'Let's pretend Friday night never happened. Shall we go back to mine?'

I take in her olive skin and jet-black hair. If this had happened six months ago, we would have been back at her place in a flash. Even though I think Fiona is an attractive woman, she doesn't come close to Pippa Browning. The hug we had yesterday is still being replayed in my head. I don't think I've ever experienced anything as powerful as the moment I hugged Pippa.

'I'm sorry, Fiona, I can't do this.'

'What?'

Leaving Fiona sat in the booth by herself, I head for the door. Karen is shaking her head with disapproval. It's still early and I need another drink, so I head to another bar.

'Whisky, please,' I say, passing over a twenty pound note. To my relief, there are a few spare tables next to the empty karaoke booth. I can sort out my head and enjoy a drink in peace. I make my way over to one of the tables and hear a shriek of laughter from the entrance to the bar. Turning around, I see Pippa Browning arm in arm with a man.

With a drunken smile plastered over her face, she whispers something to him and then erupts into a fit of giggles. My eyes are drawn to her fitted pink dress which hugs her figure perfectly. She looks beautiful. An army of butterflies break free and swarm into my chest.

Pippa spots the empty karaoke booth and drags her date towards it.

'Come on!' she slurs. 'I got to sing!'

I watch her stagger into the booth and fiddle about with the machine. There's a lot of huffing and puffing from her as she punches into the keyboard the hit she likes. Her date, a tall man with short brown hair and a shiny grey suit, stands at the opening, holding her cocktail. He's grinning like an idiot.

This should be interesting. I don't think I've heard Pippa sing. Although I do recall a karaoke machine at one of the football club's Christmas events and Dan telling everyone not to let his wife anywhere near it. The bar goes quiet as the opening tune to an eighties classic blasts out.

I watch Pippa raise the mic to her lips and start to … yell.

Her date's smile disappears as she murders a good song. He puts his hands to his ears. A throng of men stood by the bar shake their heads in bewilderment at the dreadful sound coming from the lips of this beautiful woman.

As the song finishes, I watch her date try to lead her away. Pippa is having none of it. 'I want to sing more songs,' she mumbles, tripping over her feet.

She starts singing again. I stare into my drink and pray for a power cut. Pippa's date is urging her to stop but she swipes his hand away and screams the chorus louder.

Five songs later and Pippa's mic drops to the floor. Her date marches out of the bar without her.

Her face falls. She looks like a lost little girl. Instinctively, I rush over to her aid. 'Hello, Pippa.'

She looks at me with a relieved smile. 'Mikey.'

I offer her my arm. 'Let's get you home.'

We stagger to the taxi rank and I help her into the cab.

'Chestnut Avenue,' says Pippa after I climb in beside her. In this drunken state, I think I should make sure she gets home safe.

As the taxi pulls away from the kerb, she places her hand across her mouth. She's going to be sick. 'Can you stop the cab?' I bang on the plastic window.

Somehow, I manage to open the door seconds before she pukes all over the pavement. The cab driver politely asks us to leave, which I think is fair. We stand on the side of the road and I notice she's shivering. Removing my jacket, I place it around her shoulders and give her a handkerchief to wipe her mouth. I then pull her close to keep her warm while I flag down another cab.

The new taxi sets off and the city flashes by, she stares at me. 'How are you, Mikey?'

'I'm okay, how are you?' I say, with a smile.

'I've had … too much to drink.' She giggles.

'I'm going to get you home safely,' I explain.

She hiccups and scratches her head. 'Has Liam gone?'

'Liam? Oh, you mean your date … yes, he's gone.'

Pippa goes quiet before chuckling to herself.

'What's so funny?' I ask.

'Dan wrote me something and he mentioned you,' she whispers as her chuckling morphs into hysterical laughter.

'What did he say?' My gut tightens.

'He told me to date you. Well, I won't be doing that,' she explains. 'I need someone who is … mature and sensible.'

'What?'

'You're too wild for me, Mikey Stenton, and a *tart.*' Pippa passes out and slumps against the window.

The taxi pulls into Chestnut Avenue. I point to the house with the rusty old people carrier parked in the drive.

After paying the taxi, I help her out. We stagger to the front door which is opened by Pippa's blonde friend. She stares in horror at the sight of her.

∞∞∞∞

'Look at the state of her!' the woman screeches, before turning to me.

'Thank you for bringing her home,' she gushes, grabbing hold of Pippa from me. 'I'm Emma, by the way.'

'I'm Mikey, the tart,' I snap, turn on my heel and walk away.

CHAPTER 32

PIPPA

My head is a major no-go area. It should be surrounded by orange cones and cordoned off with blue police tape. I'm struggling to lift it off the pillow without crying. My dry tongue is stuck to the roof of my mouth and my breath smells of stale vomit.

I never envisaged this would be the morning after a first date with a nurse called Liam.

Hang on, I can't remember coming to bed. The memory of last night is shrouded in a thick fog inside my head. Panic sets in. What happened after Liam and I kissed?

Forcing my sticky eyes to open, I'm greeted by the sight of my bedroom door. This means I'm lying on my side. My mind quickly runs through all the possible first date outcomes with Liam. Perhaps he's now sleeping by the side of me? What if we had sex and I can't remember the actual act?

If Dan is looking down from heaven and sees my current situation, he won't be pleased.

Stretching out my arm behind, I gingerly feel the bed for the presence of another human body. Phew. There is no one lying beside me.

Nausea envelops my body as I turn over. After throwing back the covers, I hurtle into the bathroom. Hanging my head over the toilet I start to heave; Emma magically appears at my side.

'Are you okay?' she asks, rubbing my back.

'No!' I groan, holding my hair back. 'Why are you still here?'

'I was worried about the state you were in, so I stayed. Checked you were still breathing every couple of hours and stuff.'

I glance up at her. 'Was I that bad?'

'Yes, have you got work today?'

'As it's Saturday, Mel's asked her friend to help out as I need to be here with the kids.'

'Good. Do you remember being escorted home?' Emma asks.

'By Liam?' I croak, trying to remember some detail about my date after the cocktail binge. What I do remember is feeling like I had a point to prove with Emma and Mel. This led to me letting myself go and making sure we had a wild time.

Emma shakes her head. 'Oh no, Pippa.' She chuckles. 'You were brought home by someone else.'

I stop breathing. 'What?' Straightening, I turn to face Emma.

'Nice looking, tall with brown hair. Likes wearing a ballerina outfit.' Emma stifles a giggle.

I rub my head, trying to make the events of last night reappear. The words "ballerina outfit" make the blood drain from my face.

'Mikey Stenton brought me home?' I gasp, placing my hands over my mouth.

'What happened to Liam the nurse?' asks Emma.

I shrug my shoulders. 'The last thing I remember is Liam buying me another cocktail. Everything else is a blur.'

My mind replays the hug Mikey and I shared. 'I can't believe what happened between us.'

Emma checks her face in the mirror. 'What was it like, hugging him?'

'What?' My mind drifts away. I sit down on the edge of the bath feeling light-headed.

'And?' Emma's blue eyes narrow.

I run my dry tongue over my lips. 'Nice.'

'Nice?' repeats Emma. 'You hugged Mikey Stenton, the male tart, and you found it to be nice?'

'It made me feel weird.'

Being in his strong arms made me feel protected and safe. I can remember closing my eyes and feeling like the rest of the world had been shut out.

Emma grins. 'So Mel was right. And Helen!'

Grimacing, I return to feeling sick.

'You didn't talk to Mikey in the taxi much?' Emma asks, picking up a shampoo bottle and casually reading the label on the back.

I give her a blank look. My memory is only serving up Liam buying me the third cocktail, after we'd demolished a bottle of wine in another bar. 'Why do you ask?'

Emma casts me an awkward smile. 'No, nothing, just something he said.'

'What?'

A grin takes hold of Emma's pretty face. 'He called himself a tart.'

The bathroom spins in front of my eyes. Did I call him that?

Emma places a hand on my shoulder. 'Don't worry, I'm sure it will come back to you.' Her giggle brings on a fresh wave of nausea.

∞∞∞

The kids enter the kitchen to find me slumped at the table, huddled over a large cup of black coffee.

Daisy screws up her face with disgust. 'What's wrong with you?'

Libby pokes me with her finger. 'Have you been drinking wine?'

'Mum, can I go play outside?' asks Billy, jumping up and down on the spot.

I give Billy the nod and Libby saunters after him with a football tucked under her arm.

Daisy shakes her head with disapproval at the state of me.

'Don't judge,' I groan. 'I went out for a drink.'

'With a friend?' asks Daisy, turning to yank open the fridge.

I struggle to nod my head.

'I hope you didn't sing anything,' mutters Daisy, before putting a bottle of milk to her lips.

The word 'sing' pings around my head. I sink further into the chair as a flash of memory shoots across my mind, poking through the hangover fog. The image of Liam holding my drink while standing with a worried expression on his face materialises before my eyes.

'Oh no,' I groan as another memory flashes up; the neon sign of a karaoke booth.

Daisy gasps. 'No, Mum!'

I hang my head in shame.

'How could you?' snaps Daisy. 'Please tell me it wasn't one of those songs you say are from *your era?*'

The events of last night come rushing back. I can see the mic in my hand and the words to songs rolling down the screen. There are people dotted around the bar and they're all … shaking their heads, but I don't care. I'm singing my heart out. Pissed.

'Dad said you should not sing karaoke,' exclaims Daisy, hovering over me like she is now the adult and I'm the hung-over teenager who has been doing too much partying.

'He used to tell us about the football Christmas party where you got drunk and sang karaoke. He said you had a voice like a foghorn.'

I catch sight of Dan's grinning face on one of the photos on the kitchen wall.

'Oh no,' I whimper as an image of Mikey in the taxi appears. Mikey brought me home. Liam must have left me in the bar.

It was nice of Mikey to look after me. A fragment of memory makes the fog hangover disappear.

I won't be dating you as I need someone who is mature and sensible. You're too wild and a tart!

Poor Mikey. I'm ashamed of my drunken rudeness.

A little part of me hopes this doesn't stop him coming into the coffee shop.

Daisy hands me a plate of dried toast. 'Here, eat this, you'll feel better,' she advises.

I look up and try to manage a smile.

'I take it you're dating?' asks Daisy, sliding into a chair next to me. 'You can stop telling me porkies about going out with *friends,* and Libby's school project kind of gave it away, Mum.'

Taking her hand in mine, I stare into her intense green eyes. 'You got so upset in the caravan, I couldn't bring myself to tell you.'

Daisy shrugs. 'I think I'm okay now. Just don't go out with someone who we'd hate.'

A text pings. It's my mother. Come to my house this afternoon for 5 p.m. – URGENT.

After a morning of lying still on the sofa with a cold compress on my forehead, I wearily climb up the stairs after lunch for a lie down.

Daisy wakes me later. As I haul myself out of bed, Daisy gives me some insight on dealing with hangovers. 'Try crisps and a can of fizzy drink, always works for me.'

After a cup of coffee and reading several texts from Emma about a new man she's met on *Tinder* called Scott, I decide fresh air is what I need. With a throbbing head, I encourage the kids and Maria to join me on a walk to Nana's.

As we walk, I wonder why my mother has typed URGENT on the text. Maybe there has been a crisis at her knitting group meeting or her dog, Benny, has been taken sick.

She greets us at the door with a mischievous grin. I don't think she has looked this happy since she heard my father's latest girlfriend's operation to fix her bowel problem was unsuccessful.

Spotting the children standing behind me, my mother beams. 'Daisy, go buy your sister and brother some sweets, please?'

Daisy lingers behind me on the step, shaking her head. 'I'm a bit too old for going to the shop to buy sweets, Nana.'

My mother disagrees. 'Do it please, there's a good girl,' she says, firmly.

'What's going on?' I ask, noticing the green vein in my mother's neck is bulging.

'Come and see who's here,' says my mother, clasping her hands together.

I allow her to steer me into the lounge. As we enter, I come face to face with Anthony … my childhood sweetheart.

Anthony used to be a scrawny and spotty teenager, with long brown wavy hair. Over time, he has transformed into a rugged, tanned hunk of a man, with piercing cobalt blue eyes.

He was my first proper boyfriend. We dated for almost three years but broke up after I realised just how boring our relationship had become.

Anthony put a stop to our social life as clubs and pubs bored him. He disliked festivals and holidays. We ended up spending all our time eating takeaways, watching TV at his mother's house, and having sex in his bedroom. I remember waking up once and wondering whether there was more to life than game shows, his mother's home-made quiches, and dull sex under his bed covers.

'Pippa,' Anthony says, confidently striding over. My eyes roam over his short grey flecked hair, his fitted woollen blue suit and his shiny black pointed shoes.

He leans in to kiss me on the cheek. 'Nice to see you again, Pippa,' he murmurs, staring deeply into my eyes, before placing his hand lightly on my shoulder.

I remind myself this is Anthony. The same guy who rarely went out to parties, lived on his mother's sofa watching TV, and actively encouraged me not to be sociable. He talked me out of throwing a party when my mother was in Gibraltar, he urged me to resign from the Saturday job at the newsagents, and he threw away all my cigarettes.

'How are you, Anthony?' I say while shoving my hands into my trouser pockets.

He grins. 'Life got a lot better a few minutes ago when you walked in.'

Heat is radiating out of my cheeks. 'So, what have you been up to since we last saw each other?' It must have been before Dan and I got together.

'Set up a successful business.' His eyes glint with excitement.

I run a hand through my hair. 'Oh, sounds interesting.'

He carries on. 'I've got into power lifting and won a few competitions.'

Blimey, Anthony *is* a changed man.

'Will you let me take you for dinner?' he asks.

'You're quick,' I say with a chuckle. 'We've only just met after however many years.'

Stepping closer to me he says, 'You look so beautiful.'

Feeling awkward I inch away from him.

'Helen tells me you have kids.'

'She has *three* kids, Anthony, and they're out of control,' interjects my mother, coming in from the kitchen. She's wiping a dinner plate dry with such force there'll be no floral design left if she's not careful.

My neck and shoulders are stiffening at the sight of my mother's face. There's a dreamy expression plastered across it and her eyes are fixed on Anthony. To my mother, Anthony was the perfect boyfriend. His lack of partying and love of the quiet life made him shoot to the top of my mother's good list. The day I told her Anthony and I had broken up she cried buckets.

Anthony smiles. 'I don't have any kids; I wanted them, but Deborah …' He stops himself at the mention of his ex-partner.

'When are you free?' asks Anthony.

'Any night next week,' says my mother, from the doorway, still drying the same dinner plate.

I glare at her. 'Mum, I need to sort out childcare.'

'I'll babysit.'

'Hang on, you texted me last week to say you were never going to look after them again after the incident with the emergency ladder.'

My mother casts me a sugary smile. 'For you and Anthony, I'm willing to make a sacrifice.'

'How about next Friday?' Anthony has taken my hand and planted a kiss on it.

'Fine.' The dinner plate is given an extra rub by my mother.

'Friday it is then,' confirms Anthony. 'Shall I meet you in town? What about the Italian?'

I'm sat on my mother's sofa. She's standing by her large bay window and watching Anthony climb into his car. 'Sorry, Pippa, I had to play matchmaker when I bumped into him at a garden centre.' His car engine can be heard, and she lifts her hand to give him a little wave.

'Mum, Anthony and I split up for a reason,' I say, fiddling with one of my mother's coasters.

She turns and smiles. 'You will thank me one day, Pippa.'

I sink back into the luxurious cream leather sofa. There are no grubby finger marks, no imprints of muddy footballs, no toys, books, magazines, footballs, or cracks in the windows.

My mother comes to sit opposite me. 'Dan suggested you date

someone who knows you.' She crosses her tight-clad legs and smooths out her tartan skirt. 'Okay, I know he advised you not to get back with Anthony, but we are going to ignore him on that subject.'

I take one of my mother's cushions and hug it.

'This online dating business is going to stop now Anthony is on the scene, Pippa.'

'But I don't know whether I like him again.'

My mother leans over and stares at me. 'Pippa, this man has his own business, a rental property empire, and he's a sensible man. You won't find better.'

I chew on my thumb nail.

'Anthony won't do what your father did to me.'

Her words make me sit up with surprise.

'Anthony won't have affairs. He is a trustworthy man. If I had my time again, I wouldn't have married a ladies' man like your father.'

Mikey's face flashes up inside my head. He's a ladies' man.

My mother's eyes narrow. 'Pippa, I'm worried you'll make the wrong decision. Especially if you go for the … male ballerina who Dan suggested.'

Before I have time to answer, the kids return from the shop. The sound of Libby and Billy squabbling fills the air. Daisy is talking loudly into her mobile.

'Mum, I hate my brother!' cries Libby, giving Billy a shove into the piano.

'Don't do that,' I glare at Libby.

Billy punches his sister in the arm, making her yelp.

'Come on, please behave.'

Libby whacks Billy across the head, sending him flying into the cream sofa.

'Liberty!' Booms my mother, causing Libby to freeze on the spot.

Once the kids are silent, Mum turns to me. 'Pippa, I've said it before, but your children need a good role model. Anthony has a successful business and by the sounds of it, a few sporting achievements. You won't get better than him.'

And with that, the crap-mummy guilt appears.

CHAPTER 33

MIKEY

*T*ara climbs up the slide ladder. 'Me and Keith played a board game last night. Uncle Mikey – are you listening to me?'

'Huh?' I stop pacing the perimeter of the small enclosure which contains a set of swings, two slides, and a climbing frame. 'What did you say?'

I normally give Tara all my attention, but today my mind is elsewhere. Pippa Browning's beautiful face has been with me since I woke up.

To add to this are painful soundbites from the other night's taxi journey playing continually in my head. The words *mature, sensible,* and *wild* are like flies in my mind. The phrase "tart" makes me shiver. Is that what she thinks of me – a tart?

'Uncle Mikey – what's the matter?' Tara shoots me one of her concerned looks.

Rubbing my chest, I shake my head. 'Nothing you need to worry about, Tara Twinkle Toes.'

When I think of Pippa, I get this ridiculous chest ache. Looking back, I can't recall having such intense feelings for a woman before. I've never experienced such hunger and longing for someone. With Pippa I want to spend time with her, have a laugh, talk all night and take her out to fancy restaurants. It may sound strange, but I have an urge to take her to the local boating lake and row her around the island.

Tara stands at the top of the slide. 'Don't you like the park?'

I grin at her. 'Tara Twinkle Toes, I always enjoy the park when I'm with you.'

She laughs and shrieks down the slide. Over the past few months I've grown to love this little girl more than I could ever imagine. I adore hanging out with her, making home-made pizza and playing video games on my old PlayStation which we found in Mum's attic. She also shares my love of *Star Wars* and *Star Trek*. We are always cracking little jokes and talking about where we're going to visit when we travel the world together.

I sit down on the little bench and think about what my relationship with Tara will be like when she's older. Will we still laugh and joke like we do now? Where will we be living? Will there still be the rumours and gossip about me? Before Stan died, I didn't care what people thought. The idea of women gossiping about my womanising ways boosted my ego.

A cold feeling passes over me. Zipping up my leather jacket I picture Tara hearing those rumours and noticing that the only photo Mum has of me is one where I'm a drunken beach bum, shame nibbles away at me. Is this how I want Tara to think of me?

My heart starts to beat faster. I want Tara and my mother to be proud of me. One day, my mother's cabinet will be filled with photos of Tara with me having adventures and sharing life experiences. I look up at the blue sky, dotted with a handful of white fluffy clouds. I wonder if Stan is watching all this.

My phone bleeps. To my dismay, it's another lengthy text from Sophie, telling me how hurt and used she feels. I bite my lip and delete it.

I return to thinking about Stan. My brother would never have expected me to step in with Tara and help Mum so much. He was always making comments about my party mad lifestyle and the damage it was doing to my liver. I remember he phoned me before I went on my football tour to ask whether I would help more with Mum.

A few days ago, I scrolled through Stan's old texts on my phone. Nausea curled up my throat as I read all the times Stan had mentioned Mum was struggling and how great it would be if we both made an effort to go there after work.

The text which made me want to run from my past self was Stan asking whether I would come around and organise a birthday party for Mum in the garden. I'd text back to say if he sorted it out, I would send him the money. I had a stag do to attend and might not make the party.

I clasp my hands together. I want Stan to be proud of me and … I want Pippa to fall in love with me. A tingling feeling takes hold of my body. I want that more than anything else in the world.

'What are you doing?' Tara rushes up to me. Her rosy pink cheeks and sparkling blue eyes bring an instant smile to my face.

'Thinking,' I say, reaching out my hand to ruffle her hair.

She loops her arm through mine. 'Can we go home now?'

We trudge back across the park. Tara doesn't want to hold my hand. Instead, she walks beside me, a sign she's getting back to her normal self.

Before we get to the car park, we pass a team of seven-year-olds in a football match. There are several groups of noisy parents shouting from the sidelines and a tired-looking team manager.

I look over to see Ted, the manager of my old football team. Ted's head is in his hands as the opposition has just scored a goal. I take Tara's hand and lead her over to the side of the makeshift football pitch.

'Hey, Ted,' I say, patting him on the shoulder.

'Mikey.' Ted grins and shakes my hand. 'Long time, no see.'

I point to Tara. 'Been busy with this little lady.'

Ted smiles and goes back to watching his team.

We watch a young lad with bright orange hair score a goal.

'What are you up to with this lot then?'

Ted lets out a sigh and surveys the field of children. Some look interested in football and some are tear-stained and standing on the sidelines while their parents order them to get back on the pitch. 'I've taken over this lot. Nothing too serious, just gives them a chance to have a bit of fun on a weekend.'

I chuckle. 'That sounds like hard work.'

Ted nods. 'I'm trying to find someone to help out on a Saturday morning, do a bit of training with them and maybe a practice game. You don't know if any of the lads from the senior team would mind doing some helping out?'

'With this lot?' I ask, gesturing to the far side of the pitch where two little lads are on the ground wrestling and have given up defending the goal.

'Yes, we have our work cut out though.'

Dan's words from his notebook come rushing back to me. This could be an opportunity to do something for my local community.

'I'll do it.' The words shoot out of my mouth. When I was younger, I did some football coaching exams, but got bored as the lure of Magaluf, scantily clad women, and partying was far greater than standing on a muddy pitch in the freezing cold.

Coaching these little kids would get me and Tara out of the house and it would help out Mum by giving her some respite. The more free time I can give to Mum, the better.

'Really?' asks Ted, slapping me on the back. 'You can work some of that Mikey Stenton goal scoring magic on them.'

'Don't think I can work miracles, but I'll have a go.'

Ted punches the air and then shouts at a girl from his team who's arguing with another player on the goal line.

'It'll be good to get us out of the house and Tara here can help.' I ignore Tara's scowl.

'I'll need to do the usual CRB checks and there'll be some paperwork but we can get it sorted. Mikey, this will really help me out. I'm sure this team will learn a lot from you.' Ted drapes his arm over my shoulder.

'I'll have a go.'

Ted rubs his hands together. 'Fancy staying here and watching for a bit?'

We stay until the end of the match. Some of the kids are quite good. I pointed out to Tara who, in the team, I thought was showing football promise. She listened intently while sat next to me on the sidelines.

On the way home, she turns to me. 'Uncle Mikey, could I go to football training?'

I look at her with a smile. 'Really?'

She nods. 'I love playing football at school with the boys and I begged Dad to take me to a taster session, but he was always busy with Nana.'

'Wow, my niece likes football, this has made my day!' I pull her close.

'Can we get a football and go to the park this afternoon?'

I lift her off the ground and she squeals. 'As long as you're not as good as me, Tara Twinkle Toes!'

CHAPTER 34

PIPPA

*T*he kids are off school this week. I'm kicking off my Monday by doing an afternoon shift at the coffee shop. Billy and Libby are tagging along. They've promised to take their iPads, books, and sticker books and sit quietly at the back of the coffee shop, while I work. Their reward will be a rabbit-faced fairy cake later.

My date with Anthony on Friday is on my mind. Last night's lengthy phone conversation with him didn't go well. He talked for ages about his latest second-hand vintage car and the things he's planning to do to it. When he got excited and gushed about the suppliers of spare parts, I rested the phone on my shoulder and read Emma's celebrity magazine.

I called Helen afterwards and we talked about my worries. She told me Rick used to bore her tears, but since he's started working from home and they've rediscovered each other in ways she never imagined she's now happy to listen to him for hours.

After settling Libby and Billy, I notice Libby is struggling to let go of her pink rucksack. 'You don't need to put it on the seat, Libby, stick it on the floor.'

Libby shakes her head and hugs it. 'No, I want it next to me.'

'But you look really squashed up,' I say, wondering whether I should just walk away before losing my rag over a rucksack.

Billy grins at Libby. I'm assuming this is one of their games.

I leave them to it and go to find Mel behind the counter. She's busy serving a gang of little old ladies who are desperate to try some of my little carrot cakes.

After tying on my apron, I look around the coffee shop and feel a little twang of gloom.

Lunch time is nearly over, which means I won't get to see him today. I can't believe I'm thinking like this, but for the last few days, I've been watching out for Mikey in the queue.

'He was in here looking for you this morning,' Mel says, tapping me on the shoulder.

'Who was?' My stomach tightens.

Mel laughs. 'You know who, Mikey Stenton. I think he likes you too.'

'I don't like him,' I say, turning away quickly from Mel and hiding my warm pink face.

'Liar,' chuckles Mel. 'I told him you were on the afternoon shift.'

I lift my head into the air and go clear tables, ignoring the hundreds of fluttering butterflies inside my chest.

An hour later Mel takes me aside. She looks dreadfully pale which is no surprise given she's in the early stages of pregnancy. 'I don't feel great, Pip. Can I put you in charge? Think I need to go and lie down upstairs.'

I give her arm a rub. 'Go. Don't worry, I'll be fine.'

'You need to make a batch of cakes for tomorrow.'

I cast Mel a puzzled frown. 'Why?'

'Oh ... umm ... didn't I tell you ... well ... I've been contacted by a cake blogger. She's coming to sample them ... tomorrow.' Mel backs away towards the door.

My heart starts to thud. 'What?'

Raising her hands in defence Mel leans against the door to

upstairs. 'Look, it wasn't me who told her about how amazing they are, but someone did. She's like cake blogging royalty. It would be wonderful publicity for the business if she ...'

Through gritted teeth I say, 'If she does what, Melanie?'

'Likes your cakes, Pip.'

I let out an exasperated wail. 'That's soooooo much pressure.'

Mel grins. 'It'll be fine. Pip – your cakes are out of this world. Make those little animal-faced ones again.'

'They took me hours!'

'Trust me, you make brilliant, eye-catching cakes.' Mel rubs her tummy. 'Remember, Dan said you should do something with your skill.'

As she rubs, I ask, 'Have you told Jeff your news?'

She shakes her head. 'He came over last night and all he did was moan about his kids. At one point, he said he was glad they were all teenagers and not screaming babies.'

We both go silent and find interesting things to stare at on the stone floor.

'Do you think he'll leave his wife?'

Mel nibbles on her nail. 'Not sure, I need to lie down. Are you okay dealing with the coffee shop and sorting out a batch of your best cakes?'

'How popular is this blogger?'

I watch Mel screw up her eyes. 'Small following ... of about a ... *million* cake fans. Numbers mean nothing, Pip.'

'A million?'

'She has her own *YouTube* channel and has brought out loads of books on cake making. You'll love her. She's called Flossy James.'

I place my hands over my face and groan. 'Flossy James is super famous!'

Daisy bought me Flossy's latest cake book last Christmas and I remember flicking through it and gasping at the wonderful things she creates. My little cakes won't come close to her exceptionally high standards. 'How the hell am I going to do this?'

Mel comes over and places her arm over my shoulder. 'If I feel better later, I'll come down and help.'

'Don't worry, I'll be fine,' I say, lying through my teeth. Even though the thought of Flossy James eating my cakes scares the life out of me, it would be huge for Mel's Coffee Shop. I have to make this work.

I wave Mel off with seriously sweaty armpits and turn back to the queue of customers, all eagerly awaiting a hot drink and a tasty fairy cake.

'Pip,' says Zoe, stood at the coffee machine. 'Go out the back and get started. I can manage here.'

'Are you sure?'

My cake planning and preparation is done with an ear on what's going on in the coffee shop. There's been no sign of Mikey. I tell myself to stop being silly and what Mel said wasn't true, the bit about him liking me.

The coffee shop is quieter now with only a handful of customers. I'm giving myself a break as I have two batches of cakes in the oven and a few sketches of animal faces for the icing.

Libby and Billy are arguing in the corner which I'm happily ignoring, although I'm sure I just heard Billy say the name, *George.*

Wasn't that the name of Libby's pet field mouse who I set free in the garden?

Nope, I'm imagining things again. I'm going to carry on pretending I didn't hear that.

As I wipe down a table, I hear a familiar voice. 'Hello, Pippa.'

I whirl round. There he is. My eyes take in his brown leather jacket, crisp white shirt, and navy jeans. His hair has been styled at the front and he's clean shaven. I'm drawn to his spicy aftershave and for a second, my chest feels like it's crammed full of butterflies.

'Would you both like a drink?' I ask, smiling at Tara, who is stood behind him.

He nods and we walk back to the counter.

I make him a latte and Tara a milkshake. While I make their drinks, I know he's checking out my new black fitted dress. I picked it out this morning in the hope I'd see him today.

'How are you?' His hypnotic eyes are making me lean in towards him.

I fiddle with the string on my apron. 'Fine. You?'

The boyish smile I now find myself desperate to see appears. I resist the urge to pull him over the counter and kiss his handsome face.

Oh God, I need to stop thinking like this; the man is a powerful magnet for women and he's a wild party animal. Yes, he spends his time caring for his niece and sick mother, but a little part of me still thinks he's still partying until dawn when he's not being a hero.

Libby comes over carrying her pink rucksack. She grins and struts off into the kitchen behind me.

Mikey takes his coffee cup. 'We're going to sit over here.' He points to the table near the counter.

If he thinks I'm going to lose sight of him he is very much mistaken.

I head into the kitchen to see what Libby's up to. She's bent over and peering under the large table in the centre of the room.

'Have you lost something?' I ask, checking the clock. There's only ten minutes to go before I have to close the shop, get the cakes out, order the kids a pizza, and start work on my creations for Flossy James. Another twang of gloom is set off inside of me. I won't have long to talk to Mikey.

'Mummy,' says Libby, scratching her quiff of blonde hair. She shoots me an awkward look and fidgets with her collection of football wrists bands. Why do I get the impression she's hiding something?

'I've done something which you're not going to be happy about.' She flicks her eyes to the floor.

'What?' I notice she's chewing on her finger. Another sign something is wrong.

She lifts her head up. 'George wanted to see the kitchen, but now he's run off.'

I can feel the blood draining from my face. 'What did you say?'

'I showed George the kitchen and now he's disappeared.'

'George?' In my head, I'm praying she's renamed her football George and not brought a bloody field mouse into Mel's kitchen.

'The mouse.'

'What?' I shriek. 'Why did you bring him here?'

Libby starts to tremble. 'He told me he likes coffee shops.'

'He's a field mouse, Libs, he likes fields. There is a big clue in the word.'

What the hell am I going to do?

I bend down and start surveying the kitchen floor. 'Libby, Mummy is very cross right now.' That is an understatement. I'm livid. Thoughts of Mel's business being closed down due to vermin race into my head and Flossy James spotting George scoot across the floor as she takes a bite into one of my cakes sends my stomach plunging to the floor.

Libby starts to cry. 'He said he wanted to see a coffee shop.'

'Can you please ignore what George says?' I get closer to the floor and peer under the freezer.

'Is there a problem?' A familiar voice makes me jolt.

My face is pressed against a cold kitchen floor and my huge backside is in the air. It's at times like this, I wish I hadn't spent three years stuffing my face with fairy cakes and doing very little exercise. I'm now praying Mikey Stenton isn't behind me.

'Pippa.'

He is. What must he be thinking about the size of my backside?

'Mummy's looking for my friend,' says Libby.

'Oh, I see,' says Mikey. 'What sort of friend are we talking about?'

'A small furry one,' replies Libby.

I can feel him crouch down beside me. His warm breath caresses my neck and the smell of his aftershave is making me feel light-headed.

'Does this friend have a name?' His soft voice makes me smile.

'George,' I say, turning towards him.

Our faces are now centimetres apart. The urge to kiss him is so strong but so too is the fear of angry Mel, when she finds out a mouse is roaming about her beloved business.

'That's a nice name,' mumbles Mikey, his eyes still glued to mine.

'He's there!' shouts Libby.

Mikey and I spin round to see something scoot across the floor and dive under the table.

Rising quickly to his feet, Mikey grabs a metal bowl. Sensing that catching George is going to require a team effort, I haul myself to my feet and reach out for a saucepan.

The mouse darts through Mikey's legs and heads towards me. I scream and bring the saucepan down over it.

Mikey, Libby, Billy, and Tara, who has joined the fun, all cheer as I grip onto the work surface and send a prayer of thanks to God.

Mikey releases George into the field across from the coffee shop. Libby agrees it's for the best he goes to live in his natural habitat.

He walks back to the car park and we stand awkwardly, staring at each other. Tara is tugging on his coat and Billy is threatening to hit Libby. Now is not the time for lustful glances.

'Sorry for the chaos,' I mumble, pointing at my kids.

He grins. 'I enjoy chaos.' I watch as he notices one of my sketches on the side. 'Is this one of your creations?'

'Yes, Mel has arranged for Flossy James—'

'Flossy James – as in the cake blogger?' His eyebrows rise to his hairline.

I massage my temples. 'She's coming here tomorrow. Someone's told her about my cakes.'

'Wow, who would do something like that?' he says with a grin, leaning back against the counter. 'So, you're working late?'

I feel my shoulders droop at the sight of Billy and Libby looking at me with faces of hunger. 'Yes, and at some point, I need get these two some tea and …'

Mikey grins and my hearts performs a series of flips. 'How about if I go get us some pizza?'

'Really? That would be amazing.' My mind has suddenly become awash with thoughts of boating lake dates and secluded spots for passionate picnics.

Get a grip, I think. He's only getting pizza … there's nothing romantic about pizza.

CHAPTER 35

MIKEY

I'm stood watching Pippa sat on a stool and hunched over one of her creations.

Shouts and laughter are drifting into the back kitchen. The kids are at one of the tables in the coffee shop, stuffing strips of pizza into their mouths. To my surprise, Tara quickly made friends with Pippa's two kids and now the three of them are acting like they've known each other for ages.

The kitchen smells strongly of bleach as Pippa and I mopped it after the George incident.

'Do you like my little fox?' Pippa looks up with a smile and points towards the fairy cake in front of her.

I walk over and gasp with amazement at the miniature fox, with his orange and white face, tiny whiskers, and triangular shaped ears. Dan was right about what he said. Andy's sister, Flossy, will go wild when she sees Pippa's fabulous cakes. 'Wow, he's great!'

Pippa wipes her forehead with a cloth and shrugs. 'He's okay, I suppose.'

'He's better than any fox cake I've seen.'

'Flossy James will have seen cakes miles better than mine,'

236

groans Pippa, touching the row of little farmyard animal cakes on the tray. 'I don't know why this mystery person got in contact with Flossy James.'

'Maybe Mel did because she can see how talented you are?'

Pippa lets out a laugh. 'Anyone could do what I do.'

'Anyone?' I say, with a wry smile.

She nods. 'Even you, Mikey.'

'Okay then, give me a spare cake and I'll prove to you that not everyone can produce cakes as wonderful as you.'

Pippa pats the stool next to her. She giggles as I sit beside her. I'm handed plastic gloves and an apron. 'Right, what animal am I drawing on?' I say, taking hold of a bare little cake.

Her breath on my neck sends every hair upright. 'How about another fox?'

I give her a wink. 'Let me see what I can do.'

My phone pings with a text and then pings again as I lay a dollop of orange icing onto the cake.

'You got a text,' says Pippa, gesturing towards my phone.

I grimace after checking the screen. 'It's from an ex-girlfriend.'

'Oh – is she heartbroken?'

'No, she's skint. Sophie's struggling to accept we are over, and the bank of Mikey Stenton has shut.'

My cheeks grow hot at Pippa stares at my phone. 'You gave her money?'

I nudge my phone towards her as a photo of Zack appears on the screen. His cute face and mass of cherub curls beams out.

Pippa gasps. 'You have a son?'

I shake my head. 'He's Sophie's kid, but she's not a great mother.'

Pippa casts me a puzzled look.

'When I used to go around there, he'd be screaming in his cot or left to crawl about Sophie's dirty flat, so I'd end up making sure he was okay.'

'And you gave Sophie money for him?' Pippa stares at the photo of little Zack.

I take in a lungful of kitchen air. 'Sophie doesn't buy him nappies or clothes. She never has any money, so she asked me.'

Pippa goes silent for a minute. After what feels like an eternity she speaks, 'That's a nice thing to do for Zack.'

'I'll have you know, Pippa, I'm an expert nappy changer.'

Pippa's mouth falls open in surprise. 'You actually changed his nappies?'

'Zack would be screaming in his room,' I explain. 'Sophie couldn't be bothered to look after him and his crying used to go right through me. So, I would sort the little guy out myself.'

'Oh, Mikey,' murmurs Pippa, holding my gaze, 'I never had you down as an expert nappy changer.'

I smile at her. 'I've many secret talents. What do you think?' I thrust my poor attempt at a fox cake at Pippa, who starts to giggle.

'Mikey, what is it?' She laughs at my attempt. 'I wouldn't pay for that.'

'Harsh,' I say and we both erupt into fits of laughter.

When Mel walks in, both Pippa and I are in hysterics.

'What's going on?' Mel asks, looking at us in bewilderment.

Pippa snorts with laughter and holds up my orange and white mess of a cake. 'This is Mikey's contribution.'

Mel shakes her head and grins. 'It's so nice to see you laughing like this, Pip. Mikey, you should come here more often.'

After Mel heads back upstairs, Pippa casts me a breathtaking smile. I find myself edging slowly towards her. There's something hypnotic about her gaze. I can see the rise and fall of her chest. I desperately want to cup her mesmerising face with my hands and kiss her.

'Mum,' calls out Libby making us jump.

I smile at Pippa. 'You carry on with doing your cake magic and I'll sort the kids out.'

'Are you sure? I don't want to keep you.'

I reach out and touch her shoulder. 'It's fine. Anything I can do to help, Pippa.'

By the time we all leave the coffee shop, it's past eleven. After loading Billy and Libby into the car, Pippa comes over to me. 'Thanks, Mikey, I really appreciated you being here tonight.'

'No problem. What time is Flossy arriving?'

Pippa flicks her sexy fringe and I have to lean against the car as my legs have become jelly. 'Midday, I think. Oh, Mikey, what happens if she thinks my cakes are basic?'

My eyebrows shoot up my forehead. 'Basic? Pippa, your cakes are out of this world. Believe in yourself.'

'Do you think so?'

I nod and hold her gaze for longer than necessary.

An owl hoots as our faces travel towards each other. Before our lips touch Libby bangs on the car window.

Pippa flicks her fringe. 'Right, I better go. See you, Mikey.'

I watch her climb into her car. My chest is aching for this woman.

CHAPTER 36

PIPPA

*T*he events from last night are on a continual loop inside my mind. Every time I close my eyes I'm back in the car park, staring up into his warm brown eyes, desperately wanting him to kiss me …

Mel is talking to me about the preparations for Flossy James's visit later. I stopped listening ages ago.

'Pip, are you thinking about Mikey again?' she asks, studying my face.

'What?' I say before wiping my sweaty forehead. 'No, of course not.'

Mel shakes her head. 'You've always been a rubbish liar.'

In an attempt to show Mel that I'm not stood daydreaming about Mikey Stenton, I reach for a cloth and start to wipe down the counters.

Mel laughs. 'Pip, I cleaned all the counters five minutes ago while I told you about the plans for when our important guest arrives.'

I carry on giving the counters a good clean and Mel walks away shaking her head.

Emma is our first customer. She clip-clops towards me in

gigantic heels, a huge grin plastered across her face. 'Are you ladies ready for Flossy James?'

'Think so.' The doorbell has rung again, and my heart has broken into a gallop. It could be him.

No, it's not him, it's one of our regulars.

'Earth to Pippa.' Laughs Emma, waving a manicured hand at me. 'What's got into you?'

Mel appears and starts to make Emma's usual coffee while I decide to give the counter a third wipe.

'Is she all right?' Emma asks Mel, pointing to me.

'Her and Mikey Stenton were in here last night,' explains Mel, busy frothing milk. 'You should have seen them, they were laughing and flirting like mad with each other.'

Emma laughs and takes her flat white from Mel. 'So, are you ready to impress a famous *YouTuber*?'

Mel nods. 'Pip's cakes are amazing. I can't believe someone like Flossy is coming here to my little coffee shop.'

Emma takes a sip of her coffee. 'You ladies have done an excellent job with this place. Everyone at the gym last night was talking about coming here.'

'Really?' gasps Mel.

Emma nods. 'They were all raving about those sofas and how nice it is to meet friends here.'

Mel grins. 'That's brilliant. Did you see I set up an *Instagram* page?'

'I was one of your first followers,' says Emma. 'Loved the shots of Pip's cakes. Did she help you with the camera?'

'No, she was down here too busy gazing into Mikey's eyes.'

I throw a cloth at Mel and she squeals with laughter.

Mel wipes her hands on her apron. 'To be fair to Pip, she did help me out last night. I felt really sick and could only lie on the sofa. Still can't believe I'm having a baby. How the hell am I going to manage with this place and a baby?'

Emma's sparkly blue eyes widen. 'Let's go out Friday. A celebration of this place and Mel's baby.'

Anthony's face flashes across my mind and I let out a groan. 'I can't. I've got a date.'

Emma and Mel gasp in unison.

'With Anthony.' A sinking feeling in my gut quickly follows as his name leaves my lips.

A customer comes in at the same second Emma and Mel start shouting. 'No, No, No, Pip!' They quickly hurry back out.

Emma grabs my shoulder. 'Why are you going on a date with weirdo Anthony?'

The door chime saves my life. I don't want to talk about Anthony yet. We look up as a gang of parents, with babies sat on their hips and toddlers asleep in buggies, come in.

There's an hour to go before Flossy James is due to arrive. A long queue of thirsty customers is snaking out of the door and there are tables which need to be cleared. I glance over at Mel who is steadying herself against the coffee machine. Her face is a worrying chalky colour.

'Are you okay?' I ask, touching her arm. She looks at me with red watery eyes.

'I feel so ill, Pip.'

Murmurs of dissatisfaction come from the queue and I can hear one woman complaining about the time it takes to get a coffee. I turn back to Mel. 'Go lie down. I'll sort this.'

Mel shakes her head. 'Flossy will be here soon. This is so important. Oh God, Pip, the room is spinning.'

Before I can think straight, she makes an odd sound and falls against me. 'Mel,' I gasp as panic envelops me.

'Pippa, let me help,' says a familiar male voice. I turn around to see Mikey Stenton diving behind the counter. Mel groans as we help her into the back room and onto a chair. 'Put your head between your knees, Mel,' he orders. Turning his attention to me, he rolls up his sleeves and says, 'Stay here with Mel. Get her a glass of water. I'm going to sort out the queue.' He strides purposefully out of the kitchen and behind the counter.

I sit with Mel and hold her hand until the colour returns to her face. She casts me a weak smile. 'Sorry, Pip.'

'Hey, it's okay, you need to take care of yourself.'

'Where's Mikey?'

I look up to see him standing in the doorway smiling. 'Feeling better, Mel?'

She nods. 'Still not a hundred per cent.'

'Did you sort out the queue?' I ask as he holds my gaze and my heart performs a series of flips.

'Yes, I used to work in my mate's café when I was a teenager and it all came rushing back to me.'

Mel leans her head against my shoulders, and I stroke her hair. 'Flossy will be here any minute and I feel awful.'

'Don't worry,' Mikey walks up to Mel. 'Pippa and I will sort out Flossy. First, we need to find somewhere you can lie down.'

Mel rubs her forehead. 'There's a flat upstairs. If you're sure, I'll go up?'

After settling Mel, Mikey and I head downstairs. The coffee shop is not in its best state, even though the queue has disappeared. There are dirty cups and plates at tables and litter on the floor. He turns to me and grins. 'Let's get to work, Pip, we haven't got long.'

'How come you're here?'

With a wink he goes to grab the broom. 'I knew today was a big day for you, so I popped in to show you some support.'

'Really?' My legs have turned to jelly at the sight of the two boyish dimples either side of his mesmerising smile.

We manage to get the shop back to a reasonable state. While Mikey loads the dishwasher, I make sure the cake counter is filled with my cakes.

'They look amazing,' says Mikey, looking over his shoulder. 'I hope you kept my offering from last night.'

'We do have standards here, Michael,' I say with a cheeky grin.

He brushes past me and our bodies touch for a second. 'Going to take Mel's rubbish out for her. Hold the fort, Pippa.'

Mikey's still not back when the door chimes jangle and in walks Flossy James. I recognise her instantly from the book Daisy bought me for Christmas. With her are three women who are all tapping things into their phones. Running her hand through her soft wavy brown hair, she stands to admire her surroundings. She's wearing a stylish mustard-coloured blazer, ripped jeans, and a white shirt. 'Cool place you have here.'

'Can I get you a drink?' I ask, looking at Flossy and the three women by the window, still engrossed with their phones.

By the time I have put the closed sign on the door, made everyone a drink, settled them down, and brought out a selection of cakes, Flossy and the three women have taken a multitude of photos of the coffee shop. 'This place is divine,' purrs one of the women. 'I love these polka-dot tablecloths.'

There's still no sign of Mikey which is a little worrying.

Flossy grins at my animal-faced cakes. 'Wow, they're so cool, Pippa.'

'Thanks,' I say, as my cheeks grow warm.

We chat for a while on how I've built up the animal faces and the techniques I've used. Flossy seems really interested in my designs and for a second, as she's taking a photo of a tiger cake, I have to pinch myself to make sure I'm not dreaming. Here I am, sat in front of a famous *YouTuber*, showing off my cakes. Maybe Dan was right about doing something with my baking skills?

After they've all drained their coffee cups, Flossy stands and outstretches her hand. 'Pippa, this has been great, and I adore your cakes.'

'Thank you for coming,' I gush.

'I hope Mel gets better soon. Tell her I'll be in touch,' says Flossy.

After I watch them walk away, I return to the counter and squeal with delight.

Five minutes later Mikey appears at the back door.

'What's happened to you?'

He groans. 'Mel's bins were in a state. I think there are some greedy cats around here.'

'You have been outside sorting the bins out?' This man constantly surprises me.

He nods. 'Mel's in no fit state and it was a mess. When's Flossy coming?'

'She's been and gone.'

A smile spreads quickly across his face. 'How did it go?'

'Brilliant,' I squeal.

He stretches his arms and we rush towards each other. I'm getting a strong urge to kiss the man who saved the day.

'What did she say?' Mel puts an end to my hug from Mikey and all thoughts of kissing him as she staggers into the coffee shop. 'I feel a bit better.'

When Mikey goes home, Mel and I reopen the coffee shop. 'Does he know Flossy James?' Mel asks.

'Why do you ask?' I say, wiping down a table.

She sits down on one of our stools. 'I looked out the window upstairs earlier and I saw him hugging her. They looked like they knew each other.'

My heart sinks.

'Really?'

Mel nods. 'They were laughing and joking with each other.'

I start to scrub the table. 'I should have known. He's probably slept with her.'

CHAPTER 37

PIPPA

*A*nthony and I are meeting in town. He's booked a table at a new Italian restaurant. Even though I have reservations about him, I'm starting to think Anthony is my only relationship option.

Daisy walks past me as I coat my lashes with black mascara.

'You're going on a date, aren't you?' She leans against the door frame of the downstairs bathroom and watches me.

I take a deep breath. Maybe Daisy will help sort out my muddled mind. 'Yes, with Anthony. I used to go out with him when I was a teenager.'

She frowns. 'Anthony? Not the one you used to go out with before Dad? The one who you and Dad joked about being boring?'

I cast her an awkward look and turn back to the mirror.

'Dad used to say you needed a bit of fun, after Anthony, when you met him in the pub all those years ago.'

Why did Dan tell her all about Anthony and why has it stuck in her mind?

'He's mature and sensible,' I add, recalling my mother's words.

'You mean dull,' adds Daisy. 'I'm not happy about you dating, Mum, but please don't date someone who's boring. That's the last thing we all need.'

'People change!' I snap, dismissing Anthony's text this morning, which contained five photo images of the kitchen in one of his rental properties which needs tiling. Anthony was keen to see how the morning light made the room look before he chose the tiles.

Daisy places her hands on my shoulders. 'Think about this carefully, Mum. You don't want to spend the rest of your life with a dull man.'

'Keep your voice down, Libby and Billy will hear you.' I apply blusher and think about what Daisy has just said.

My mother arrives to collect the kids. They're going back to sleep at her house for the night. I love how Anthony makes my mother get out of her comfort zone and actually have them overnight. She bounds into the house with a jubilant look. 'Are you excited, Pippa?'

I shrug my shoulders. 'Excited is not the word I would use.'

Taking my elbow, my mother steers me into the living room for one of her lectures. 'Listen, Pippa, Anthony is a good man and I want you to consider something …' She gives me a warm smile.

'What's that?' I ask, stealing a glance at myself in the mirror. My God, I look like a clown.

'Women at a certain age have to take what they can get.'

'What do you mean by that?'

My mother smooths her grey hair down. 'Pippa, you're mid-thirties and I hate to say this, no spring chicken.'

'Thanks for reminding me.'

She sighs. 'I'm just saying that if a nice, sensible man like Anthony comes along, you should go for it.'

Shifting her weight from one sensible walking shoe to another, my mother continues. 'I just think that at your age, you should be grabbing hold of certain opportunities which come your way. These opportunities might not come again.'

'You never married again after Dad ran off with …' I stop as my mother doesn't like to hear Denise's name.

'Nothing suitable came my way, Pippa,' she explains. 'But, if someone like Anthony had popped up, I would have grabbed him with both hands.'

'Do *you* fancy Anthony, Mum?'

'Oh, behave. You also have to remember, you do have … baggage.' My mother picks fluff from her woollen jumper.

'Baggage?'

She looks up and smiles. 'Children. It can't be easy taking on another man's kids. When you find someone who's happy to get involved with looking after moody teenagers, animal-mad girls, and energetic football-mad little boys, you have to hang onto them.'

Her face tilts to one side. 'Dan wanted you to date someone you knew.' My mother's hot hand squeezes my shoulder. 'He also made reference to a man having to take on your children. Ignore the bit about the ballerina, he wasn't thinking straight.'

Dan's red notebook appears in my mind. He did say our children were a bit of a handful. I only have to think back to the field mouse incident in Mel's Coffee Shop.

'Anthony is solvent and sensible, Pippa. Men like him don't come along that often. You might not find another Anthony.'

∞∞∞

Anthony looks handsome in his grey woollen suit and crisp white shirt. He sits across from me in the restaurant and carries on telling me how successful he's becoming in the house rental market.

'I have a portfolio of three houses,' he says. 'All rented out. I'm attending an auction next week to buy a fourth.'

I stifle a yawn. Since we arrived, I've not talked once.

'I love the thrill of making a small profit,' gushes Anthony. 'It gets me going.'

I raise an eyebrow at him. In my mind, I'm replaying the conversation with my mother. She might have a point about hanging onto someone like Anthony. The chance might not come up again. I could very well find myself alone in my forties and fifties. Alone with just my kids to keep me company …

He places his warm hand over mine and leans in to tell me how beautiful I look. 'You don't need to wear so much make-up for me,' he says, studying my face. 'You're naturally beautiful.' After taking a mouthful of wine, he smiles. 'You could come with me to next week's house auction.'

Maybe the thrill of a property auction is what we need to fire us both up?

He strokes my leg with his shoe underneath the table. 'Just think about how exciting it'll be for you to see me in action.'

I sit and take in what I'm hearing. Here is a man, striving for success as a landlord. He is solvent, mature, and he has extensive knowledge of the housing and second-hand car markets. Anthony has also told me he is in bed before ten every night and he can't remember the last time he got drunk.

Mikey Stenton's face flashes up inside my mind. I've spent most of my week thinking about what Mel said. Every time I start to think he's a nice guy something happens to make me doubt him. Dating him feels like it would be a thrill-seeking emotional rollercoaster. At theme parks I never go on the big rides.

After draining my glass of wine, I make the decision to embrace all that Anthony has to offer.

Outside, while we wait for a taxi, he kisses me. His lips are dry, but I let him carry on.

'I can't wait to show you my property portfolio.'

I smile and glance over Anthony's shoulder. Mikey Stenton is stepping out of a pub. Anthony peppers my neck with kisses, I stare at Mikey. Our eyes lock onto each other and he stops in the middle of the street. He looks so handsome in his smart tweed jacket, shirt, and dark jeans. In a flash we are back sat on stools in the rear of the coffee shop, laughing over his rubbish attempt at a fox cupcake.

A taxi arrives and Anthony bundles me inside. I watch Mikey get smaller and smaller.

∞∞∞

'I want to make love to you,' whispers Anthony as he lies beside me on the sofa. He's just given me a lengthy account of his life, since we broke up at seventeen. I've been staring up at the ceiling thinking about Mikey Stenton.

I wake up and realise what he's just said. 'Not on my sofa.'

My new family furniture has to be respected.

'Why not?' he moans, pulling me closer and pressing his face against my cheek.

'It's our first date … we can't go too far.' I try to escape his clutches and sit up.

He starts to kiss my neck. 'We went out with each other when we were teenagers.'

'I can't get carried away on a first date.'

Anthony places his hand on my thigh.

'No.' I try to dismiss the image of Mikey Stenton in my head.

'Let's seal our relationship,' Anthony whispers, running his fingers over my hips.

'Okay, but not here … it doesn't feel right!' I'm imagining Mikey Stenton running his hands over body.

'Why?' Anthony is now panting in my ear.

'Not here.'

'I'll book us a hotel room,' Anthony whispers, undoing the hook of my dress.

'Stop it,' I say, swatting away his wandering hand.

Anthony sits up and wipes a layer of sweat from his brow with the back of his hand. He turns to me. 'We need to make up for lost time, Pippa.'

I haul myself up from my sofa and button up my dress. 'Yes … okay, but not here.'

'I think I'll book us a room in a nice budget hotel I know.' Anthony runs his hands through his sculptured hair.

I give him a puzzled look. 'Budget hotel?'

'We don't need to waste money on anything fancy. All we need is a good-sized bed.'

'But I like fancy hotels.' Anthony and I have different views on romantic nights in hotels.

'One of my properties is near the one I have in mind, so in the morning I could show you around the house?' He takes my hand and kisses it.

'What about your place?' I ask, trying to steer him away from the low-cost hotel room idea.

He fiddles with his shirt cuffs. 'I'm currently on the sofa at Deborah's and she wouldn't be happy if we went back to hers to seal our relationship.'

I stare at him. 'Deborah?'

He nods. 'My ex.'

'But I thought you have a vast property empire?'

Anthony pulls me into his arms. 'I do, but all my properties are being rented. As I said, all we need is a bed. You'll be impressed with the hotel, it's clean and spacious.'

The thought of Anthony booking a room so that we can have sex sends an uncomfortable feeling over me. Surely I'm worth more than a budget hotel room?

He strokes my cheek. 'Trust me, Pippa, after a night with me, you'll be begging me to marry you.'

Breaking free from his hold, I wander over to the living room window to think.

The thought of spending the rest of my life with Anthony sends tears rushing into my eyes and a lump to rise in my throat. They are not tears of joy either. My mother's words echo in my ears. *Women at your age have to grab hold of opportunities like Anthony.*

CHAPTER 38

PIPPA

'Mum, wake up!' chants Libby. 'Football training.' I groan into my pillow. Why did I agree to this? Dan Browning, once again, you have a lot to answer for.

Once Anthony left, I fell into the comforting arms of a bottle of pinot grigio. My head is now throbbing and there's a sour taste in my mouth.

'Can't Nana take you?' As my mother had the kids last night, she could have done me a favour and taken them to football.

'She said no, I asked her.' Billy rushes into my bedroom and tugs on the duvet.

I rub my puffy eyes. 'What was her excuse?'

'She's never having us to sleep over again as Libby brought George's wife too.'

The mention of that bloody field mouse's name makes me sit bolt upright in bed. 'Please tell me you have not homed another poor mouse out of the garden?'

Libby fiddles with her quiff. 'George's wife said she wanted to see Nana's house.'

'Libby!' I scream, making my throat burn and head hurt.

She kicks a football towards Billy. 'I didn't put George's wife in Nana's bed, I promise.'

'What?'

'She ran off under Nana's dressing table. Daisy caught her.'

I haul myself to my feet and *whack* … a ball knocks me back down. Billy grins at his sister. Even though my blood is close to boiling point over the mouse incident and being hit in the chest by a ball, I can feel Billy's glee at the sight of the old Libby.

I turn to my daughter who flips the football into the air and then hoofs it across my bedroom. 'For goodness' sake, Libby, stop kicking that ball!'

'Come on, Mummy,' shouts Billy, fist pumping the air.

As Billy runs out of the bedroom, I grab Libby's elbow. 'I told you the other night after the coffee shop incident not to bring a mouse inside ever again.'

Libby heads the ball across the room 'She doesn't know where her husband, George, is Mummy. He was last seen outside the coffee shop after Mikey let him go.'

Picking up the football I storm out of the bedroom. 'No more mice, Libby.'

We arrive at the park. Cars are jammed into all the parking spaces and finding a space is proving tricky. Billy and Libby are out of the car before it's stopped moving and I don't have time to go batshit crazy at them. I watch them charge across to where the training session is starting.

An older man is shaking his head as I climb out of my car. I've created my own space and parked our rusty old people carrier almost diagonally and blocking someone's truck.

Smiling sweetly, I say, 'On a Saturday most people are relaxed about parking.'

I walk over the grass towards the team and head towards the throng of mothers gathered around the coach. Circling the mothers is a ring of excitable boys and girls, all jumping up and down.

I don't know what to do so I stand on the sideline and wait for the crowd to disperse.

Libby smiles at a familiar blonde girl standing near them. After a second glance I recognise Tara. The mob of mothers parts to reveal Mikey Stenton dressed in a tracksuit.

Our eyes meet as a red-haired mother, wearing a T-shirt two sizes too small, thrusts herself in front of him and asks whether he'd give her son a private coaching session. Her son, she claims, is showing premiership potential and is only six years of age. I hear Mikey refuse a private session.

As usual, Mikey is at the centre of all the female attention. Every female parent, apart from me, has dressed up for the football practice event in skinny jeans, white T-shirts, and shades.

He instructs the children to start doing some jogging and sidles over to me.

'Hello again,' he says, with a warm smile. 'This is a nice surprise.'

'Hi,' I reply, seeing Billy talk to some of the other children while Libby stands on her own. 'What are you doing here?'

'Ted, the manager, was struggling to find someone to look after this lot so I decided to help out.' Mikey's arm brushes against mine. 'You recovered from meeting Flossy James?'

Irritation prickles my neck. I nod and look away. How can he ask me about her when he was all over her outside the coffee shop? This man has no shame.

'Seen any more of George?'

'We've not seen him since you let him go. Libby tells me George's mouse wife was in my mother's bedroom last night.'

Mikey chuckles and walks away.

'Nice evening last night?' he asks, returning after shouting instructions to the children about the warm-up game he wants them to play. His eyes remain focused on the children.

'It was okay,' I mumble, loosening my scarf. The memory of

kissing Anthony and seeing Mikey over his shoulder has rushed into my mind.

'You looked like you were having a nice time.' He gives me a sexy wink.

'He was just an old friend.' I turn to face him and we survey each other's outfits. Him, a muddy black tracksuit, football socks stuffed into football boots. Me, a pair of old jeans and my navy striped T-shirt with scarf.

We are interrupted by a gang of kids desperate to play a football match.

After a series of kicking games, Mikey splits the children into two teams. Billy and Libby are on the same team. My heart beats faster as Libby comes over to me, yanks Dan's old Cardiff City shirt out of my handbag and puts it on. She races back onto the pitch running her hand through her quiff.

The whistle blows and a crowd of excited players rush towards the boy who has the ball at his feet. A mother next to me starts screaming at her son and then turns to me to say, 'He's destined for the premiership.'

Before I can reply, Billy breaks away. Sprinting up the right side of the makeshift pitch with the ball, he skilfully weaves past a kid picking his nose and a girl checking her phone. In a moment of Browning magic, Billy spots Libby charging up the left-hand side and kicks the ball high into the air. I'm robbed of breath as my youngest daughter leaps into the air and confidently heads the ball into the back of the net. The goalie didn't have a chance. Tears prick my eyes as I watch Libby and Billy run to hug each other.

Mikey comes over to me and pulls me into an unexpected hug. 'Danny Boy would be so proud.'

Wiping away tears of happiness I smile, leaning closer to Mikey.

Libby goes on to score five goals. At times it is like watching magic at work. Every time she scores, she makes me weep more by racing round pointing to Dan's shirt. Billy scores two and by end of the match my cheeks are damp and hot. The other team storm off to their parents after the whistle has gone.

Looking up at the fluffy blue clouds, I hope Dan is sat on one watching. This single parenting lark is hard, and I've made so many mistakes since he died, but seeing my kids today has made my chest swell up.

All the parents and children disperse quickly, leaving me stood with Mikey. Billy has run off to play in the trees with Libby and Tara.

'Will you help me lock these away?' asks Mikey, pointing to the giant net of footballs and then to the green shed like building.

We reach the shed and he opens the door. I step inside, hauling the net of footballs. Mikey is behind me. When I turn around, we gaze into each other's eyes. I'm drawn to him. It's like there's something invisible pulling us closer together.

Inside, he takes my hand and a surge of electricity powers up my arm. In a second, we come together in a passionate embrace. His strong arms wrap themselves around my body as he treats me to a warm and sensuous kiss. Every single bone in my body has turned to jelly. His arms circle my back and my hands dive deep into his chaotic brown hair. We pull each other closer and I find myself letting out a soft moan as he kisses my neck.

My brain wakes up, mid-kiss. This is wrong. I should not be kissing Mikey Stenton.

It feels so right, but I'm not right for him. As my mother correctly said, I have *baggage*, and at times my kids are feral. When they're not climbing down fire ladders, kicking footballs through windows, and refusing to listen to me, they're cutting all their hair off and stalking their love interests. He's a single man who doesn't need to date a woman with three spirited children.

I don't dress fashionably, I can't handle my cocktails, after three children my breasts are not things I want to take photos of, and I don't think I can cope with dating someone as adventurous as him. Mikey would find me dull and we'd end a few weeks later.

Every time I see him, he has a huge following of excitable women. The memory of Mel telling me about him and Flossy hugging each other nudges me. Then there's the ex-girlfriend sending him texts of her breasts and asking him for money. No, I don't think my little heart could withstand the torment this man brings with him.

Dan's red notebook appears in my head. He recommended Mikey, but he was clearly confused and not thinking straight due to the chemo.

In a flash, I pull away, gasping. 'Oh … I'm so sorry.' I wipe my mouth. 'I don't know what came over me.'

He grins and tries to reach out for my hand. I bat it away. 'Mikey … I can't.'

'Why not?' he asks, taking a step towards me.

'We're not right for each other. I can't … I'm sorry.' I need to get back into the fresh air. My reaction to Libby and Billy's football performance has made me get carried away. 'I'm sorry.'

Diving out of the shed, I call Libby and Billy. We walk hurriedly back towards the car.

Anthony's face appears in my mind and I groan. We're supposed to be spending a night in a hotel next week and here I am snogging Mikey Stenton in a football shed. Knowing him, he probably does that to all the football mothers.

I *can't* start a relationship with someone like Mikey Stenton.

CHAPTER 39

MIKEY

*A*s I drive back to my mother's house, Tara tells me all about her new friendship with Libby. At the traffic lights, the sight of Tara's beaming happy smile brings tears to my eyes.

When my car turns into the high street, Tara becomes distracted by a new stationery shop which has opened. I allow myself to think about what happened in the football shed.

I've never been kissed by a woman like that. Yes, I've kissed a lot of women in my time but not one who electrified my entire body. As her hands ran through my hair and her body pressed against me, I made the decision to not kiss anyone else for the rest of my life. When you have been kissed by Pippa Browning, everyone else fades into insignificance.

Her voice echoes inside my head. 'We're not right for each other.' What does that mean? She turned me down. I relive the terrible sinking feeling again, when she pulled away, flicked her fringe at me in that sexy way and told me we were not right for each other.

Tara and I enter Mum's house. Before I can hang our coats up,

Tara has raced off upstairs. She and Libby are now friends on *Snapchat* and she wants to message her.

My phone rings as I hang up my coat. It's Sophie. My shoulders tense at the sight of her number. When will she learn we're finished?

'What?' I place the phone to my ear.

'I need to talk to you.'

'Why?' I lean against the doorframe in the hallway and kick off my trainers.

'I'm pregnant and it's yours.'

Her words hang lifelessly in the air. I grip onto the doorframe and steady myself. My mother's choice of complicated floral wallpaper spins before my eyes.

'What?' I snap.

'I'm three months gone and it's your baby, Mikey. I wasn't on the pill.'

'I'll be over now.' I grab my car keys. Mum comes out of the kitchen. She takes one look at my face and freezes. 'Are you okay?'

I rub my face. 'I've got to go sort something out.'

The drive to Sophie's flat is long and tedious. Everyone is on the roads and there are snaking queues of cars at all the traffic lights. Nausea bubbles away inside of me.

Sophie opens the door to her flat in silence. On seeing me, she walks away into the kitchen diner. I stride after her.

'I'm pregnant.' She hands me a scan photo. The sight of the blurred baby outline on the photo makes my legs weaken. Wiping my sweaty brow, I try to get a hold of myself.

'Are you sure it's mine?' My voice wavers.

Sophie nods and goes to scoop up a grubby faced Zack from his playpen.

'But I thought you had a boyfriend?' I recall our last conversation.

She watches Zack chew on his saliva coated finger. 'I do, but you got me pregnant.'

I stare in disbelief at the scan photo. 'But I was too drunk the last time we were together.'

Sophie shakes her head. 'We did enough.'

My stomach nose dives towards the floor. The memory of the wedding is patchy. All I remember from when I got to her flat is changing Zack. After he settled, Sophie and I did mess around on the bed and … shit – maybe she's right?

I rise from the sofa, still holding the scan photo. 'So what happens now?'

Sophie rolls her eyes. 'Dunno. I need some money though.'

Zack starts to cry as I pace the room. My mind is frantically working out what I should do. If it's my child, then I need to take responsibility. The thought of my child being raised with parents who live apart, is not something I want to consider.

Somehow, I need to make Sophie, Zack, and the baby a part of my life. Tara's face appears in my mind and an uneasy feeling passes over me.

'I'll move in here and Tara can come stay a few nights,' I announce. Sophie looks at me in surprise.

'What … who?' she asks, popping Zack back in his playpen. She turns and reaches for a packet of cigarettes.

I swipe them out of her hand. 'I'm helping to look after my brother's daughter. She's eight.'

Sophie's face changes to one of disgust. 'You can move in, but I'm not having some brat live here.'

The word "brat" causes my shoulders and neck to stiffen. Tara is not going to be labelled a brat. 'Please don't refer to her like that!'

Sophie snatches the cigarettes back out of my hand. After sliding one out, she places it in her mouth. 'You and the kid are not moving in here.'

I pull the fag out of her mouth and crush it with my hand.

'You're not smoking in front of Zack. We've discussed this. It's not good for his lungs. Plus, that's my kid you're carrying.'

'Mikey, stop it!' she screeches, stamping her foot.

Anger courses through my body. We've talked before about her smoking with Zack in the same room.

I survey her flat. Clothes are strewn across the sofa, sweet wrappers over the floor, empty drink cans on shelves, and ashtrays overflowing on surfaces. 'Do you think you should tidy this place up?'

She looks away and drums her manicured pink nails on the work surface.

'I need to go home.' I turn and make my way out of her flat.

She follows me. 'You haven't given me any money.'

'Why do you need cash?' I stand on her doorstep and let my eyes linger over the thick layer of foundation starting to crack on her cheek. Her limp brown hair hangs, almost lifeless, over one side of her face.

'I want to buy our baby something.' She smiles and fishes out my wallet. 'Oh, and I'm off out tonight with everyone from the club.'

Snatching my wallet back, I glare at her. 'Who's looking after Zack? You're not going out drinking in clubs when you're carrying my child.'

She casts me a dark look. 'I'll do what I like,' she hisses, yanking back my wallet. 'Zack'll be okay.'

Frustration and anger rise inside of me. I barge back inside her flat, grabbing her arm as I pass. 'You need to change your ways. This isn't going to work if you're going to carry on with your old life.'

She pushes me away. 'Get out!'

I hold my ground. 'No – you promise me you're not going to go out and get pissed tonight.'

'You were never this bothered about me before, coming to my door at all hours and wanting to get your dirty way with me.'

Her words make me flinch. My old friend *shame* makes an appearance inside my gut.

'You weren't carrying my child then.'

She passes Zack a dirty teddy bear. 'Give me some money then and I won't!'

I pass her thirty quid. She grabs the money and rewards me with a sugary smile.

The scan photo is still in my hand. I offer it to her. 'Take it.'

She walks into her bedroom and shuts the door. Zack starts to howl. I pick him up and wait until he quietens down. 'Sorry, little man,' I whisper, before laying him down in his playpen.

As I drive back to Mum's house, I'm numb with shock. In the space of a few hours my life has been torn apart. Sophie's face flashes across my mind. Why did she have to fall pregnant?

Of all the people in the world I could have got pregnant, why does it have to be her, my cash-hungry *Tinder* acquaintance, who sits at home in a dirty flat, leaving her baby son to cry his heart out. Sophie, the woman who wears so much make-up I'm actually scared of what lies underneath her crusted mask.

Why was I so stupid not to realise that something like this might happen? Is this a punishment for being an arsehole all these years? I think it is. This is karma for all the girls I've messed about.

At the lights, I hit the steering wheel with frustration. How the hell am I going to explain this to Tara? Sophie's label of 'brat' echoes inside my head and makes my gut tighten. The look of disgust on Sophie's face when I brought up Tara will forever haunt me.

Pippa Browning flashes across my mind and what she said to me in the shed.

She has a point. We aren't right for each other. I'm an idiot and not worthy of her attention.

CHAPTER 40

PIPPA

*I*n the queue for coffee this morning, Mikey glances up once to say a brief hello. He's unusually quiet and withdrawn. His head is bent over his phone and he is furiously tapping out a text.

I watch him take his drink and walk away. I must have hurt his feelings. The thought of making him sad makes my chest ache.

He stands by the door to the coffee shop, letting a few tired-looking office people in and helping a woman with her buggy inside. There's something preventing him from leaving.

'What's up with him?' Mel asks, staring at Mikey. 'Blimey, Pip, what did you do to him in that football shed?'

There has been a lot of messaging on our *WhatsApp* group over the weekend. Mainly to do with what happened at football practice. Mel and Emma didn't hold back with their views on the situation; to my surprise they both think I've made a mistake.

My phone pings from the shelf behind us. I groan. 'It'll be Anthony texting to confirm he's booked a room in his budget hotel for Friday night.'

Mel is still looking in Mikey's direction. He's leant against the wall by the door and in between reading his phone and opening the door, he keeps glancing up at me. 'I think you should go and see him, Pip.'

'Really?'

She places her hand on my shoulder. 'Go easy on him.'

I head towards him and he gestures for us to go outside. We leave the coffee shop and turn into the car park shared by the little row of shops and bars.

'Listen, I'm sorry about what happened on Saturday,' I say. 'I don't want it to ruin our friendship.' My body begins to tremble.

He rests against the brick wall and holds my gaze. 'Don't be silly, nothing could do that.'

'Are you okay?' I notice the dark circles around his eyes.

He nods and pushes himself away from the wall. My heart breaks into a gallop as he walks towards me.

'Will you do me a favour?' He chews on his lip, giving me the impression he is thinking about what he wants to say to me.

'Anything.' I'm drawn to the boyish smile which is spreading across his handsome face.

'Will you kiss me one last time, Pippa?'

The request takes me by surprise. 'What?'

He reaches out and cups my face with his hands. 'You were right. We shouldn't be together, but would you please kiss me, one last time?'

'One last time,' I murmur, unable to drag my eyes from his.

He nods.

All my self-control is swept away on the breeze as I allow myself to fall into his arms. Our lips come together with such passion and energy, a few seconds in and I'm locked in a lustful paralysis.

This time, he breaks away first. He strokes my cheek with his thumb and places a delicate kiss on my forehead. 'Thank you,' he whispers.

I smile as a hot blush takes over my face and neck.

He turns and walks away.

Mel takes me aside when I return to the coffee shop. 'Well, what happened?'

I shrug. 'He asked me to kiss him one last time. What do you think he means?'

Mel's eyes widen with surprise. 'One last time?'

I shake my head. 'Do you think he's leaving?'

'Pip, what the hell are you doing?'

I let out a long stream of air. 'I don't know.'

'Why are you going to the hotel with Anthony?'

'Because, as Mum says, he's solvent, sensible, and a good role model for the kids.'

Mel's brown eyes narrow. 'Pippa, this isn't about them. It's not about your mother, it's about you.'

I can't think. My head is awash with thousands of thoughts.

I go into the back and throw myself into an elaborate cake making session. I can only think properly when there's a piping bag with a petal nozzle attached to my hand. The sight of buttercream roses always lifts me, encourages a smile, and once my fairy cakes are made, my world will seem less complicated and muddled.

Mel appears as I take my first batch of cakes out of the oven. 'You okay?'

I nod and pop them onto the wire rack.

'Look, Pip, this is your life and I shouldn't be sticking my nose into it. If you want to go with Anthony on Friday, then fine. Go for it.'

She comes over and throws her arms around me. 'I just care for you, Pip, and I don't want to see you make a silly decision.'

I rest my head on her shoulder, close my eyes, and he's there, asking me to kiss him, one last time.

CHAPTER 41

PIPPA

*T*he radio is blaring out an eighties hit which normally would have me singing along to it, but today I am in a world of my own. Surrounded by my baking utensils I am sat at the back of the kitchen wondering why I haven't seen Mikey all week. To say it's been torture in the coffee shop is putting it mildly. Even Mel has been watching out for him each day. She even asked one of the girls who works in Mikey's office where he is. The girl said he was off work and no one knows why.

'What's the matter, Mum?' Daisy asks, sauntering into the kitchen in her gingham PJs.

I swallow back tears. 'Just feeling a bit mixed up.'

Daisy takes the stool next to me. 'Come on, talk to me.'

It's time for me to tell her about Dan. 'Your dad wrote me a notebook, as well.'

Daisy stirs my baking mixture. 'What did it say?'

I reach over to my handbag and retrieve it. She wipes her hands on a tea towel and opens it. While I create beautiful yellow rose flowers with delicate petals, Daisy reads through her father's instructions.

'Well?'

Daisy is chewing the inside of her cheek. 'I was wrong to have a go at you about Dad and dating, wasn't I?'

I force out a smile. 'It's okay, I understand it must have been difficult seeing me on that dating site.'

Daisy jumps off her stool. She rests her head on my shoulder. 'I miss him so much.' In an instant, we're both hugging each other, our eyes brimming with tears.

'Reading his words, Mum, it is like he's sitting beside us.' Daisy traces a circle on my arm. 'They're all the things Dad would say.'

Taking a deep breath, I return to putting the finishing touches to a delicate rose. 'Chemo made him do strange things like write me instructions on how to fall in love again.'

Daisy lifts her head. 'Nah, that is Dad on those pages. I mean, he was ill when he wrote us our notebooks, but he knew what he was doing.'

'Do you think so?' I ask.

My daughter nods. 'I know why he chose Mikey Stenton too.'

I step back in surprise. 'What?'

'He's fun, isn't he?' Daisy twists her black hair into a ponytail and nimbly braids it in front of me.

'What do you mean?'

Daisy leans against the work surface. 'There would never be a dull moment with Mikey, Mum. Even I know that.'

I try to return to my cakes, but all I can see in my head is Mikey's face. 'But he's a bit of a ladies' man.'

Daisy raises her pencilled black eyebrows. 'He used to be a ladies' man, you mean.'

I laugh off her suggestion. 'What?'

'Do you remember when he used to pick Dad up for football training?' Daisy clambers back on her stool.

I cast her a puzzled look.

'Dad would always be upstairs getting changed and searching

for his lucky goal scoring shorts. Mikey would be in this kitchen, stood over there.' She points towards the back door.

I try to recall Mikey when Dan was still alive. On football nights the house would be a crazy and noisy place. Dan would be excited at the prospect of playing his beloved game and hanging out with his mates. Billy would usually be grizzling, and Libby would be having a tantrum in the corner. The kitchen would be strewn with mess and I would be in a world of my own, tidying up carpets full of Lego, cars, and bits of Barbie dolls. Mikey would have stood among the chaos and I would have probably cleaned around him.

'I knew he fancied you then,' states Daisy, with a cheeky grin.

'What?'

'Honestly, Mum, Mikey only had eyes for you. Dad and I used to joke about it in private. I remember Dad telling me about some football party you both went to and Mikey had spent the entire evening mesmerised by you.'

I try to keep a straight face but fail. Uncontrollable nervous giggles come from nowhere. Could this be true? Mikey Stenton, the legendary tart, only had eyes for me at that event?

'Dad picked up on this?'

'Yes. Dad thought it was funny. So, I think there's more to this recommendation than Dad being ill due to the chemo.'

A shiver passes through me. I'm in new emotional territory. Perhaps Dan *had* been thinking straight when he wrote to me?

'So, you think Mikey Stenton has fancied me for years?'

Daisy nods. 'Mum, he's crazy about you. I can tell.' She touches my hand. 'He wouldn't forget about Dad either.'

I wrap my arms around her. She's right. Mikey knew Dan. He would make sure Dan's memory lived on.

'Can I have a party on my birthday?'

My teenage daughter has mastered the art of asking for stuff when I'm at my weakest in life. She senses my emotions are running wild and knows now would be a good time to ask for anything.

'Yes, all right,' I say quickly, not really giving the subject much thought. My mind is frantically trying to sort out my feelings for Mikey based on this new knowledge.

'Really?' Daisy's face brightens.

'Well, you have been good lately and you have been through a lot with Tom.'

Daisy grins. 'Yes, Tom and I are just good friends. Thanks, Mum, you're the best!'

As she heads back upstairs, I return to my cake mixture. My brain gets a chance to digest what Daisy said. As my heart starts to gallop at the thought of Mikey secretly fancying me, back rush all the reasons why I shouldn't date him.

Anthony's face appears in my mind as I stir the mixture. He's a good man and has a kind heart. Okay, he might be a little dull and have some odd ideas about romantic nights away but surely I can change him?

A knock at the door makes me jump. To my surprise, Emma and Mel are stood on my doorstep. Mel's eyes are red and puffy.

I usher them both into the lounge.

Mel sinks onto the sofa. 'Jeff wants a paternity test.'

'What?'

She gives me an awkward look. 'The baby might not be his.'

I gasp and stare at Mel. 'What?'

'You know I go to the gym a lot, well, there might be someone there who I slept with before I flew out to Spain.'

'Oh no.'

Emma comes over to sit on the opposite side of Mel. 'We're going to get you through this.'

I rest my head on Mel's shoulder and wonder whether she'll ever start leading a life which is not filled with drama. 'Definitely.'

We stand for a group hug. Emma plants kisses on the tops of our heads. 'Love you both.'

Emma sits back down and scratches her blonde head of curls. 'Right, Pip, let's talk about Mikey.'

I take a deep breath.

'Do you fancy him?' asks Emma.

'It doesn't matter now.' I cross my legs. 'We both knew it was wrong.'

Emma's glossy pink lips break into a smile. 'You're avoiding the question. Do you fancy him?'

'Maybe a little. Nothing serious or anything.'

They both laugh. 'You are such a crap liar, Pip.'

'Daisy told me something interesting tonight. She reckons Dan suggested I should date Mikey because he's always fancied me.'

Emma and Mel stare at me.

'Apparently, Dan used to joke with the kids about Mikey fancying me when he came to take him to football.'

Mel grabs me by the arm. 'Pip, this is important.'

I shake her hand away. 'Mikey is different to me. I couldn't date someone like him. He's wild, reckless, and has a bad track record.'

Emma leans closer. 'Pip, listen to how stupid you sound. Why are you going through with dating Anthony? Don't tell me it's because Barbara made some ridiculous comments?'

'I'm not being stupid. It's common sense.'

Mel shakes her head. 'Absolute bollocks, if you ask me. Mikey's like a different bloke lately. I've never seen any man change like that.'

'Nor me,' says Emma. 'I think we got Mikey Stenton all wrong.'

CHAPTER 42

MIKEY

*A*fter a few sleepless nights spent finding the bottom of a large bottle of whisky, I've come to the conclusion that, in time, I'll grow to like and possibly even love Sophie. I have to focus on making things work between us.

Saying goodbye to my feelings for Pippa was one of the hardest things I've ever done. Kissing her outside the coffee shop nearly killed me. I knew I could somehow survive the rest of my painful life with Sophie, the baby, and Tara, if Pippa gave me one last kiss. After everything in the football shed, I never expected her to be in my arms so quickly. It was so powerful; I struggled to drive home.

Tara and Mum are unaware of the situation with Sophie. This makes things a little easier for me. I've taken a week off work to sort out my life. Lying to Mum isn't easy; she didn't believe this was about me using up a week's annual leave.

When Tara is at school, I go around to Sophie's. She's never in when I get there and every day this week, I've returned without seeing her. I keep the scan photo in my wallet and while sat on Sophie's flat doorstep, waiting for her, I stare at our baby. This is my baby. I'm going to become a father. Life with Sophie isn't going to be easy, but I know I can make things right.

I've texted her a million times to ask whether I can move in. She keeps saying no as I would *do her head in.*

Earlier in the week, I texted to suggest we go out for a meal on Friday. She accepted and asked whether I could transfer some money so she could get a dress. The amount she wanted made me take a sharp intake of breath. It's not like she's in maternity wear yet. I reluctantly did so, and she text back to say the pregnancy hormones had made her breasts swell. Nausea collected in my stomach and I stuffed my phone away.

Mum's looking after Tara while I take Sophie out for dinner. They both look up from a board game as I walk into the living room wearing a smart navy suit jacket and jeans.

'Look at you, Michael!' gushes Mum, giving me one of her twinkly eyed smiles. 'I hope she's worth it.'

I give Tara a kiss goodnight. 'Be good, Tara Twinkle Toes.'

Sophie is stood outside the pub when I meet her. It's been raining heavily, and she doesn't have an umbrella. Her tight red mini dress is damp in places and droplets of water are falling from her black hair.

Leaning in, I kiss her on the cheek and detect alcohol vapours on her breath.

'Have you been drinking?'

She smirks and giggles. 'Yeah, naughty me.'

'For God's sake, you're pregnant.' Anger bubbles up inside of me. 'Who's looking after Zack?'

'The neighbour, and I'll drink when I want!' she snaps, hobbling towards the French restaurant in her giant stilettos.

A waiter ushers us to our table. The restaurant has a rustic interior to it and its intimate, homely feeling was one of the reasons I chose it. Once seated, I calm myself down. Sophie is soon to be the mother of my child and a stepmother to Tara. I need to make this work.

Sophie's eyes survey my suit jacket and open-neck shirt. 'You look like my dad,' she scoffs, before taking a large bite out of a bread roll. I force out a smile and bury my face in the menu.

The restaurant is well known for its classic French dishes and I thought the delicious food might help spark some much-needed romance between us.

The waiter comes over to take our drinks orders. I ignore Sophie's demands for a vodka and coke and instead order her a lime and soda.

We sit in silence for what feels like an eternity. Around us are tables full of smiley couples who are either laughing at their partner's jokes or lovingly serving food on forks to their beloved.

I reach into my jacket pocket and take out the scan photo. I gently thumb the edges as Sophie sighs with exasperation.

'What have you done today?' I'm urging myself to try to make things right between us.

Sophie shrugs her shoulders. 'Nothing. Zack whinged all day. Oh. Abby came around and we drank ...'

Her voice fades away as she catches sight of my face tensing. 'What have you done today?'

'Collected Tara from school. She's joined an art club, so she brought home her first painting.'

Sophie stifles a yawn and stares at the couple opposite who are holding hands and whispering sweet nothings to each other.

I seize my chance to get closer to Sophie, reaching over and squeezing her hand. 'I'm really excited about the baby.'

She removes her hand and rolls her eyes.

The waiter arrives to take our food order.

'I'm not hungry,' Sophie whines, as she rummages inside her black handbag.

'You're pregnant, you have to eat, Sophie.'

She turns to the waiter and asks whether she could just have the onion soup.

While we wait for our food, I gaze at the scan photo. 'I wonder if it will be a boy or a girl?'

Sophie shrugs and takes out her phone. She starts to scroll through whatever is on the screen.

'It's exciting,' I say, 'once you get your head around having a baby, you do start to think about how amazing it is to make another human being.'

'This is really boring talk, Mikey. Babies are not all they're made out to be,' she snaps, turning away from me to text a message.

The waiter brings over her onion soup. Sophie takes one look at it and pushes it away. 'I need a drink.'

'Eat your soup.'

She throws down her napkin, letting it fall into her soup. 'I want a drink.'

The eyes of the couple at the table next to ours are focused on Sophie and me. This is turning out to be the nightmare evening I'd imagined. I try to grab her hand, but she rises quickly and staggers to the bar.

She sits back down with a grin. I watch her take a gulp from a vodka and coke.

'Please stop drinking.' I reach out again for her hand. 'Do it for our baby.'

Sophie scowls. 'Will you stop acting like my dad!'

'I just want us to be a family,' I hiss, noticing more couples are becoming interested in my heated conversation with Sophie.

Sophie drains her glass and stands up.

'Can we talk please?' My shoulders and neck are stiffening.

She shakes her head. 'I'm heading down the club in a bit. You're boring me.'

'Sophie,' I bark, snatching her phone away.

'Give it back!' she snaps, causing the restaurant chatter to disappear. All eyes are now on us.

'Not until you promise to talk to me.'

'I don't want to play happy families.' She swings her handbag over her shoulder and summons the waiter to get her coat.

'This is not fair,' I hiss, as my entire body becomes engulfed in a red rage.

'Look!' She drunkenly props her elbow on the table. 'I just want you to be like Gary and pay for your kid. I don't want none of this happy couples rubbish.'

I grip onto the table with both hands. 'It's my child too and I'm not going to just give you money so that you can go clubbing.'

Sophie snatches her coat from the waiter and puts it on. 'This is getting dull.'

I watch her turn on her heel and laugh. 'I'm going – bye, Dad!'

After stuffing a handful of notes into the bewildered waiter's hand, I race out after her.

She's tottering along the rain-drenched pavement, festooned with puddles, towards a dance club. I know because it's the one she frequents most evenings.

Grabbing her elbow, I steer her round.

'What is wrong with you?' I cry out. 'Why are doing this to me?'

She jerks her arm away and hobbles through a puddle. 'Get your hands off me!'

'Sophie, please!' I'm now shouting at her.

'Go away, Mikey,' she snaps, hurrying away.

I race after her. As I approach, she spins round to face me. 'Leave me alone, go home to your brat!'

'Don't say that about Tara.'

Sophie runs her hand through her black hair. 'This isn't how I expected things to be.'

I can't help but let out a sarcastic laugh. 'What did you expect?'

She shrugs. 'Not like this.'

'Like what, then?'

'You wanting to start playing happy families, taking me out for dinner looking and acting like my dad.'

I bite my lip and lay my hand on her shoulder. 'I'm trying to do the right thing.'

Her face softens and I instantly feel protective of her. She is carrying my baby. Together we've created something so wonderful and precious. 'Shall we go home?'

She nods and we stand on the edge of the pavement to hail a cab.

Her flat stinks of damp clothes and cigarettes, when we arrive back. A leftover pizza in a box greets me as I sit down on her sofa. By the side of my feet lies an empty bottle of vodka.

'Did you drink all that?' I demand, holding it up.

Sophie hiccups and flops down onto the sofa next to me. Her manicured fingers slip underneath my jacket. I can feel her hot breath on my neck. 'We used to have such fun,' she purrs. 'Do you remember those days, Mikey?'

'Where's Zack?'

She giggles. 'With the neighbour.'

I close my eyes and pretend I'm sat with Pippa Browning.

A knock at the door makes her jump. She shoots up and staggers into the little hallway.

Outside her flat is a young man dressed in baggy jeans, a black bomber jacket, and a red cap. Sophie leans against the doorframe and talks to him a low voice.

'Sophie, who is it?'

She turns around and smiles. The man in the bomber jacket takes this as his signal to barge past her and come into the flat.

'Hi, mate, I'm Darren.' The man gives me a nod, before slumping onto one of the chairs.

Sophie grabs an ashtray for him and perches on the chair arm. She offers him a cigarette from a packet which has magically appeared from her handbag.

I watch her place one in her mouth. Shifting uncomfortably in my chair, I watch her suck on a cigarette.

A grin spreads across Darren's face. 'Who are you?'

'Mikey, Sophie's partner.'

Darren raises his eyebrows and glances at Sophie. She bursts into a fit of giggles.

'I need a wee,' she mumbles and heads towards the bathroom.

Darren and I avoid eye contact. We both find cracks in the wall to focus on.

Sophie returns some time later, clutching a bottle of vodka. She winks at me, unscrews the top, and lifts the bottle to her lips.

A surge of anger rises up inside of me. In a flash I'm on my feet. I can't sit and watch her do this to herself and our unborn child.

'I need to get out of here.' My head is thick with anxiety.

Sophie grabs me by the arm. 'Don't go.'

'I'll stay if you stop drinking and smoking,' I hiss, avoiding Darren who is grinning at us.

Sophie rolls her eyes. 'You are so boring, Mikey.'

I've heard enough. She follows me towards the front door.

'Please stay,' she squeaks, in a small voice, as I reach for the door handle.

'Yeah … stay, Mikey,' shouts Darren, who has now moved to the sofa. 'We can get pissed!'

I turn to Sophie. 'Who is he?'

She smiles, hiccups, and says, with a giggle, 'He's my boyfriend.'

I stare in bewilderment. 'You said you no longer had a boyfriend.'

Sophie shrugs her shoulders. 'I was lying.'

Yanking open the front door; I pull Sophie outside. Anger courses through my veins.

'What is going on?' I bark, holding her roughly by the arm.

Sophie laughs and places a hand over her mouth.

'Talk to me!' I take out the scan photo. 'Think of our baby!'

She grabs hold of the door to steady herself. 'God, I'm so drunk!'

'What are you doing to us?'

I thrust the scan photo in her face and point to the image of our baby.

Her face darkens. 'Go home Mikey, there is no *us*.'

'We're having a baby,' I shout, as blood rushes past my ears.

She rests her head against the door frame and closes her mascara-clad eyes.

'Sophie!'

I watch her straighten and smooth down her shiny black hair. 'I can't be arsed with this. There is no baby.'

'What?' My heart grinds to a halt.

'I made it up, Mikey – I thought you would just give me money and stay away.'

I start to tremble.

Darren appears in the doorway with a huge grin plastered across his face. 'Has she been a bad girl again?'

'The scan photo?' I mumble, staring down at the baby image in my hands.

Sophie throws back her head and laughs. 'It's my sister's, you idiot!'

'What ... so there's no baby?'

'No,' she says, raising her eyebrows at me.

I want to scream at her. Something inside me stops my hands from grabbing her shoulders and shaking her.

'Did you think she was up the duff?' jokes Darren, flicking his cigarette stub into the night air. 'She already has one rug rat; she doesn't need another.'

My eyes remain fixed on Sophie. 'Why did you do this to me?'

She leans against Darren. 'We were skint.'

'When were you going to tell me there was no baby?' My voice is thick with emotion.

She shrugs. 'Dunno.'

As I hail a cab all I can hear are Sophie's words 'you idiot!' echoing inside my head.

I'm an idiot. She was right about that.

CHAPTER 43

PIPPA

*a*nthony drives us to the hotel he's booked. I listen to the rhythmic swish of his windscreen wipers and silently ask myself, repeatedly, whether I'm doing the right thing.

Even though I've been harbouring feelings for Mikey Stenton, there's little chance things will progress. He even said himself the kiss we had shared would be our last.

'You feeling okay?' Anthony reaches over to squeeze my thigh.

'A little tense.' I give my aching neck a rub.

'I'll help you relax, baby,' Anthony whispers, moving his hand over my thigh. Instinctively, I swat it away.

'What's the matter?' He pulls the car into a lay-by. 'You didn't complain when I did that on Friday night?'

I run my hands through my hair. 'I'm okay, just had a bad day with Daisy.'

The plans for her birthday party tomorrow night have started to fill me with dread. The day has been spent trying to persuade Daisy to go out to dinner with some friends, after reading horror stories on the internet about carefree parents who allow their teenagers to throw a party and have been left with a ransacked house.

We have argued the entire day about her plan to cram drunken seventeen-year-olds into our family home.

Anthony smiles. 'I'll take your mind off things.' He leans over and starts to kiss my neck. 'Then I'll show you my property empire.'

'Let's just get to the hotel,' I say, moving away from him and edging closer to the car door.

When we arrive at the hotel, all I can hear in my head is my mother telling me that women at my age have to grab opportunities before it's too late.

The room was what I expected. Basic furnishings, which include a double bed, a chair, and a lamp shade.

Anthony has been busy preparing for our night of passion; on the table are two bottles of prosecco and two wine glasses.

He pulls me into his arms the second the door is shut. 'Do you want some wine now or afterwards?' he whispers.

'Now,' I say quickly, hoping the wine will either dampen his spirits or change my mood.

We sit on the bed next to each other. He pours us both a glass. 'To the start of our beautiful relationship, once more.' Clinking his glass with mine, he grins and lays back on the bed.

I grimace and look away.

We work our way through a bottle. I don't feel like doing anything remotely sexual, so Anthony switches on the TV. To his delight the football is on. He drapes his arm around my shoulders, kicks off his shoes, and sits on the bed, engrossed with the match.

My brain is heavily soaked in prosecco. Anthony senses this and starts rubbing my shoulders. Soon his fingers are fiddling with the zip on the back of my dress and his breathing has quickened. I once again remove his hand.

Anthony leans into kiss me. In a second, I'm kissing Mikey Stenton. By closing my eyes and imagining Mikey, a warm tingling feeling starts to envelop.

It suddenly hits me. 'Anthony, this is wrong. I don't want this, us.'

I rise from the bed with an overwhelming sense of relief.

'What do you mean?' he questions. 'I thought we could go back to where we left off all those years ago?'

I straighten my dress and smooth down my hair. 'I'm sorry, Anthony. My mother talked me into starting our relationship again and for a short time, I thought it was the right thing to do. Tonight has proved to me that I don't have any feelings for you anymore. Thanks for everything. I'm sorry, but I need to go.' I grab my bag and race out of the door.

'Pippa, wait!' he shouts from the door as I scuttle away down the corridor.

The receptionist orders me a taxi. It takes forever to turn up and I'm forced to sit awkwardly in the foyer next to a sweet vending machine, which is out of order.

When the taxi arrives, I climb in feeling a wave of relief wash over me.

The taxi driver speeds into town. I lay back against the warm leather seat and watch the city lights flash past the window. My hand grips onto the door handle. I've finally realised who I want: Mikey Stenton.

It's the craziest idea I've ever had. He's unsuitable for me in so many ways, but there is something about him. I can't stop thinking about him; I get a tingling sensation every time he touches my hand and now I understand what Dan means about the invisible thread.

My mother has to accept I need to make my own decisions in life. This is something I have to do.

As the cab sits at the traffic lights, I turn my head and notice Mikey standing outside a restaurant. This is a sign. My heart breaks into a gallop. I was meant to go to him.

Impulsively, I order the taxi driver to pull over while I fumble in my clutch bag for some money. I want to run to Mikey and tell him about the feelings I have for him. The prosecco fuels my confidence.

My cheeks become hot as a giddy feeling builds up inside me. As I raise my head to pay the taxi driver, I notice he's talking to a woman with long brown hair. I struggle to catch my breath as I watch him walk away with her. They look deep in conversation.

Blinking away hot tears, I silently curse myself. I should have known there was someone else in his life. This is why he had called our kiss the last.

Through blurry eyes I nod at the taxi driver and ask him to carry on.

'You were wrong about him, Dan,' I mutter under my breath.

When I arrive home, my mother meets me at the door in a fluster. Her face is red and the green neck in her vein is bulging.

'What's wrong?' I ask, closing the door behind her.

My mother wipes her glazed forehead. 'Daisy and I had an argument. She stormed out.'

'What was it about … your argument?'

My mother puts up her hands. 'Hang on, I thought you were staying in a hotel with Anthony?'

'Don't ask. I've called it off between us.'

My mother steadies herself by placing a hand on the wall. 'That's sad news, Pippa. After all the lengths I went to.'

I stride into the kitchen. 'I need to do things for myself.'

After sinking into a chair at the table, I turn to see my mother at the door. 'He was perfect for you.'

Shaking my head, I unearth Dan's notebook from my handbag. 'In your head, maybe, but not for me.'

'Are you letting Daisy have this party tomorrow night?'

I nod, as a shadow of unease glides across me. 'Yes, but I don't want to.'

'Are you going to be here?' she asks, starting to pace the room.

'No – Libby and Billy are coming with me to Mel's so I can bake some cakes.'

My mother stares at me in disbelief. 'Do you not think you should be here?'

'Look, she's a day away from seventeen, I need to be able to trust her.'

The front door opens and then slams, making us both jump. Daisy comes to stand in the doorway to the kitchen.

'Mum, you're back,' she says, leaning against the wall. 'Did you not like boring Anthony?'

I smile and shake my head.

'Thank God for that, you had us all worried.' She sighs, kicking off her boots. 'I think you should start dating Mikey.'

My mother raises her hands and lets out a frustrated wail. 'No, Pippa, you must not date that man.'

Daisy turned to my mother. 'Nana, I think you should leave Mum's dating choices to her.'

'What?'

Daisy places her hands on her hips. 'You heard. Leave Mum alone. If she wants to date Mikey Stenton, then let her. It's her life.'

Once my mother has left in a huff, I explain how I left Anthony, after making the decision to be with Mikey. I struggle to take a breath remembering what I saw from the taxi.

'I caught sight of him coming out of a restaurant with a woman. They looked close.'

Reliving the moment again makes my chest ache.

Daisy shakes her head. 'It might have been a friend. Don't rule him out.'

Later, I lay in bed and stare up at the ceiling. My mind insists on replaying the image of Mikey putting his arms around that woman. Wiping my wet cheeks, I turn onto my side and hug Dan's notebook tightly. 'What shall I do?' I whisper into the darkness. 'This is all your fault, Dan Browning.'

CHAPTER 44

MIKEY

'Uncle Mikey, why are you grumpy?' asks Tara, coming to stand by the sofa and placing her hand on my arm.

'I'm not grumpy,' I snap, uncrossing my legs and rising quickly from the sofa.

'You've been in a mood all day,' she moans.

She's right. Ever since last night's episode with Sophie, I've been in the darkest of moods. I feel broken and lost.

Deep down, I'd started to bond with the idea of Sophie having my child. It sounds daft, but I'd become connected to the scan photo, stared at it for so long, it had left an imprint on my brain.

Everything was a silly scam to get some cash out of me. There was no baby. I'd been conned and tricked. Feeling like a fool, I'd come home and drunk shots of whisky by myself.

'I'll cheer up.' I ruffle Tara's hair. 'How about a game of Monopoly?'

When Tara has gone to watch TV in bed, I return to the living room after saying goodnight.

Keys in the door and voices in the hallway signal Mum and Keith are back.

'Hello, Michael.' Mum walks in, resting on Keith's arm. Even though I don't want to admit it, when she's with Keith, she looks amazing. There's a glow to her face and she can't stop smiling.

She stops. 'What's wrong, Michael?'

Keith offers to go and make us both a cup of tea. For the first time in my life, I find myself having a heart to heart with my mother. In an uncontrolled gush, everything comes out; Dan's notebook, Pippa, Sophie, and the baby that never was.

Mum sits on the sofa and rubs my arm. 'So, what are you going to do about Pippa?'

I shrug my shoulders. 'She said it. We're not right for each other.'

'Michael, there are some things in life you have to fight for.'

I hang my head. 'No, I've lost her.'

My mother leans towards me. 'Dan wrote those instructions for a reason.'

I watch as she pushes my unruly fringe out of my eyes. 'He could see that under all that bravado, there is a good and decent man.'

I try to hide my smile.

Her face becomes serious. 'I mean it, Michael. Dan could see what I'm seeing now. These last few months, you've changed beyond all recognition and I've never been so proud of you.'

I wipe my nose with the back of my hand.

'Go after her, Michael. Fight for her.'

Before she can say another word, I leap up, grab my jacket, and fly out of the door. As I race down the street, the black cloud hanging over my head starts to lift. Mum is right. I need to fight for her. My mind buries the thought that I've never fought for anyone in my life.

As I jog up to the high street, I feel energised and filled with a sense of optimism. It's been raining again, and puddles are everywhere. A bus roars past, sending a wave of spray against my legs. I carry on running. Pippa is the only thing I care about.

I weave past a group of pub goers and late commuters. My heart is racing.

As I reach Pippa's house, I can hear loud music thumping out of the living room. The windows are hanging open and two lads are fighting on the lawn. In the doorway are a mass of boys trying to push open the door. They're leaning on it, while a girl is screaming for them to get out.

Something is wrong. Pippa wouldn't allow this chaos.

I charge up the path, shouting, 'Clear off!'

The boys turn around.

'You heard me, go!' I glare at them and they all leg it into the night.

Daisy opens the front door with a look of relief. 'Oh God, Mikey, help! Mum's going to kill me. I never invited all these.'

I stride past her and into the lounge which is heaving with bodies. In the corner, a youth with headphones is blasting out a dance tune from Pippa's stereo.

Everyone shouts as I turn the music off. 'Get out, this party is over!'

A steady stream of disgruntled teenagers leaves Pippa's house. Daisy sits with her head in her hands on the sofa.

I'm clearing up a load of beer bottles when a car pulls up outside. Pippa and Emma's voices can be heard in the hallway.

She's standing in the doorway to her lounge, staring at the chaos. Behind her are Billy, Libby, Emma, and Mel.

'What's going on?' Pippa asks looking at Daisy and then me.

Before I get a chance to say something, Daisy stands up. 'The party got out of control. Tom Ridge and all his mates showed up. They were trying to break the door down and then Mikey turned up. He saved me.'

'What?' gasps Pippa. 'Tom Ridge – I thought you and he were good friends?'

Daisy fiddles with her hair. 'Mum, I had the party to impress Tom, but I've learnt my lesson. He's bad news.'

Pippa shakes her head in bewilderment.

'Mikey was amazing. I'm sorry, Mum.' Daisy hangs her head in shame.

'Right, come on, kids, let's go and clear the kitchen,' suggests Emma, beckoning at Daisy.

They leave Pippa and me. Under the glow of the living room light she looks so beautiful; her hair is slightly tousled, her eyes are glistening, and there's a hint of a blush blossoming over her cheeks.

I instinctively reach out and offer her my hand. She refuses to take it.

With my mother's words in my ears, I begin. 'Just hear me out. I know you don't think we're right for each other, but I disagree, Pippa Browning.'

She rubs her chest. 'But I saw you … last night with that woman,' she murmurs. 'I was in a taxi.'

I shake my head. 'That was Sophie.' A wave of nausea washes over me. I stuff my hands into my pockets. 'You know, the ex-girlfriend who was –'

'Asking you for money?' Pippa interjects.

'She told me she was pregnant to get more money out of me.'

Pippa casts me a look of horror. 'She did what?'

I flick my eyes to the floor as shame nibbles away at me. 'She used her sister's scan picture. Over the past week I'd actually come round to the idea of being a father. After you saw us, I was going to move Tara and me in with her.'

'I thought you and Sophie had broken up?'

I nod. 'The old me would have run a mile, but I've changed. It would have been hard, but I would have forced myself to love Sophie for the sake of the baby.'

'Really?'

Running my hands through my hair, I take in a big breath. 'Sophie admitted it was all a trick. It broke my heart.'

'Oh, Mikey.'

I turn towards her. 'What you said in the shed came back to me. We weren't right for each other, because ...'

'I didn't mean it like that.'

'Well, after what happened with Sophie, I questioned whether I was right for you. But the thing is, I can't stop thinking about you. I want to be a part of your life. I love your kids and I don't mind chaos.'

She's still staring at me.

'My brother dying forced me to stop being an arsehole. I have people in my life who I want to look after: Tara, Mum, and you.'

'Really?'

I walk towards her. 'This evening, I was feeling sorry for myself and I didn't think you would ever be mine. My mum told me to fight for you. Pippa, I've fancied you for years and I'll never stop.'

'But the cake blogger, Flossy James. Mel saw you outside hugging her.'

'Flossy? She's the sister of Stan's best mate, Andy. I've known her for years. She's got a girlfriend called Kate, who is hilarious.'

Pippa's eyes widen. 'Oh, I thought you and Flossy were ...' Her voice fades. She scratches her head. 'Hang on ... was it you who told Flossy James about my cakes?'

'Yes, it was me. The world needs to know about your fantastic cakes.'

'You did that for me?'

'I'm in love with you, Pippa Browning. I can't keep away from you. It's like there's an invisible piece of string drawing me closer to you. I must have put on a stone eating all your cakes. I only want to put football nets away with you, and I'll happily give up my evenings to rescue Daisy, Libby, Billy, Mel or Emma.'

Before I know it, Pippa is in my arms and we are locked in a passionate kiss. My body has become consumed with a wonderful tingling feeling. We break away and I nestle my face into her soft brown hair.

She flicks her fringe in that sexy way I've come to love. 'Do you really mean the bit about being in love?'

'I started falling in love with you all those years ago when I used to stand in your kitchen lusting after you in your yoga pants.'

Pippa breaks away. 'But you're a ...' Her voice tails off.

I pull her back to me, placing a delicate kiss on the bridge of her nose. 'I was a wild tart. You will be glad to know that I've changed.'

Wrapping my arms around her I whisper, 'I would do anything to be with you, Pippa.'

She leans her forehead against mine and we both close our eyes. 'Dan arranged all this, you do know that, don't you?'

Stroking her cheek, I think of Dan's notebook. 'He wrote to me, before he passed away.'

'He did what?' she asks, taking a step back from me.

'I got a notebook from him and inside were a set of instructions on how to make you fall in love with me.'

Pippa shakes her head in amazement. 'He wrote me instructions on how to fall in love again, with you.'

I smile. 'Did they work?'

She steps back into my arms. 'Do you want to find out?'

We lean in for a long, lingering kiss. I break away and murmur, 'Yes, please.'

'So, what happens now, Mikey Stenton?' she whispers, giving me a seductive smile and bringing up her hands to caress my neck. A delicious wave of arousal is gliding over me.

'Let's do things properly. I want to date you,' I say with a smile.

'What?' she asks, with a look of surprise. 'No ...'

'All that physical business can wait.'

'Really?' Her eyebrows arch sharply.

I lean in and pepper her neck with tiny kisses. 'I want us to take our time. I want to do things differently with you. I want to take you on romantic dates, talk to you, and go on adventures with the kids.'

'For how long are we waiting before we …' she asks, before letting out a soft moan at my kisses.

'A month, maybe?'

I hear her giggle. She lifts her head. 'After what happened in the football shed. Are you being serious? We're going to wait a month?'

'It is not going to be easy, actually it's going to be torturous for me … but why not?'

She grins. 'You'd do that for me?'

'I'll do whatever it takes to prove to you I'm not the man everyone thinks I am. Pippa Browning, I only want to be with you.'

Flicking her fringe, I start to doubt myself.

'So, what are we going to do in the meantime?'

'I've heard more nets need to be put away at the football club.'

She laughs and I catch a twinkle in her beautiful eyes.

CHAPTER 45

PIPPA

'*M*ikey, are you there?' I call out of my bedroom window and into the darkness below.

There's a rustle of leaves and the sound of someone cursing. 'Yes … ouch that hurt … just climbing up now, my love.'

I giggle as his handsome face appears out of the darkness. He climbs off the emergency ladder and pulls himself through my window.

With arms wrapped around each other, we fall onto the bed, laughing like a pair of naughty teenagers.

Since that Saturday evening when he rescued Daisy and confessed his feelings for me, we've not spent a single night apart. We've talked for hours about Dan, Tara, Stan and his mum. We've laughed until our sides hurt and we've watched films cuddled up until we've both fallen asleep.

Dan's emergency fire ladder has been given a new lease of life. After he's put Tara to bed and said goodnight to his mum and her boyfriend, Keith, Mikey comes over to mine. He leaves early in the morning so that he can be there for Tara when she wakes up.

Something inside tells me Mikey and I are for keeps.

'Good evening!' he whispers, kissing my neck. 'Tonight is the big night.'

We have somehow managed to stick to his rule. Sleeping in the same bed at night, fully clothed, has proved tortuous. So too has kissing at the rear of the coffee shop, kissing behind my garden shed, kissing in the old football shed, and kissing in the pub.

There was a boating lake picnic, which got out of hand, but not because of us. As we were kissing each other on the pebble shore of the little island, fully clothed, I might add, there was a rustle of leaves. To our surprise, a man's naked bottom poked through. This was followed by a familiar voice purring, 'Rick, you're a rock star!' I don't think Mikey will ever forget meeting my sister and brother-in-law for the first time.

He's kissing me passionately. Our clothes are flying coming off. Mikey and I are now almost in just our underwear.

What happens if I don't live up to all the many women he's slept with?

Mikey stops. 'What's the matter?' he whispers. His warm finger strokes my cheek. 'Hey, Pippa, talk to me.'

My heart is thudding. 'You're so experienced and I'm worried I won't be ... um ... any good,' I say, in a quiet voice.

Placing his hands on my bare shoulders, he smiles. 'But I never loved any of them. This is different. I'm madly and totally in love with you.'

Running my hands through his wild brown hair, I still can't believe this handsome man has fallen in love with me. 'Really?'

'One hundred per cent. I'm bloody nervous too.'

'Oh, come on,' I laugh. 'You? Nervous?'

He pulls me closer. 'You're my dream woman. I might be terrible.'

I press my forehead against his. 'This is going to be interesting.'

Out of the corner of my eye I catch sight of the red notebook sticking out of my handbag. I smile and silently thank Dan.

'We don't have to do anything, Pip,' Mikey says peppering my shoulders with kisses.

Flicking my fringe, I laugh and drag him onto the bed.

THE END

A MESSAGE FROM LUCY

Dear Reader,

Thank you for reading my debut novel. I do hope you enjoyed meeting my characters.

Instructions for Falling in Love Again began as a spark of an idea when my husband was training for the London Marathon. He was raising money for the Leukaemia & Lymphoma Research charity and celebrating being ten-years cancer free. Shortly after we got married, he was diagnosed with lymphoma, a cancer of the lymphatic system and spent a year having gruelling treatment.

In order to fit his marathon training around our busy family life, he created family wall planners in an attempt to organise me and the kids. My husband is *Mr Organised*. Me, I'm *Mrs Go with the Flow*. He also left instructions for us stuck to the fridge and all around the house while he was pounding the streets.

He soon ditched the wall planners as none of us were taking much notice of them, or his advice, and so he resorted to carrying around a little red notebook with his plans written inside. This ignited that spark and Pippa was born.

I loved writing Pippa's story because I know I'd definitely

need a set of instructions for falling in love again. I've been married for a long time, and I know the dating scene has changed a *lot* since the early nineties! I mean, the word *selfie* didn't even exist then, never mind having dating apps on your *mobile phone*! I also think I'd crave that reassurance I was doing the right thing, which is ultimately what Pippa needed.

If you enjoyed Pippa's story as much as I loved writing it, I'll be eternally grateful if you could take the time to leave a review. Reviews are so important to authors because they help us to see that the blood, sweat and tears were worth it.

I love speaking with my readers, so please do come and say hello and keep up with all my news. You can find me on:

Twitter: @LucyMitchAuth

Facebook: @lucymitchellauthor

Blog: LucyMitchellAuthor.blog

Thanks again,

Lucy x

ACKNOWLEDGEMENTS

To Huw, Seren, and Felicity, thank you for your love and support. For taking on the ironing so I have time to write, making me endless cups of coffee, buying me a lot of chocolate, listening to my story ideas, giving me feedback on my story ideas, passing me sheets of kitchen roll when I am an emotional mess about my writing, and for telling me to get a grip when needed.

To my amazing parents who have always encouraged me to follow my dreams. Thank you for sending me to John Smeaton High School in Leeds all those years ago. It was in Mr Barrand and Mr Townsley's English classes where my passion for writing fiction first began. Also, thank you for keeping all the funny letters I used to send you when I was at university, recording the emotional highs and lows of my student life.

To my sister, Vez, and nieces Bella and Chloe. Thanks for the shopping trips, ladies! Had some of my best book ideas while we all tried on clothes in New Look.

To my wonderful father-in-law, Jeff, thank you for your words of encouragement and support.

To Catherine and Sue, thank you for reading countless drafts, telling me to get a grip over Messenger, pestering me to do something with this story, encouraging me to follow my dream over a glass of wine in the Nag's Head and spending Sue's birthday night in a posh hotel proofreading my novel. You two are amazing x

To Paul Gilbert, thank you for having a stern word with me in the Olway and telling me to get my writing act together.

To Liz Baker, thank you for your encouragement and wise words.

And finally, to Kristine, my wonderful mother-in-law, who is sadly no longer with us. Kris, you once told me to follow my writing dream. This was over a ham sandwich, a cup of tea, and a slice of cake. Well, I took your advice.

I did it x

A NOTE FROM THE PUBLISHER

Thank you for reading this book. If you enjoyed it please do consider leaving a review on Amazon to help others find it too.

We hate typos. All of our books have been rigorously edited and proofread, but sometimes mistakes do slip through. If you have spotted a typo, please do let us know and we can get it amended within hours.

info@bloodhoundbooks.com

Printed in Great Britain
by Amazon

36178880R00179